LOVE
UNSPOKEN

the flawed love series
book 2

Lisa DeJong

Yvette –
" The Teaser Queen "

Lisa
DeJong

Edited by Chelsea Kuhel

Cover by Mae I Design

Formatting by Formatting By KassiCoop

This book is dedicated to all those who I have loved and lost. You're never forgotten.

PROLOGUE

THAT PICTURE BLAKE PAINTED me of my house at Christmas time—I set it in the corner of my room after he left. For the rest of that day—and the day after—I stayed curled in a ball staring at it as tears rolled down my cheeks.

I fucked up. I made too many assumptions and read too much into Pierce's words.

Blake is not an angel, but he's definitely not the person Pierce made him out to be. I can't help but think about what this Christmas would have been like if I'd just waited at home for him. If he'd come in with the painting ... how different that day would have been. Who does that for someone? Who spends all day painting a girl a picture of home when she can't be there for Christmas?

It would have been a turn in our relationship. Instead, I took the curve too fast, not watching where I was going, missing the turn all together.

Somewhere along the way, the little game we liked to play turned into something more. Something a lot like love—a better love than I've ever felt before. And now it's gone.

I won't get a chance to kiss him every morning.

I won't get to tell him I love him before bed.

And I think what hurts the most is that I won't get a chance to help him through the suffering. He needs someone, but it won't be me—not after everything that has happened.

Everything he told me about Alyssa plays over and over in my head. To think about what it must have been like for him to watch Alyssa change over the years. To watch her fall into such a dark hole that he couldn't even see her anymore ... at least not as the same person she used to be.

And to have been the one who found her ...

I can't imagine the weight of the guilt he feels every day that he wakes up without her. I wonder if certain places or things remind him of her. I wonder if he sees any of her in me.

Are we different? Are we the same? And if we are, would he still feel the same way about me if I wasn't.

It's not his fault ... it's not hers either.

I brought back all the emotions he's been trying to bury. Not only that, but I threw them in his face in the worst way possible. He was doing the best he could for me, and all I did was doubt him.

He ran because of me, and now all I have left is a picture of home. It's beautiful—it's a memory to keep for years, but he missed something when he painted it: he's my home.

I want to go *home.*

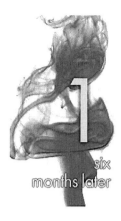

1

six months later

"ARE YOU DONE WITH THE MOOD board for the 5th Avenue project?"

I jump, not having heard him coming up behind me. He's good at that. Too good.

"Almost. I just need to decide what color to pull from the window coverings for the walls. Any suggestions?"

His strong hand squeezes my shoulder. It might faze me if he hadn't done it hundreds of times before. "Gray would be the safe choice, but if it were me, I'd cover the walls with wood planks. A rustic, aged gray that will balance the bold furnishings."

Ideas like that are how he got to where he is. "Do you think Wade will go for that?" I ask, remembering how hard the man is to please.

"He might balk at first, but it'll grow on him, especially when he realizes no other hotel in New York has anything like it."

I nod, picking a gray colored pencil from the table to make the idea come to life. That's what my job is after all — turning a blank white board into something people will stare at ... something so detailed they actually envision themselves in the space. It's also a distraction from the proximity of Pierce's body and his strong masculine scent.

1

Even though it's been a few months, I still can't get the thoughts of the one night we spent in New York out of my head. It's further complicated because I'm working on the New York boutique hotel—the same one Pierce didn't want any part of.

"How's this?" I ask, shading between the dark gray lines. He leans in closer, his chest brushing against my shoulder. I shut my eyes on instinct but quickly recover. "What if we give it an illusion? Make the planks appear woven."

I hate and admire his ability to visualize what I can't. Some day I hope that I'm half as good as he is at this. "I like it."

For a couple minutes, he just stands there watching me. It used to make me uncomfortable, but even this seems normal now. I try to pretend he's not there, but his warm breath tickles the back of my neck. High buns may be in, but on days like this, they aren't a good idea—not when your powerful, sexy boss is literally breathing down your neck. The one you kissed—almost slept with.

"Did you have lunch?"

I shake my head. "Not yet." Unless Reece kidnaps me from my desk, I usually grab a protein bar from my drawer. Attacking the cafeteria alone is like wandering aimlessly into a high school dance without a date.

"Come with me."

I don't answer right away. I can't. My mind is in a constant tug-of-war with my heart. I just ... I want *him* still. After the pain, the months of silence ... I want him. As long as I remember him, he'll always be a part of me.

"Don't let him take you down with him. You're better than that ... you're better than him," he says softly, his warm breath hitting the back of my neck yet again.

"It's not about him. It's—"

"Then have lunch with me."

My teeth grind together in an angry rhythm to keep my emotions at bay. Pierce painted Blake as a monster when he's not even close, and a part of me hasn't forgiven him for that. "I need to finish this."

He pulls the pencil from between my fingers. "If it makes you feel better, we'll discuss the project over a sandwich."

Blake's been gone for almost six months, and I blame Pierce. I blame him when I should blame myself. I should have trusted him. I knew him better than to make assumptions.

"Fine, I'll take a short lunch then I have to get back to it."

"Don't be that way, Lila. Have you done anything outside these cubicle walls since you started on this project?" he asks, crossing his arms over his strong chest.

I pull my sweater from the back of my chair and slip it on. "No reason to."

"It's called inspiration, Lila."

He walks. I stay close behind, drawing the eyes of everyone we pass.

"There's enough going on in my head. I don't need to add to it," I mumble, watching his expensive leather shoes to avoid the stares.

The elevator opens, and five sets of eyes stare at us. Being Pierce Stanley's friend sucks sometimes. He walks to one corner, and the group automatically clears to the other.

As soon as the door closes, he leans into me. "I liked the old Lila better."

So did I, I think.

"She's still here," I whisper, half-heartedly.

"I know," he replies. "We just have to find her."

I don't have an answer for that. I know she's still in me. Who I used to be is part of my history—she's not going anywhere. She's just buried under a heavy pile of heartbreak.

I fall hard.

I love harder.

Blake left, and when he did, he took a piece of me with him. I've tried to get the old Lila back the last few months but it's as if I can't see anything in front of me ... not when I can't stop thinking about what I once had.

Pierce nudges my shoulder. "We can get off now."

Shaking my head, I come out of the fog. I've been caught up in it so much lately that I don't know what it's like to just be.

We walk side by side to the little café I've gone to with Reece before.

"I didn't think people came here for business meetings," I say as I walk through the door he holds open for me.

I look back. He smiles. "I left business back at the office."

Damn him.

"This should be quick then," I chide as we walk up to the counter.

I order a club sandwich and a bottle of water. He gets the same with a cup of soup and follows me to a small table in the back corner. My heart beats faster than usual. Pierce pushes me. My friends push me. Life is easier when I can hide away inside my own head. I've done a good job of it.

"Actually, I do have one piece of business," he announces after enjoying the first bite of his soup. "I talked to Wade earlier."

"I'm sorry I missed it," I reply, sarcastically, twisting the cap off my water.

He laughs, scrubbing his hand over his jaw. "You almost make that sound believable." He pauses, some of the playfulness from earlier disappearing. "He wants us in New York next week for a few days to meet with his team."

Thoughts of the last time we were in New York flash through my mind, and they have nothing to do with Wade. New York City will never be just a place to me; it's a page in life's scrapbook.

"And if we don't?"

"That's not an option."

Great. "I don't know if I can have the mood board done by then."

"If I asked you to, you'd have it done this afternoon."

I open my mouth to argue, but I think better of it. He's right ... always. "What days are you thinking?"

"Leave Monday. Come home Thursday afternoon."

"Why so long?"

He shrugs. "We have a scheduled meeting with him late Monday afternoon then he's hosting a meet and greet for everyone Tuesday evening. This is Wade's new baby; failure is never an option for him."

"I still don't get why you even want to work with him."

He leans in, his bright eyes just inches from mine. "If I only worked with people I like, you wouldn't have a job. Getting to where I'm at required a lot of sacrifices, and my sanity happens to be one of them."

'Do you ever get bored? I mean ... you've accomplished so much. Have you reached a point where you feel like you have enough? I'd think at some point the success would give you the power to retain your sanity. Be more picky about the projects you take on."

"You're missing the point. Money is nice, but I don't do this for the money; I do it for the challenge. I want to be the best," he says, taking another spoonful of the steamy broth.

"I think you're already there," I say quietly. In the six months I've been working with him, I've been captured by his brilliance. And through every step of the way, he's been a steady force. If he's stressed, I never see it.

"There is one challenge I haven't completed. It's not over yet, and I'm not going to give up."

I pull my water to my lips, sipping it slowly. He says little things like this sometimes when we're alone. He's not afraid to show his cards, but I'm not ready to let him see mine ... or to even play the game.

"I think we should get back to the office, especially if I have to complete the board by next week," I say, standing to dump my mostly uneaten sandwich in the garbage.

"Why do you do that?" he asks, sneaking up behind me.

I keep walking. "Do what?"

"Run. Why do you keep running from me?"

I ignore him until we're outside, away from the crowd. "Because you're the one who helped tie the rope around my heart and squeeze it until it was broken in two. If you would have been more honest with me about what happened with Alyssa, he'd still be here."

He presses his hand against my back, guiding me down the street. "I've been waiting to hear you say it."

"That's it," I say, spinning on my heels to face him. "What the fuck do you want from me, Pierce? Is there a mass conspiracy amongst men to make my life a living hell?" I attempt to keep my voice low, but the rage within me makes that almost impossible.

The asshole actually smiles. "No, but if we're ever going to move forward, you have to let out that anger. This is a nice start."

I point my finger at him. "I swear, Pierce, if you weren't my boss, I'd have some very choice words for you right now."

"Keep it coming." He smiles again.

Without another word, I spin around and hurry back into the office building. If he talks, I don't hear him. If he walks closely, I don't feel him.

FOR THE REST OF THE DAY, I do a good job avoiding Pierce. He must have gotten the point because he sent his secretary over with my flight itinerary for next week. He's pretty official for someone with a private jet.

Reece comes around the corner as I'm pulling my purse over my shoulder. "What's the plan for this weekend?"

"Same old." I smile, but it's with sadness. Rainbows only form after rainstorms if the sun shines. I've lived in the clouds for far too long to even believe in the rainbows.

"Why don't we go hang out at Charlie's tonight? Dana is working, right?"

Truth is, I hide out there some days after work when I know Dana isn't working. Charlie saves a seat at the end of the bar just for me. He keeps the drinks coming until I've had enough, and then he calls a cab to take me home.

Sometimes when things get really bad, I just need familiarity. Charlie's gives me that.

"I'll join you for a drink or two then I have to go."

She shrugs, a huge smile pulling at her lips. "I'll take it."

"Train or taxi?" I ask, starting toward the elevator.

"Taxi, please. I don't feel like dealing with the crowd."

"Bad day?"

She groans, pushing the button for the first floor. "I spent all day drawing and redrawing the same floor of a twenty-two story office building. The rooms were too big, then too small, then the asshole forgot to tell me about the conference rooms that were supposed to be at each corner."

"Did you get it done?"

She laughs sarcastically. "That's a big no. I'm going to work on it this weekend, and hopefully it will be in an acceptable state by Monday. Then, I only have twenty-one floors to go. Yay me!"

"If it makes you feel any better, I have to present the board I've been working on in New York next week. Thinking about it makes me want to vomit, so it's probably a good thing we're drinking tonight. Make sure I drink just enough to forget about it, will you?"

We hail a taxi and continue complaining about our upcoming week as it drives through rush hour traffic, moving only a few feet between stops. It would be annoying if I was alone, but the company makes it tolerable.

"If you want to get out of going to New York, I'll gladly take your place," she remarks as we pull in front of Charlie's.

"Would you give up your baby, Reece?"

She lifts a brow. "That's an odd question since I don't have a baby and all. Or even a man to make a baby with."

"You're missing the point."

"It's the end of a very long week. I'm not in the mood to read between the lines."

"Point taken," I say, handing the driver some cash before climbing out of the car. "What I was trying to say is I've put so much into this project that I'm not willing to give it up ... not for anything. From beginning to end, it's been mine."

"Ah, well, I can't say I've fallen in love with my current project yet, so I'd gladly give it up."

We walk into Charlie's, taking in the usual Friday crowd. It hasn't changed much. Heads still turn when I walk in. It's hard to escape when the ratio is ten men to each woman. They haven't quite figured out that they have a ten percent chance of getting laid on a good night.

"Hey, pretty ladies. Are you looking for a place to sit?" asks one of the regulars at the bar as we walk by. He's harmless enough, but I learned when I worked here that it's best to ignore him.

"What the hell are you two doing here?" Dana asks when she sees us coming. I don't see her often anymore, and I feel like the worst friend in the world when I do.

I wrap my arms tightly around her. "I missed you."

"And we need to get drunk," Reece chimes in behind me.

"Well, you're in the right place. What can I get you?"

"Shots," Reece blurts before I get a chance. "Charlie will let you do one with us, won't he?"

Dana gestures to Charlie then leans over the bar, whispering something to him.

He nods and lines three shot glasses on the bar, filling them with an amber colored liquid.

"What's that?" I ask, tracing my fingertip along the rim.

Charlie grins. "Fireball. Have one, and I promise you'll be begging for a second then a third."

"Let's do this, girls!" Dana shouts, holding her glass in the air. Reece eyes me, watching until I pick mine up. "1 … 2 … 3"

I tilt my head back, pouring the liquid down my throat. It burns a little at first, but for the most part, it just tastes like cinnamon gum. It would be easy to disappear with the entire bottle and not know what hit me until I wake up the next morning.

"Again," I choke, slamming my glass on the bar. I need to forget, even if it's just tonight.

He fills my glass. "Let me know when you're ready, and I'll call you a cab."

I wink, hoping the other two don't pick up on my regular habit.

After the third shot, the night blurs.

My head aches as I attempt to open my eyes. Drinking has become a form of self-punishment. The more pain I cause myself, the less guilt I feel. It's my way of seeking repentance.

Deep down, I know repentance will never be found at the bottom of a bottle, though.

The first thing I always do on mornings like this is try to recall what happened the night before.

I remember laughing. That was all Dana's fault.

I remember arguing. Reece was on the receiving end of that.

And crying ... the water works always start after the fourth or fifth drink.

Someone moans next to me causing me to squeal as I jump out of bed. "Damnit, Reece! Are you trying to kill me?" I scream, recognizing her as my departing gift from the bar. At least it's not a nameless man.

"Please stop screaming. My head is going to explode any minute," she says quietly, circling her temples with her fingertips.

"You scared me."

"Sorry," she mumbles. "I don't even remember how we got here, but I'm glad it was just you I woke up to."

My head pounds, forcing me back to my pillow. "We're never doing Fireball shots again. Ever."

"Trust me. I'll never suggest it." She turns her head so we're lying face to face. It reminds me of the sleepovers I had when I was younger. "What time is it anyway?"

I pinch my eyes closed, despising the bright sunlight that shines through the crack in the curtains. "Don't make me look. I'd have to turn around, and I can't commit to that right now."

"At least it's Saturday."

"No doubt. The mood board may just have to wait until tomorrow."

She sighs. "I've seen that thing a hundred times at least. It's perfect ... brilliant actually. Leave it alone."

"It's not really that. I have to be able to sell it to a group of wealthy, intelligent businessmen. What if they hate it?" I speak as quietly as possible, trying not to disturb the raging demons in my head.

"What does Pierce think?"

"He says he loves it."

"Then you have nothing to worry about," she says, curling the pillow under her head. We lay in silence for a few minutes; it's nice to spend time with someone who doesn't need to be entertained the entire time. "Are you ever going to be able to let him go?"

It takes a moment before her question registers. Between the lack of sleep and pounding hammer in my head, things aren't adding up easily. "I never had him, Reece."

"But you thought you did. Perception became your reality."

"I know. I keep waiting for him to come back and say he made a huge mistake by leaving."

"Has he called yet?" she asks, hesitantly.

It's been a sore subject—me not being able to get ahold of him. I want to know that he's okay if nothing else. "No."

"After everything you've been through the last year, you may not believe this, but there's someone better out there for you. Someday, you're going to meet a guy who'll stay by your side unconditionally."

"That scares me actually," I whisper.

"Why would that scare you?"

"Because to get to that point, I'm going to have to trust someone again. I just don't think I can."

She stares me straight in the eye. "There is one guy you trust." My lips part, but she starts up again before I can say anything. "Maybe it's time for you to give Pierce a real chance."

I open my mouth to argue, but nothing comes out. If Blake hadn't walked into my life, Pierce would be the one lying beside me in bed right now. I don't doubt that for a second.

"I screwed up any chance we had a long time ago," I say sadly.

"You don't really believe that, do you?"

I think about the benefit. The night in New York. Frozen hot chocolate on Christmas Eve. I had chances but I gave them all up for Blake.

"I don't know. I mean … I've done things. He's done things. I don't know."

"Promise me one thing," she says. "Promise me you'll keep an open mind. I can't stand to see you like this for much longer, and you'd hate to meet the guys I'd set you up with."

I laugh which only makes me wince due to the massive headache last night gifted me. "Are you going to lend me one of your many book boyfriends?"

"Well, I'm not willing to give up any of them, but have you met the new guy in accounting?" she snorts. "The one with gold, wire-rimmed glasses and a hideous comb over complemented with a whole tube of gel."

My nose crinkles on instinct. "You mean he's bald?"

"Oh, he's not bald. I just don't think he's made time for a haircut lately." She giggles. "And, this is the best part, he wears white tube socks with black dress shoes and slacks."

"He's all yours," I say, closing my eyes to ease my headache.

"It's your loss. I bet he's hung like a horse."

"Why don't you find out? I think you spend too much time worrying about my love life." I yawn, feeling myself drifting off to sleep.

Reece leaves shortly after noon, giving me back my quiet apartment. This is how it was supposed to be when I moved here last fall, but I liked the way it was when Blake was here more.

He took away my lonely. I would rather fight with him than be here like this, and the worst part is, I can't even tell him.

His second chance has been a phone call away the last several months.

My cell phone rings, pulling me from the internal prison I've locked myself in.

I look down at it and smile, swiping my thumb across the screen. "Hey, what are you up to?" I ask, fiddling with the bottom of my yoga pants.

"Just thinking about you. Weekends are quiet here; I'm ready to come home so we can take on Chicago together." Mallory comes home in two months, but that seems like an eternity from now.

"What? You don't think I'm already lighting this place up?" I ask, rolling my eyes at my own question.

She laughs. "Yeah, I'm sure you are. What did you do last night?"

"Reece and I went to Charlie's. And for your information, I got drunk and woke up in bed with someone."

"No way," she blurts. *Would it be that much of a surprise?* "Was he at least cute?"

"He was a she."

"Holy shit!"

"Mallory."

She laughs. "Sorry, you're throwing me for a loop today. Are you sure you're the same Lila I've been talking to the last few months?"

"I avoided the mirror this morning, but I think so." I pause, wondering how much of this she's taking seriously. "Aren't you going to ask me about her?"

"Who?" she asks.

"The woman I slept with last night."

"You're starting to scare me."

"You don't have to worry too much. It was just Reece."

She sighs. "For a second, I thought I was going to have to catch the next plane back to the states to fix you."

"Am I fixable?" I ask quietly, thinking back to what Reece and I talked about this morning.

"I don't think you're broken."

"Maybe I'm not broken, but a part of me is missing."

I rarely bring him up, but today he's on my mind. He takes up so much of it, there's no room for anything else.

"I wish I could tell you it will all be okay, but I can't, Lila. I know my brother, and once he makes a decision, he usually doesn't turn back." She takes a deep breath. She hates being in the middle, and I hate putting her there. "I've talked to him. He's doing better than he was, but I wouldn't wait for him to come back. I don't know if he'll ever come back."

"Thank you for telling me ... that he's doing better, I mean. I've been spending a lot of time worrying about him."

"He doesn't want you to wait for him," she whispers.

LOVE UNSPOKEN

My lungs constrict, making it hard to breathe. "Did he say that?" My voice shakes with each word.

"No, I'm telling you as your friend and because I know my brother. I just want you to have a chance at happiness. You're not going to get it from where you are right now," she pleads.

"I know."

There's a long awkward pause—a rarity for the two of us. I can't take it because it gives me too much time to think. I don't need any more time for that.

"So what are you doing this weekend?" I ask, filling the void.

"I have a project to finish, and then I think I'm going to go to go for a hike or something. It's too nice to be stuck inside. You?"

"I'm going to New York with Pierce on Monday to present the board I've been working on for months. I should probably pack then I'll spend the rest of the weekend talking myself out of running away." My stomach hurts just thinking about it.

"From what I know about Pierce, he wouldn't put you in this position unless he thought you were ready."

"I'm just nervous. It wasn't long ago I was selling furniture; it's hard to believe sometimes."

"When you are stressing, think about everything you've overcome this last year. You've got this," she says in the same tone my mom would use if I were talking to her right now.

"Thank you. I think I needed this today."

"Are you sure I made you feel better?" she asks.

"I'd be lying if I said I felt better, but I do have more clarity. I probably needed that more than anything," I admit. I've been living my life by walking through it with my eyes on the ground. It's time I look up and get a glimpse of what's going on around me. I've been given the biggest opportunity of my life, and I'm going to be there for it.

"You better call me next week and let me know how it goes."

"You'll be the first to know," I answer back before letting her go.

The next week is going to be interesting.

14

"ARE YOU READY FOR THIS?" Pierce asks when the plane reaches cruising altitude.

"This isn't my first rodeo," I answer, thinking back to our last trip to New York, and the most unforgettable night I wish I *could* forget.

"It's your first big project."

I laugh. It's my first project period. How many people get to say their first interior design project was a multi-million dollar hotel in New York? "You said I could handle it. I got it handled."

"I know you do," he says, his voice softer, "but just in case, one of these will help."

He passes me a flute of bubbly champagne, and I accept without hesitation. Truth is, my stomach is in more knots than the necklace I left in my purse last week. Pierce would never say it out loud, but this project is going to net him some serious cash if it's successful. He's placing his bet on me, and the pressure is eating me up.

I sip, getting a taste of the cool, bubbly liquid. The rest goes down easily after that. I lift my glass for more.

Pierce's warm hand wraps around my forearm. "Take it slow, Ms. Fields. I need you to be able to walk off this plane."

I laugh for the second time in less than ten minutes. "You haven't called me that in months."

15

He smiles, subtly sliding his hand toward my wrist. I don't think I was supposed to notice, but I do. "It's been months since I've seen you like this. Brings me back to when you were Ms. Fields."

"Mr. Stanley."

"Hmm?"

"Lila can hold her liquor far better than Ms. Fields ever could." I pause, watching his smile widen. "Now, can I have another glass, please?"

His hand slips from my arm. He pulls the champagne from the bucket, refilling my glass. "Must I ask about your recent improvement in liquor retention?"

"I'd blame Reece and Dana, but I think we both know the real answer to that. You're a smart guy."

The amused look he had seconds ago falls away. That happens a lot more than I'd like it to around me.

"This is the point where I'm supposed to change the subject."

I nod, sipping more champagne.

"What do you want to do while we're in New York? Believe it or not, I don't have anything planned outside of our commitments to Wade."

I shrug. "You don't have to entertain me, Pierce. A soft bed and a movie sound like heaven tonight."

When he doesn't respond, I look up to see his eyes glued to me. I've seen them like this before—in the moments before he kissed me in New York and when he showed up at my apartment on Christmas Eve.

They're begging.

I want to cave.

I want to love and be loved.

You know when you look in someone's eyes and all you see is truth. They stare right at you—right through you. He does that to me, and he may not realize it yet, but I do the same to him. I've never been more honest with anyone than I've been with Pierce. Honesty is easy when someone has seen the worst of you, and yet, they still stick by you. I trust him more than I've ever trusted anyone, but it's hard to be loved by one man when your heart is with another.

16

If only the heart wanted what it should.

His voice cuts through the silence. "There's this one place outside the park that I like to visit when the weather is nice. Will you come with me for lunch before we step foot into hell?"

I bite my lip, rolling it back and forth between my teeth. Pierce is like a wrapped piece of chocolate being set in front of me: once unwrapped, there's no way I'm going to be able to resist.

"I don't know if that's such a good idea."

He tilts his head, peering over at me. "How's it any different than the lunch we had the other day?"

Because New York is our place, I think to myself. "Pierce—"

His index finger touches his lips, halting my words. "You think too much."

"You don't think enough."

He laughs—deep and throaty. "Lila, if you had a thirty-second view into this head of mine, you'd get dizzy." He pauses, his eyes dancing between mine. "Especially now."

"This is exactly what I was talking about. We've teetered on this line before, and I can't take another chance like that. Not now."

"It's just two people enjoying a meal together."

"It was the same the last time we were in New York."

He shakes his head. "You have an answer for everything, don't you?"

"Almost everything," I quietly answer.

I don't have an answer for Blake.

The plane lands smoothly, pulling up to a waiting black town car. If I do this ten or twenty more times, I might not require champagne to make it through. The driver pulls our luggage from the plane as Pierce and I make our way down the stairs and slide into the back seat of the car.

I fixate on the cityscape while Pierce rattles off an address. Memories of the last time we were in New York creep up to the forefront of my mind ... and everything that happened in the weeks that followed. I wish it would all just go away.

"Have you ever been to Madison Square Park?" Pierce asks after a few minutes of silence.

"I've only been in New York with you so if we didn't go, I haven't been there." The answer comes out sharper than I intended it to but yet I don't apologize.

"I guess it's going to be your first time then," he says as the car pulls in front of a lush green lawn guarded by a wrought iron fence and mature trees. It looks foreign in the city.

"What are we doing here?" I ask, looking over at him.

"Having lunch." He opens his door and steps out without looking back.

I follow behind, walking as quickly as I can in my heels to catch him. "If I'm not mistaken, I declined your invitation."

He laughs, turning back to look at the street. "Looks like our car already left. Do you want to sit on the bench over there and wait two hours for it to come back, or would you like to have lunch with me?"

"This isn't fair."

He shrugs. "Life rarely is."

Without another word, he starts walking down the paved path again. I stand with my hands clenched, debating my next move. I hate giving in, but I'm also not keen on being left alone in New York.

"I'm not very happy with you," I say as soon as I catch up.

"I don't think you have been for months. Why would that change now?"

He's right. What happened on Christmas Day put a fence up between us.

"Where are we eating?" I ask, changing the subject.

"Shake Shack." He sounds like a little kid who has just been promised ice cream with sprinkles.

"And it's in this park?"

"Yep"

I stay close behind him taking in the colorful flowers and smiling children that we pass by. Before long, we reach what I can only describe as a fancy concession stand. It's a nicely appointed metal building surrounded by a crowd of suits and families alike.

"This is where you wanted to have lunch?" I ask, breaking the silence.

He lifts a brow, lips curling. *Why is he so hard to stay mad at?* "This place has the best burgers and fries in the country. Just wait."

"What do you suggest?" I ask, staring up at the menu board.

He points to an empty table. "Grab us a seat, and I'll order. If you don't like it, I'll let you run the show for the rest of the trip."

Now, it's my turn to lift my eyebrow. "You'd give me all the control?"

"No, that's just how confident I am that you're going to love it."

"We'll see," I taunt as I watch him walk away.

The wait seems like forever, and I have to admit all the food that passes smells amazing.

"Is this seat taken?"

I look up to see Pierce smiling down at me. "It depends. What's in it for me?"

"My company and this," he answers, setting a basket of the most delicious smelling food in front of me.

"Consider the seat yours." I pick up a piping hot fry and pop it in my mouth. It burns the roof of my mouth, and as I struggle to cool it off, Pierce slides a cup in front of me. I sip it, tasting chocolate ice cream; it's a perfect compliment to the salty fry.

"Better?" he asks.

"Much."

For the next few minutes, we eat in silence. The burger is cooked to perfection, the juice soaking through the bun. It's messy but worth it.

I catch him watching me every now and then but divert my attention to the people that walk by.

"Why don't you just yell at me and get it over with?" His words are so out of the blue I practically choke on my food.

"I'm not mad anymore if it makes you feel better," I reply, going back to people watching.

"I'm not talking about this."

Now he has my attention. "What are you talking about then?"

"You blame me," he says, pushing his food away.

I open my mouth to ask what he's referring to, but I already know. And he's right … if he hadn't said some of the things he did about Blake, I would have approached things differently that day. He can't take it back nor can I.

"You have to know, Lila … you have to know it wouldn't have worked out whether I told you or not." He stops, playing with the corners of his napkin. "I wish I could go back. I wish I would have chosen my words better, but it's done. I'm sorry."

Tears pool in my eyes, not because I'm thinking about Blake but because Pierce just proved himself to be a better man than I already knew he was. I built a short wall between us because I did blame him for some of what happened with Blake, but at the end of the day, it was all me. I didn't trust Blake enough to not draw the wrong conclusions.

"I don't blame you," I whisper so he won't hear the tears in my voice.

"I feel like you do."

I shake my head, looking up to the sky as if it holds all the right answers. "I'm not happy. I wouldn't say I'm depressed, but I'm not happy. My friends keep telling me it's time to move on, but I don't know how."

He leans across the table, holding my hand in his. "You have to forget. You have to have moments where you think about something other than him."

As I look down, I notice his watery eyes. "Is that what helped you get through what happened with Alyssa?"

Now he's staring up at the sky. "It took a long time, but I buried myself in my work—kind of like you do—and after a while I realized that wasn't enough. You're just putting off what needs to be done."

I wait for him to look at me. "And what's that?"

"Live. You have to live the life you want … look forward instead of back."

"And how long did it take before you were able to do that?" I ask, swallowing the lump in my throat.

"I'm still working on it. It's a constant search for happiness."

LISA DE JONG

I think long and hard before what I say what's on my mind. It's something I've wanted to say to him for a while. "Her death is not your fault, and it wasn't his either."

There's a long silence again. Maybe I overstepped my bounds, but I needed to say it.

"I don't want to argue," he finally says, "but that's something I'm still working through. My opinion might change down the road, but it's something I struggle with."

This is a point I'm not going to push. Alyssa was his sister. He knew her all her life, and I can't imagine what it was like when she took her own life. I can't imagine.

I pick the remnants of our lunch up and throw it in a nearby trashcan. When I get back to our table, I don't sit down, but I hold my hand out to Pierce instead. "Ready?"

His eyes widen. "Where are we going?"

I shrug. "You'll see."

We passed a playground on the way in. It reminded me of when I was a little girl. I used to swing for hours, dreaming of what the world had in store for me. It was a form of meditation; I always felt like the weight of the world was off me when I was done.

I pull him straight to that playground, finding two empty swings.

"You have got to be kidding me," he remarks, his hands on his hips.

Grinning, I say, "I played your game. It's time for you to play mine."

"I could fire you, you know."

"But you won't."

I sit on the swing, kicking my heels off in the sand. Pumping isn't easy with long legs and a pencil skirt, but the emotional benefit hasn't changed. "Aren't you going to join me?"

"You look a different kind of beautiful with that smile and the wind blowing through your hair. I might just stand here and watch."

"Pierce, if you don't get on that swing right now, I'm taking the next plane out of New York, and I'm leaving you to deal with Wade all by yourself."

21

He throws his hands in the air, showing mock fear. "I'm not scared of Wade, but I don't want you to leave so you win."

If I look ridiculous on the swing, he looks outright crazy. He does his best to get it going, and I can't help but laugh.

He smiles genuinely, lifting his legs in the air. "For the record, I didn't really think you would leave if I didn't do this. It just looked kind of fun."

"While we're on the record, that different kind of beautiful comes from within ... because you make me happy. I like how happy looks on you, too."

"Are you flirting with me, Ms. Fields?"

"Take it how you want," I laugh, pumping my legs faster until I'm a few feet higher than him.

For almost an hour, we play that game—trying to see who can go higher while reminiscing about our childhoods. For once, I'm just in the moment.

"I CAN'T BELIEVE I LET YOU talk me into stepping foot into Wade's conference room again."

The elevator door closes, lending me a few seconds to smooth my red pencil skirt and straighten my black blouse. I read in an article not long ago that said wearing red to a business meeting shows strength. Since a suit of armor would look ridiculous, this is all I got.

"Quit fidgeting," Pierce says, coming to stand a few inches in front of me. "If you looked any more beautiful today, he wouldn't hear a damn word you had to say."

My eyes cautiously float up to his. He's got that look again. "Stop doing that. Besides, now I have sand stuck to my legs, I smell like a French fry, and the sweat from our little park workout probably washed all my make-up away."

The corner of his mouth turns up. "Stop doing what?"

"Looking at me like that ... flirting."

He presses his hand to the elevator wall causing the sleeve of his suit to brush my cheek. "I don't know any other way to look at you, and I definitely don't understand how the truth got confused with flirting. Besides, I think you did a little flirting back at the park yourself. My memory isn't the best, but I do remember that; I practically framed it."

The scent of him. The closeness of him. The memories. It hits me all at once—a long lost desire pooling between my legs ... something I haven't felt in months. This could be so right ... could be. Without another thought, I lean into him until my chest is pressed to his. His warm breath hits my lips and then we collide. It lingers, neither one of us wanting to let go ... neither one of us moving. I'm lost. We could be on a deserted island. We could be on packed sidewalk with the whole world walking by. We're nothing but two lost souls found in a moment.

Just as he starts to press for more, the elevator dings, forcing us to slowly pull apart until I see into his eyes again. "We need to talk about this later," he says, leaning in just enough that I think he might kiss me again. Or maybe I just want to get lost again.

The elevator doors open, and his hand is wrapped around mine pulling me forward.

I want to kiss him more, but there's a little voice in my head telling me to stay away. Yet, the more time that passes, the more I wonder what is holding me back, and the guilt starts to wash away. Blake left me. It was his choice ... not mine.

Wade's conference room hasn't changed. The arrogant look on his face hasn't either. "It's nice to see you again," he remarks, eyes scanning the length of my body—from my sleeveless blouse to my fitted skirt, not stopping until they hit my black high heels. Pierce did the same thing when I walked on the plane earlier today; his stare just didn't leave a sick feeling in my stomach.

"Likewise," I answer, struggling to pull my lips into a smile. "I didn't think I'd be back."

Fingers curl against my back. "Behave," Pierce whispers behind me. I almost forgot that he's standing there. Chess only has two players after all.

"I knew you'd be back," Wade chides, holding his hand out to me as he steps closer. I take it, wrapping my fingers tightly around his, not because I want to feel his snaky skin, but because I want to show the power I possess. I'm not the same Lila I was when we last met. A metal shield around my heart keeps it from breaking or bending. It's left my mind to think without interruption, and I could care less if I offend this guy.

When I let go of his hand, Pierce still has hold of my shirt, keeping me from moving forward. "I see you're starting out with your regular pleasantries," Pierce remarks, his comments pointed at Wade this time.

Wade holds his hand out to Pierce. He accepts, and I'm finally free. "Oh, come on, Stanley. You should know how I am by now. Quit acting like anything I do surprises you."

Pierce laughs. "It doesn't but don't consider that a challenge."

Wade's eyes briefly meet mine then he smiles at Pierce. "This is strictly business. Who has time for surprises?"

"Let's get started then, shall we?"

I nod and make my way toward the expansive conference table, taking a seat on the opposite side of the table than I'd sat last time. Maybe it will bring good luck.

Not surprisingly, Pierce takes a seat right next to me, and Wade sits at the end of the table next to him.

"So, what's the plan for the next couple days?" Pierce asks, never one to mince words.

Wade unbuttons his suit jacket and leans back in his chair. "I figured you would be tired tonight so we'll start going over your ideas tomorrow and Wednesday. I want to show you the site and have you meet with some of the suppliers I've been using locally. And don't forget the get together I've arranged at my place tomorrow night. Cocktails. Appetizers. You know the drill."

Thank God for the little black dress I threw in my suitcase last minute.

"Lila and I would like to have some time in the space to talk and go over some final details before we present them tomorrow. Can we get in there tonight?"

Wade reaches into his suit pocket and slides a key card across the table. "That should get you in." His gaze drifts to me. "I'm excited to see what you've got planned. Pierce told me you took the reins on this one."

For the first time since we walked in, my hands sweat. Though my heart is guarded, my head controls my perfectionism, and unfortunately, that's never going to shut off. Clearing my throat, I say, "I did. I think you're going to like it, especially if you're tired of the ordinary."

He leans in, his elbows resting on the table. He's as close as he can get with Pierce between us. "That's why you're here."

"Good choice." Somewhere along the way, I learned to fake confidence, too.

"If you don't mind, I think we'll be going," Pierce interrupts our exchange. "We have some work to do yet tonight."

"Just work?" Wade asks, lifting a brow.

"Just work." Pierce stands. His shoulders are stiff, and I can tell that even though this hasn't been so bad, he'd rather be anywhere but here.

"Well, it was good seeing you again."

As Wade walks us out, his assistant hands us a carefully put together itinerary for the next few days. It's so thorough that I'm surprised it doesn't tell me when I'm going to get to use the ladies' room.

"Remind me again why I agreed to do this with him?" Pierce asks as we climb into our waiting car.

I stifle a laugh. He was so nonchalant about this before we left Chicago, but in reality, Wade crawls under his skin like a blood-sucking insect, eating away at him until he can no longer ignore it. "I think it had something to do with money. Lots of money."

"Next time, remind my forgetful ass that he's not worth it. I need something to drink. Would you like to join me?"

"Give me one reason why I should."

"Because I asked you to ... because I want you to."

I'm tempted to look over at him, but I can't. Not when I already feel his eyes burning into the side of my face. I know exactly how he's looking at me—the same way he does when we're alone. And, after what happened in the elevator earlier ... I just can't.

"Can I take a rain check?"

"No, but I'll compromise."

I chance a look in his direction. "A cup of coffee?"

He shakes his head. "That's not going to cut it tonight." He pauses, his deep green eyes staring into mine. "One drink in the hotel bar then if you want to go to your room, you can go."

"You're kind of pushy."

"And you're kind of beautiful."

I snort. "Kind of?" *Oh my God, I can't believe I just said that.*

The look I tried so hard to avoid minutes ago is there — eating away at my conscience resolve. "Lila, I don't think you can handle the weight of my thoughts. If you want to skip drinks, we could discuss them."

"Drinks sound good," I answer back quickly, rubbing my fingers together to control the nervous butterflies in my stomach.

He laughs.

The rest of the ride is quiet. The day is winding down as the city's business people make their way down packed sidewalks. We barely move, but as long as it's quiet, I could sit and stare at the view for hours.

But then my mind flashes to the past. It's been doing that a lot the last few months when it has nowhere else to go. I hate thinking about it. Even though some things were good, my mind has a way of focusing on the bad. Chicago wasn't an escape for me; it was just another stepping-stone in the journey of life. Love and hurt and everything in between — it just follows you wherever you go.

Warm fingers curl around my bare knee. I flinch, but then reality comes into focus again. "We're here."

We're at the same hotel we stayed at last time. Memories emerge, but I bury them. *This time is different.*

"Do you always stay at the same place?" I ask, chewing on my lower lip.

The driver pulls his door open, but his eyes remain on me. "I've only had one bad experience here."

His eyes linger. Mine are stuck to them. "Why would you want to come back?"

"Because I think everyone deserves a second chance." With that, he slides out of the seat, holding his hand out to me. I take it, leaving our fingers entwined as we walk up the sidewalk into the hotel I fell in love with last winter. Nothing

27

about it has changed except for the way I feel once inside. There's no shock and awe ... just memories.

Pierce uses my hand to pull me to his side. "Do you need to change, or should I have someone bring our bags up?"

"It's just one drink, Pierce. I think I can handle it in this."

He turns, acknowledging the older gentleman who's handling our bags. "Can you make sure those make it up to our rooms? The red one belongs to Ms. Fields, and the other is mine."

"Sure thing, Mr. Stanley. Anything else I can do for you?"

"No, and thank you," he says, passing the man a couple twenties he had rolled between his fingers.

He guides me to the right where a dimly lit restaurant sits, piano music faintly echoing through the doorway. It's the same one we had dinner in the last time we were in town. "Would you rather sit at the bar or get a table?"

"Bar," I answer without hesitation. If we do everything the opposite of how we did it last time, the results should be different, right?

We take the last two seats at the bar, each ordering a glass of red wine. Pierce defies my wish for drinks only, ordering a caprese salad for us to share.

"I agreed to a drink, Pierce."

His lips curl. It's so hard to stay mad at him when he does that. "What kind of guy would I be if I gave you alcohol, but didn't feed you?"

"Let me think ... one who stuck to his word."

"Nope," he says, holding a fresh piece of mozzarella close to his lips. "An asshole."

I follow his lead, taking a bite of tomato and cheese all at once. "I didn't realize how many assholes I'd met in my life until you just defined them for me."

"If I had it my way, you'd never have to deal with another."

There he goes again, laying it on thick. I put my wine glass to my lips, remembering what he did to them earlier. One side of my brain is telling me it would be okay. He'd never hurt me like Blake, not intentionally. But the other side—the one I've chosen to listen to—is telling me he could tear down the cage I've put around my heart.

Love feels so good but hurts so bad. If I didn't think I could love him, the only question would be his room or mine.

Pierce is worth more than one night.

"Weren't we supposed to go check out the hotel building tonight?" I ask, desperately trying to change the subject.

"Shit," Pierce mutters under his breath. "If we can't do it tonight, I'm afraid we won't get to without Wade around, and you know how that goes."

"Do we have time yet tonight?" I ask, enjoying yet another bite of salad.

He looks at his watch and signals to the bartender. "It's only a couple blocks from here. We can walk."

I look down at my four-inch heels and shrug. I've put miles on them before.

After charging our drinks to his room, he grabs my hand again, and we start down the quiet street. The sun is setting over the horizon, and I wonder what it would look like if we were near the ocean right now. I've always wanted to see the sun set over the ocean.

"Have you ever watched the sunset over the ocean?" I blurt as we cross one of the many busy streets.

"I've seen it a few times. Why do you ask?"

I shrug, trying to keep pace with him. "I've only seen it in pictures. I've always wondered if it looks even better in person."

He stops suddenly, coming to stand in front of me. "You've never seen the sunset over the ocean?" he asks.

I shake my head, feeling slightly embarrassed. I'm not a world traveler, and just being in New York is a big deal to me.

The corner of his mouth turns up, and his eyes glimmer the way a little boy's would if he were about to create mischief. "We're not going to worry about the 5th Avenue project tonight."

"But—" Before I can continue, he's on the curb signaling an available cab down the street.

"We can run there tomorrow, but I have other ideas for us tonight."

LOVE UNSPOKEN

I slip into the waiting cab, watching Pierce follow. I'd argue, but I learned a long time ago that it doesn't get you far with Pierce Stanley.

I sit quietly, watching parts of New York I've never seen go by. Maybe when this project is over, I can come visit with the sole intention of exploring—trying different restaurants, walking through museums, seeing all the different neighborhoods. From the little bits of it I've seen, New York is full of inspiration.

Pierce nudges my shoulder. "We're here."

I glance over at his smiling, handsome face. The way he is with me ... the way he's always trying to make me happy, it's not something I've experienced before.

He holds his hand out to me. "We need to hurry, or we're going to miss it."

I slide out of the seat behind him getting my first glimpse of the ocean. "Where are we?" I ask, mouth gaping.

"Chelsea Pier."

We walk hand in hand to the end of the pier. We're not the only ones here, but we might as well be because the silence lends to the sounds of nature. With a slight breeze, small waves hit against the pier. A few white pelicans fly overhead while a pod of them float on the water right off the deck. With the sky glowing from a deep purple to orange, they look even more beautiful.

Once we reach the end of the pier, I let go of Pierce's hand to grip the railing. The wind blows against my skin as I close my eyes, breathing in the scent of the ocean. There are places—moments—that you just wish you could stay in forever.

Everything is perfect ... and nothing else matters.

Pierce wraps his arms around my waist, momentarily resting his chin on my shoulder. "Is this what you had in mind?"

"This is the way life should always be," I mutter, my eyes locked on a small sailboat coming into the harbor.

"I agree," he whispers, pressing his lips to my cheek. "It's definitely better than work."

"This would top just about anything," I answer honestly.

His hands fold over my stomach, pulling me even closer. "Is this okay?"

30

LISA DE JONG

I nod. There's nothing I would change about this moment. Not a thing.

And we stay like that until the sun seemingly disappears into the ocean, slowly painting black where the purple and orange once lit the sky.

"That was one of the most beautiful things I've ever witnessed," I say, covering his hands with mine.

"I'm glad I was able to give it to you," he says quietly, lips pressed against my hair. "About earlier—in the elevator— that wasn't just a moment. I want to kiss you every time I look at you. I've been patient, Lila. I've been waiting for your heart to mend. There's no one else, and I'll hold on to the idea of us unless you tell me it's never going to be."

His words touch me in a place I thought had become untouchable.

He's flowers just because.

He's candles and rose petals.

He's the meaningful diamond and a house in the burbs.

He's a perfect now and forever after.

"I want us," I say, leaning my head back against his shoulder. "I just need it to happen slowly ... naturally. Like this ... this is perfect."

"I agree."

We stay just like this for a while. Maybe it's the surroundings or maybe it's being locked in his arms, snuggled against his strong body, but I feel weightless for the first time in a long time.

"As much as I don't want to, we should probably get going," he says. "It's getting late, and we have a big day tomorrow."

"We can't just tell Wade to screw off and explore the rest of the city?" I ask, only half joking.

"You have no idea how much I'd love to tell that asshole to fuck off, but we made it this far. Might as well show him what you got because you really did knock it out of the park."

I laugh nervously, only reminded of what's to come. "You don't have to lie to make friends, Stanley."

31

He loosens his grip around my waist, spinning me in his arms. "I don't need friends, Ms. Fields. I really only need you."

I open my mouth to respond, but he cuts me off. "I'm moving too fast," he says, brushing my hair away from my eyes. "I'll stop."

"Thank you for this."

He winks. "It's just the beginning."

ON THE WAY BACK TO THE HOTEL, he holds me close in the back of the cab, rubbing the backs of his fingers up and down my arm. His touch lulls me until my cheek rests against his chest. I watch the lights go by until the cab comes to a stop in front of the hotel.

"Can you walk?" he asks, still brushing his fingers against my skin.

"I'm just tired. I'll be fine."

He wraps his arm tightly around me as we make our way inside the hotel, not letting go until we're standing in front of the door to my room.

"Lila," he whispers so close I feel his warm breath against my lips. That little touch is all it takes before I'm leaning into him, curling his crisp, white shirt between my fingers. Without another thought, I stand on my tiptoes and press my lips to his. It's just a touch—a soft, lingering, sweet touch—but then his strong arms wrap around me, and he pushes for something more.

His teeth tug at my lower lip then he presses me tightly against him—hips, heart, lips—and his tongue begs for entry. It feels like forever since I've been kissed like this, and desire grants him a key.

I remember everything about Pierce and how we got here. There's something about a man who can kiss a woman and tell her everything he's feeling at the same time.

Pierce leaves nothing unsaid.

Seconds...minutes...hours could have gone by with us locked in the same place. For the first time in a long time, I feel alive—like there might be something left in this life besides sadness and loneliness.

My lips are numb by the time he finally pulls away. My fingers instinctively trace where his mouth was. Powerful yet sweet. Firm yet tender. Everything he is. It takes everything I have in me to not pull him in for another.

His thumb comes up, tracing a line under my lower lip. "That was the best night I've had in a while," he whispers, chest heaving up and down.

"That was the best anything I've had in a while."

"If you'd let me, I'd make every moment feel just like that one."

"Pierce—"

His finger moves up, pressing against my lips. "Don't consider it an invitation. Consider it a reminder."

I nod, enjoying the feel of his fingers against my sensitive skin. "You haven't been forgotten."

"Good," he says, the corner of his mouth curling up. "We should get to bed. I have a feeling Wade is going to keep us busy tomorrow."

"I can hardly wait."

"Your sarcasm is one of the things I like about you. I never know what is going to come out of that mouth of yours, yet I expect something."

"Can you guess what I'm going to say now?" I ask staring up into his mischievous eyes.

"No, but I know I want to hear it."

I lift up on my tiptoes and kiss him softly. It wasn't meant to linger, but it does. I feel stuck to him and don't want to let go. I pull away hesitantly. "Good night."

Turning my back to him, I fumble with my key card. It's not a hard task by any means but I can feel his eyes burning into my back.

LISA DE JONG

"Do you need help with that?"

A shiver runs down my back as his warm breath hits my neck. "I'd be okay if you weren't staring at me."

"Here," he says, slipping the key out from between my fingers.

He unlocks the door easily, holding it open for me to go inside. When the door clicks shut, he's standing in my room, staring at me.

"What are you doing?" I ask, startled.

He leans back, resting the sole of his expensive shoe against the wall. "You don't really want to sleep alone in this big room do you?"

"Pierce—"

He shakes his head. "Let me hold you. Nothing else."

Words want to fall from my lips, but I consider them carefully. There have been way too many forks in the road for me lately, and I'm getting so tired of having to pick my way. "Can I trust you?" I finally ask, feeling my heart pound against my chest.

What he's offering could be the start of something perfect, or it could just be the next in a line of bad decisions I've made.

Without words, he walks to me, cupping my face in his cool hands. I can do nothing but look at him. He's gorgeous and successful—a dream for most women.

But, is he my dream?

He kisses me tenderly on the forehead then stares down into my eyes. "I think you should let me stay and find out."

I nod, mostly because I'm not ready for the night to end. Because I do trust him. Because he's never been anything other than good to me. And mostly because I want him to stay.

"Go get changed for bed and do whatever it is you do. I'm going to run across the hall and grab a few things."

"Here," I say, handing him a key. "I want you to trust me, too."

He smiles, his lips curling up in that way that gets me every time. A woman could fall in love with that smile, shower in it forever, and he'd never have to say a word.

35

My heart beats rapidly as I fumble through my suitcase looking for pajamas. The silk camisole I usually wear during the summer months doesn't feel right, and it's literally all I brought for bed. Pierce might get the wrong idea if I go there.

After a couple minutes of staring at the pile of clothes I'd brought with only a business trip in mind, I decide on a pair of black cotton running shorts and a tank top that says "Catch Me If You Can" which I'd planned on wearing for my morning workout. Not that I ever crawl out of bed early enough to make that happen.

There's a knock at the door just as I finish brushing my teeth. *Here goes nothing,* I think to myself after one last look in the mirror. *It's time, Lila. It's time to let him go.*

When I see him standing outside the bathroom door, I'm startled at first, but then I remember the key I handed him, and all the fear washes away. His hair is mussed up, probably from pulling his clothes off. My eyes wander down, passing by the smile I'd just admired minutes ago to his muscular chest. No shirt. *Fuck me.*

My gaze passes the sculpture I probably admired a little too long down to his black athletic shorts. Great minds think alike, I guess.

"Are we going to stand here all night or are you going to let me take you to bed?" he asks, his voice sounding tired.

I find his eyes, and my voice at the same time. "I'm too tired to stand here so I guess we'll have to go with the second option."

He grins. "Good."

Dear God, help me.

Without warning, he lifts me into his strong arms and starts toward the bed.

"What are you doing?" I ask, feeling my nerves kick into overtime again.

"I read your shirt and decided to accept the challenge."

He sits me on the edge of the bed and pulls the covers back. "If we were running—like really running—you wouldn't be able to catch me."

"Really?" he asks, lifting a brow. I bet he runs, and I bet he does it often.

He motions for me to crawl under the covers. I continue my meaningless chatter. "Yeah, I run a few times a year at least. Usually when I'm pissed off and need time to think."

I slowly make my way toward the pillows. "I went out for cross country in high school and didn't make it past week one. It wasn't that I couldn't do it, I just didn't like to be told to run and where and how long. But if I really want to, I can run. I can run really fast. Once — "

"Lila," Pierce interrupts, "Tonight, I'm going to lie in this bed next to you. I'm going to wrap my arms as tightly around you as I can without smothering you. I may cover your legs with mine, and I may bury my nose in your scented hair just to remind myself who I'm with if I wake up in the middle of the night and think this is just another dream. If you'd like, I'll even give you another goodnight kiss, but Lila, we're not going past that. I want to take this slow. I want to know that you're with me every step of the way. Are we clear?"

I nod, speechless. He always seems to know exactly what to say even when I don't know what it is I need to hear. He's the period to my sentence, and sometimes I can't believe that he wants anything to do with me after what I put him through.

As I lay my cheek on the pillow, I watch him climb in next to me, taking a second to push the button that turns the lamp off. Only the city lights illuminate the room now. We lie facing each other. No words, just eyes reading the other's thoughts. The position makes it impossible to think of anything but this. We might as well be in our own little world.

I think we are.

"What are you thinking about?" he whispers, gently caressing my jaw line.

"You. It's hard to consider anything else. What about you? What are you thinking about?"

His eyes close briefly, and when he opens them, they speak of something different — hope, desire, hesitancy — it's all there. "Have you ever dreamt of something knowing it would never happen?"

I pause, thinking back to things I probably shouldn't be thinking about right now. After Blake left, I dreamt for days that he'd come back. I prayed for it, but he never did. And then there's the whole idea of happily ever after … I think that's all a dream now too. The whole exercise of thinking makes me feel like the Lila who has existed the last several months so I push it all away. "Of course," I whisper.

"Have any of them come true?"

I shake my head. "No."

His fingers move up, tracing subtle lines across my cheek to my lips. "Mine is right now. It's amazing and scary at the same time."

"Why is it scary?"

He replaces his fingertips with his mouth, giving me a kiss that feels like a gust of air against my lips. He pulls away just enough to speak. "Because I'm afraid I'm going to wake up tomorrow morning, and it's all going to be a dream again."

The pit that's been lodged in my stomach since Blake left puts an end to its short-lived vacation. I'm at a point where I can't make promises to myself, let alone someone else.

"I'm incapable of commitment right now, Pierce."

"Can you promise me a chance?"

"I wouldn't be here right now if I couldn't," I answer honestly.

His warm lips brush my forehead. "That's all I need."

I run the backs of my fingers along his bare shoulder. "We should get some sleep. I don't want you to strangle Wade tomorrow."

He chuckles, kissing my forehead yet again. "Now that I know I have a chance with you, I'm not going to do anything that might land me in prison. It would be better to hire someone else to do it after we leave town."

Now, it's my turn to laugh. He's obviously put a lot of thought into this. "Okay, it's obviously past your bedtime, Mr. Stanley. You're starting to scare me."

"Can I kiss you once more?"

"Please," I say without hesitation.

It happens like a kiss in the movies the director wants you to savor. He closes the distance between us slowly, increasing the anticipation … increasing my desire. His breath hits my lips first then it finally happens—his mouth presses to mine. There's no movement. There's no attempt to reach deeper.

It's everything. I feel it in places I didn't think were capable of being touched anymore. He's answering a prayer I didn't even know existed.

And when I'm completely lost in it, he pulls away. It's as if I lost the covers on a cold winter morning.

I want him back.

"Turn around," he instructs, laying his head back on the pillow.

I comply without question, my trust fully gained by the magic of a kiss.

His arm wraps tightly around my stomach, pulling me into his warm body. "Goodnight, Lila."

"Goodnight," I whisper, feeling myself drifting. Sleep hasn't been this easy since ... well, since *he* left.

AS I START TO WAKE, I feel a warm body curled against mine — one arm firmly wrapped around my stomach and another along the top of my head. I smell Pierce's cologne, and the dream I'd thought I had becomes real. All the memories of last night come flooding back, and a smile pulls on my lips.

I slept with Pierce. Literally just slept. The bed shifts behind me, his arm pulling me in closer. "How did you sleep?" he asks, nuzzling my hair.

"Great. I don't think I moved an inch."

"You make these little sounds when you sleep," he says softly, still nuzzling.

"Like what?" I ask, keeping my eyes closed in an effort to stay in the moment.

His warm breath brushes against my ear. "You *mmm* in your sleep. It's soft and sweet like the purr of a kitten," he whispers. The way his words hit me he might as well be between my legs because I feel him there.

"Is that it?" I ask, rubbing my thighs together.

His hand slowly moves from my stomach to the outside of my thigh. "I think so. It lulled me back to sleep." He reaches mid-thigh then moves his hand back up.

"Pierce," I breathe. Control is something a woman thinks she has until a man touches her, especially in the morning when they are laying skin to skin with nothing else in the world to distract them. Too bad my fucking heart doesn't control my libido.

"I can't do this with you now. It has to be the right time, or it will never be right." He's struggling to hold his voice steady. If I wanted him, he'd be mine.

His hand slips down again. "Touch me," I say, all remaining strings of control slipping from between my fingers.

His fingers still, but I hear him breathing. I hear his struggle even without words. "I can't," he whispers brushing his lips against my neck.

"Please. I wouldn't ask if I wasn't ready."

Another pause then his fingers find my bare stomach, tracing circles around my belly button.

"Please," I whisper again, begging.

His fingers curl against my skin. He's fighting—his heart beating against my back, his breathing growing increasingly heavier. I wiggle against him, trying to make his decision easier. Desire wins out when his hand dips beneath the band of my shorts and panties all at once.

"Is this what you want?" he asks, trailing a delicious line of kisses down my neck and shoulder.

I moan, his fingertips circling my sensitive skin.

It's the only answer he needs before he presses deeper ... harder. I've starved myself of lust over the last several months—to the point where I didn't know what I was missing—and now I could orgasm all day and night and not feel as if I've had enough.

He shifts, suddenly, sending me on my back without his strong body to hold me steady. With the light shining through the curtains, he stares down at me and sees everything. There's too much there I'd rather he not unravel ... so much I don't want him to know.

Closing my eyes, I rest my cheek against the soft pillow much like I'd been a couple minutes ago.

His hand stills. My eyes shoot open. He looks down at me, irritation written all over his face in simple English. "Look at me when I'm touching you. I don't want there to be any confusion about who's doing this to you ... who's making you feel this way."

I read between his words. He doesn't want me thinking about Blake, and I'm not, but I'm not thinking about him either. I'm selfish, and he knows it.

I nod hesitantly, staring up into his bright eyes. Over the last several months, I've developed a deep admiration for Pierce. I know what he can do—how he could be with me—and I could easily fall much deeper.

I could love him.

I don't want to love him ... I don't want to love anyone.

Yet, I need this. I need him.

He could make me love him.

Our eyes hold as he presses one finger inside me then another. Everything is so intense—what I feel emotionally ... physically. I can't take it, but I can't stop it either. Gripping each side of his face, I pull him down for a kiss. He's a master at that too, gently brushing his lips to mine then pressing his tongue between them as his fingers push in further.

I feel it ... the heavenly tingle that occurs right before I fall apart. It's my favorite part—the beautifully painful ache that sweeps my body before I climax. Pierce makes it almost impossible, though. I fight it, but he wins. I come hard around his fingers, back arching to control the trembles that take over the rest of my body. Instead of breaking the kiss, he swallows my screams.

It's amazing. It fills a void I didn't realize I had, but I could still go again ... and again ... and again. He's that good.

He breaks the kiss, looking down at me while his fingers are still deep within me. He's putting the puzzle pieces together again, and I don't like it.

He leans in for a kiss but stops just short. "You've never looked more beautiful than you do right now. Sensuality stripped you bare, and all I see is you." He kisses the corner of my mouth then whispers, "Just you."

His fingers work again. The second orgasm rolls through my body soon after followed by a third.

"Pierce," I gasp, trying to catch my breath. "We can't do this anymore, or I'm not going to be able to walk today."

The corner of his mouth turns up. "It's worth it though, isn't it? I'd carry you on my back just to do this a million times over."

God, help me.

"How about you?" I ask, turning to my side to get a better look at him. He looks just as satisfied as I feel, and I barely touched him.

The fact that his fingers are still buried inside me doesn't go unnoticed.

"We should probably get ready for work."

"Pierce—"

"Lila, the first time I come with you, I want to come inside of you. I control your pleasure, and I control mine."

"It doesn't seem fair."

His fingers slip out of me as his hand slowly slides back up to my stomach, trailing the evidence of my desire along the way. "Watching you, being with you like this … it's enough for me. More than enough, actually."

In defiance, I brush my hand against his smooth stomach then let it slip further until my fingers are wrapped around his impressive bulge. His hand wraps around my wrist, pulling my fingers away. "I'm glad you follow directions a little better than this at the office, or we'd have a big problem."

"You have a big problem, Mr. Stanley. A very big problem." *In fact, it's the biggest problem I've ever come across, and I can't help but wonder how it would feel inside me.*

He smiles. "If I play my cards right, I'll have a resolution soon enough."

Is he right? I don't know if I want him to be. I'm walking a dangerous line, not that I haven't done this before a time or two.

"I slept with him last night," I tell Mallory as soon as she picks up her phone.

"With who? With Pierce?"

"Yes," I reply, pacing back and forth across my room. Pierce left a couple minutes ago to shower and get dressed. I finally feel as if I can breathe again.

Long pause. Damn her ... she's giving me too much time to think.

"Are you there?" I ask, needing something to fill the silence.

"I wish you hadn't done that, Lila. You're not ready for this ... you're not ready to put your heart on the line again."

I shake my head, knowing full well that she can't see me. "It's not like that. I mean ... we didn't..." I pause, trying to grab hold of my thoughts. "I meant we slept together in the same bed."

"That's it?"

"And he gave me three orgasms, but not in the way you think."

She sighs, quiet once again. "Promise me something."

"What?"

"Don't. Not in New York. I don't want you getting hurt again."

"I won't do anything my heart won't allow."

"Damnit, Lila. Just listen to me on this one. Besides, your heart is broken which makes it an unreliable instrument."

She's right, yet she's so wrong. The fractures haven't healed. The bruises are still visible by those who know me. But the scars will always remain. The marks Derek made on my heart still show through from time to time. Blake was in my life for a short time, but he did the most damage; nothing will ever quite be the same, but that doesn't mean life can't be good. Besides, she's one of the people who have been encouraging me to move on.

"I need this," I finally answer back. It's true.

"Just promise me something, Lila."

"What?" I ask, pulling a dress from my closet.

"Don't take it any further this week. It's too new, and I don't want to see you jump into another relationship. You need to walk slowly this time."

I blow my bangs away from my face, looking to the clock. *I really need to get going.* "I will try really hard not to have sex with Pierce this week. Is that what you want to hear?"

"I'm so convinced," she answers back, sarcastically.

"Good because I really need to get in the shower."

"You're difficult."

I laugh, untying my robe with my free hand. "But you still love me."

"Behave, Lila."

"Bye, Mallory."

Before she can get another word in, I end the call and step into the steamy shower, letting the hot beads of water hit my skin. I haven't felt this alive in months—this aware. Pierce woke me up in more ways than one.

"Jesus Christ, Lila. Are you trying to bring attention to yourself or your designs?" Pierce asks when I meet him in the lobby.

"What?" I ask, throwing my arms up.

He motions the length of my body. "That dress. Are you trying to distract Wade or drive me crazy?"

I glance down at my form-fitting red pencil dress and four inch red pumps. Power was all I had on my mind this morning. "Is it too much red?" I tease, tucking a long curl behind my ear.

He steps close, placing his hand on my lower back to pull me into his body. I feel exactly like I did just over an hour ago when we were lying in my bed, and he wouldn't have to do much to get this dress off me so we could do it all over again. "That dress wraps around you the way I want to be wrapped around you, and if the stares in this lobby are any indication, it's not a dream I'm alone in."

Leaning in closer, I whisper in his ear, "But you're the only guy in the room who really knows what's under this dress."

He hardens against my stomach. I want to feel that so badly. I want him to erase some of the marks that have been left behind, to wash away my bad memories.

"Lila," he breathes, holding me even tighter.

I stare up into his bright eyes. "Yes?"

"There's going to be consequences for this later."

I bite my lip. He twitches. "I'm up for the challenge."

A throat clears behind us, breaking the stare but not the physical contact. "Mr. Stanley, your car is waiting."

"Just wait outside. I need ten more seconds with Ms. Fields here."

"As you wish," he answers before disappearing.

"Can we go now?" I ask when the driver is out of earshot.

He shakes his head, letting go of me to adjust his suit. "You're going to be the death of me."

And, you're going to be the life of me, I think as we make our way to the car.

PIERCE WAS RIGHT. Wade's eyes stayed on my legs through the entire meeting this morning. He made sure to get a seat right next to me during lunch with a small group of investors, and now as we walk through the hotel building for the first time, I can't help but notice his gaze fixed on my backside every time I turn to ask a question.

For me, a man will never be attractive if he tries to undress me before he woos me. He has zero chance at winning me over, and I'll never see him as anything but a creep.

"Can I use that ladder?" I ask, wanting to get a look at the lobby from a different angle—one that a person might have coming down the soon-to-be glass staircase.

"Of course," Wade says. "Let me help you. I don't want you to fall in those heels."

Pierce practically growls at him; it's not the first time today. "I've got her," he says, standing behind me. He knows by now that my interest in Wade is below zero, but he's also well aware that Wade's intentions aren't good.

The space is huge with an industrial feel—a blank canvas really. "I think the design plan is perfect for the space. I can't wait for you to see it," I say, carefully climbing back down.

"I'm excited for tomorrow." Wade smiles, hands tucked in his pockets.

I smile back, feeling an interesting mix of excited and nervous. "Me too."

"So, what time can I expect you at my place tonight?" he asks, eyes dancing between me and Pierce. It's been such a long day, I almost forgot about the little get together Wade planned.

"We have a few things we need to do beforehand, so we'll plan on nine o'clock."

"Perfect," Wade answers, walking us out to the street.

I wonder what we could possibly have to do, but Pierce knows way more than I do, so I just go with it.

"Do you want a ride?" Wade asks, pointing to his black Escalade. At lunch, we went three blocks from his office, yet he still insisted on taking the car.

Pierce shakes his head. "We're staying just down the street. We'll catch you later."

After Wade is safely tucked away in his oversized ride, I turn my attention back to Pierce. "What do we have to do before the event?"

"That dress was a bad choice. A really bad choice."

"That doesn't answer my question. What do we have left to do?"

He wraps his arm around my waist, pulling me close as we walk down the street. "If you'll let me, I'd love to take that dress off you. What happens after that is up to you."

My heart flutters. A tingly sensation runs down my spine. Watching Pierce talk business in his charcoal gray suit wasn't easy for me today either. Every time his hand touched me, I thought of this morning, and when he'd lift his hand to make a point, all I could think of was what those fingers can do.

He may think I'm the mouse, and he's the cat, but I think it may be the other way around.

We walk quickly back to the hotel, past the bellboy, straight to the elevator. It seems like forever before it opens, and when it finally does, we're the only ones inside.

Sometimes I think before I act. Sometimes I don't. I'm not sure my head's all in the game, but every other part of my body is.

As soon as the door closes, I slip my fingers in his waistband, pulling him to me. He stares down at me, eyes hooded, and I can't stop. I don't want to stop.

"Are you taking my dress off in your room or mine?" I ask. He said we were going to move at my pace, so I'm moving us right along. Might as well get a speeding ticket; it's been a while since I let myself have a little fun.

"Mine," he answers before pressing his lips to mine. His kiss is punishing—meant to leave me wanting more. I let go of his slacks, running my fingers over his impressive bulge. He moans against my lips just as the elevator opens.

"Just a second," he says, pulling me in front of him as we walk down the hallway. "You have no idea what you're doing to me, Lila. No idea."

I think I do because he's doing it to me, too.

He splays one hand over my stomach and uses the other to unlock his door. As soon as we cross that threshold, there's no going back.

I have a second of control left before I lose it all.

All I've ever wanted is for a man to make me feel this way, but it's scary, too. I'm opening myself up again. Time heals all wounds, or that's what they say. Time might make them better—might ease the pain—but it can't protect you from new cuts or hide old scars.

I enter his room, making my choice. My back is pressed against the wall. He uses his strength to lift me as he stares down into my eyes. So fierce ... so beautiful. He slips my left heel off then right, trailing a line of kisses down my throat.

I've been starved of affection, but he's given me permission to lust again.

I thought this would feel wrong, but it feels so right.

I've held my breath for too long, and it feels so good to breathe again.

He holds me securely in his arms, carrying me to the oversized king bed. I bury my head in the crook of his neck, relishing in his masculine scent. He's amazing in every way. Every. Freaking. Way. He sets me down, using his long fingers to pull my zipper to my lower back. One sleeve falls down my arm then the other, leaving me standing in nothing but my white lace panty set.

His finger lifts my chin until my eyes are even with his. "You're stunning."

He kisses one cheek then the other. "Sometimes, I have to ask myself if you're even real."

Then his lips fall on mine — soft and tender. "And, now I know you are."

His words wrap around my heart, squeezing tightly. He could break me, but he's worth the risk.

I fumble with the button on his pants as he kisses me deeply. My lips are numb by the time I have him stripped to his black briefs. Our lips part, eyes meeting. He grabs my face in his hands. "Promise me this is real."

"This is real," I whisper.

My bra falls to the floor.

"And you're not running?"

I shake my head. "I'm not going anywhere."

I'm lying on the bed with him between my legs. He trails a hot path of kisses around my belly button to my breasts, sucking and nibbling until I want to scream for him to be inside me.

"Pierce," I moan, his lips pressed against my neck, slowly working their way up to mine.

He looks down at me, tracing a line around my lips with his fingertips. "The wait," he whispers, trailing his finger between my breasts, around my belly button then between my legs. He circles once then slides his hand back up to my stomach. "The wait makes it even better."

My breath hitches as he sits back on his heels. I can't hold the weight of his stare, not with the day's light shining through the curtain. Closing my eyes, I hear the sound of paper ripping. For the first time since we entered the room, I feel nerves creeping up. If left for too long, they would suffocate me.

"Look at me."

Opening my eyes again, I see Pierce. All the doubt melts away as I watch him slip my panties off.

I feel the realness. The connection. Even if this isn't forever, it won't be a regret. I want this … I want every part of him.

He kisses me tenderly, easing my nerves as he enters me. He does it slowly all the while keeping his lips on mine. He fills me completely—body and heart. Over and over.

"Amazing," he says as he picks up pace. "You're absolutely amazing."

I wrap my legs around him, creating even more friction. He pushes in quickly then pulls out slowly—not all the way but enough for me to crave more.

"Oh my God," I pant as the first orgasm hits.

"Jesus," he groans as I pulse around him.

He pulls my nipple between his teeth. I whimper. He thrusts into me harder. My fingers tangle in his hair, pulling at it until his mouth is back on mine.

Pierce is desire, but he could be love. I feel him everywhere—places I haven't been touched in a while.

His lips suddenly halt as he pushes inside me one last time, whispering my name over and over again. And for several minutes, we stay like that, our heavy breaths mixing.

My mind wants to wander off to the last time someone touched me like this, but I focus on the feel of his skin against mine—his heart beating against mine. Making comparisons between what I can and can't have would be worthless.

"Pinch me," Pierce says, breaking through my thoughts. His voice is huskier than usual.

"What?"

"Pinch me."

And, I do … on his bare ass.

"So, I wasn't dreaming," he mumbles, lying his head on my chest.

"I hope not," I say softly, curling his hair around my fingers. It's nice just to lay like this with the comfort of a man's warm skin. "Do we have to go to that party tonight? I'd much rather lay here with you."

He rests his chin on my chest, staring at me. "If you put another dress on, we'll have something to look forward to later."

All I can do is grin. There's no reason to worry about the past when what I have now is pretty sweet.

Those *things* we had to take care of before Wade's get together ended up being sex, a short nap, and showers. I can't complain.

My phone rings just as I'm about to head back over to Pierce's room.

"Hi," I answer, using my free hand to slip my black heels on.

"Hi. What are you up to?" Mallory asks. "You sound out of breath."

"Just getting ready to go to an event for all the people working on the New York project."

"Oh, God. I need to tell you something."

"Why do I have a feeling this isn't going to be good?" I ask, holding my clutch as tightly as possible.

I can practically hear her pacing on the other end of the phone. "The guy you're working with—Wade I think it is—he called Blake for the same project." There's a long pause ... too long.

"And?" I ask, my voice practically shaking.

"He accepted," she whispers.

"I can't ... I haven't. Shit."

"There's more," she interjects before I get too far in my ramblings. "I just talked to him. He's going to an event tonight, too. He didn't say where, but—"

"It doesn't matter," I finally say, looking over at the digital alarm clock. "There's going to be a lot of people there. I probably won't even see him." *I don't believe a word I'm saying, but it makes me feel better.*

"I just thought you should know."

"Thank you," I answer quietly, suddenly searching for any reason not to go. This day has been so perfect. Why does my perfect always get ruined? "Can I ask you one thing?"

"Of course."

"Why did he come back now? After all this time, why now?" I ask.

"Ask him. He didn't tell me, but I think we both know why he's back."

With no more time to waste, we say a quick goodbye. I was sort of looking forward to tonight, and now I can't wait for it to be over with. The timing of it all couldn't be worse. After debating telling Pierce, I decide not to because, knowing Blake, he won't even show up tonight. Or, if he does, we won't see him.

At 8:33, I open my door to let Pierce know I'm ready only to find him standing in the hallway with his back against his door. He looks edible in a black suit and tie. He's all I've thought about the last hour with exception to the last few minutes. Seeing him now brings him back to the forefront.

"Ready?" I ask, grinning big to mask my nerves.

His lips part as he starts toward me, wrapping his arm around me to pull me to his chest. "Maybe we should skip the party. I can think of something else I'd rather be doing."

He could convince me with a kiss.

"I already offered that, remember? Besides, we can have the best of both worlds. Let's go have a drink or two, and then we can come back, and you can do what you said you were going to do." *I need to know if what Mallory said is true,* I think to myself. My affections lie with Pierce, but Blake has my curiosity

He grins. *Fuck me.* "I'll be thinking about it the whole time we're there. Remember that when I'm staring at you."

I swallow hard. Just thinking about it makes me want to push him into my room, but this is business. Business and pleasure can't be mixed, but they can be stacked. "One hour. We'll stay one hour then come back here."

"What are we waiting for then?" he asks, grabbing my hand. "The quicker we get there, the quicker we get back here."

By the time we step outside to climb in the waiting car, it's dark outside. This is when I love New York the most—seeing the city lights.

As the car pulls away from the curb, Pierce's hand grips my thigh. The sleeveless black cocktail dress I'm wearing leaves him lots of room to explore, and he does—his fingertips tracing circles on my inner thighs.

For once, I close my eyes to the passing lights. It's nice to have someone who helps you forget. There's a lot I'd like to forget right now. "How long is the ride?" I ask, resting my hand on his knee.

"Just a few more blocks."

I run my hand up his thigh—all the way—until I feel just how much he's affected by the simple touches between us. "That's too bad."

He leans in, whispering against my ear, "One hour, Ms. Fields."

He presses his fingers between my legs. My breath hitches. I look up to see if the driver is watching, but he isn't.

"One hour," he repeats before pulling his hand away.

The car pulls up in front of a well-appointed brick building on Park Avenue. I wouldn't be surprised if Wade owned the whole damn thing.

My knees are weak as I step onto the sidewalk, probably a mix of Pierce and needing to eat and who I might see once we're inside. I hope Mallory is wrong because if she isn't, I have no idea what I'm going to do. "These things make me kind of nervous," I admit.

"Stay close to me, okay?"

I nod, letting him lead the way to Wade's top floor penthouse.

WE'VE BEEN HERE FOR ten minutes, and I already want to evacuate. It's a room full of people I don't know ... people who I feel are better than me. I'm a frog on a Lillie pad while everyone else in the room owns a pond.

When we first stepped inside, I scanned the room for any sign of him and was relieved that he was nowhere in sight. It wouldn't be unlike him to not show for something like this.

I smile, walking through the room with Pierce as others greet him.

"Stanley, I haven't seen you in ages. Where have you been?" It's the fourth person who has stopped him since we walked in. I haven't even made it to the appetizers yet.

He squeezes my hand. "I've been working on a few projects in the Midwest. You?"

"I just got back from Paris. Did a renovation on a nineteenth century."

"That's exciting," Pierce states. I've learned the differences in his tone when he does and does not like someone; this is someone he'd rather pass by. "Royce, I'd like you to meet Lila Fields. She's my new partner."

"Nice to meet you," Royce smiles, holding his hand out to me.

"Like wise," I respond, dropping Pierce's hand to accept Royce's.

As they continue in conversation, my mind drifts off. My eyes scan the room, full of well-dressed men, many with beautiful women on their arms. A few of them look lost like me, but most own the room like professional socialites. *This could never be my whole life*, I think to myself.

And, as I continue scanning, I see him.

He's here. The man who stole my soul is standing across the room with his back against the wall. My eyes are locked on him, but his eyes dance around the room like I'm not here. Maybe to him, I never was. Maybe he's looking for the next one — the girl he'll show the world to then disappear.

I look beside me — at Pierce — and I feel sick that any part of me even wants to go across the room. I feel sick because there's a man here who I know could make me happy — who does make me happy — and yet I'm willing to throw it all away. He looks away from Royce, eyes instantly finding mine. He smiles, and I return it the best I can because for just a few more minutes, I need him to think that nothing has changed. And, maybe nothing has.

"I'm going to find the restroom," I whisper to Pierce.

"I'll come with you."

Shaking my head, I say, "No, you stay. I'll be right back."

He nods, hesitantly, and I wait for him to turn his attention back to Royce before blazing a path through the crowd, anxious to prove to myself that this isn't a dream.

The shield cracks.

My heart races.

His eyes still roam, taking in everything … everything but me.

I'm not going to let him out of my sight … I'm not going to let him hide from the anguish he's buried me in the last several months. He has nowhere to run. Even if he did, I wouldn't let him, not this time.

A few long strides and I'm standing in front of him, staring into those familiar pained eyes. When you love someone, it's impossible to look at them and feel hate. You may want to feel it. You may think you feel it, but love and hate can't co-exist. I hate that I love him, but I can't hate him.

And, I want to hate him. It would make it easier to love someone like Pierce who deserves my heart. This man stole it months ago, and I don't think he has any intention of returning it. Sometimes I don't know if I want it back.

But then, I think of the last few days — few months actually — and I realize another man may be winning it back for me. Maybe it's not gone forever but simply misplaced.

His hair is a little longer, but he's the same. The way he stands ... the way his fingers curl around a beer bottle. He's exactly the same.

"Blake," I whisper, afraid of what he'll say, what he'll do. Still afraid he'll find a way to run away, and I won't be able to catch him.

He stares at me like he's never even met me, or maybe he's spent the last several months trying to forget me. I can't say I haven't tried to do the same. There's not enough alcohol in the world do erase him.

"Does he make you happy?" he finally asks, practically staring through me. He sounds so broken, so sad.

"Who?" I ask, caught off guard by his question.

"Pierce. Does he make you happy?"

My eyes well with tears I've left unshed ... tears I left for him to see. "Yes," I whisper, doing my best to hold them in. He deserves to watch every single one of them run down my cheek but not here ... not now.

He nods, reaching his fingers up toward my cheek before quickly pulling them back away. And just as quickly as he came back into my life, he's gone.

It's really over.

If any part of him wanted me, he would have fought for me.

"There you are," Pierce says, wrapping his strong hands around my shoulders. Through the corner of my eye, I see Blake standing in the doorway. He nods then disappears. He left for me this time instead of just leaving me, but there was so much I wanted to say.

I take a deep breath and pull myself together before Pierce has a chance to see my face. He'll know I'm not okay. "Actually," I groan, rubbing my fingertips against my temples, "can we head back to the hotel? I'm not feeling well all of a sudden."

His warm hands run down my bare arms then slowly slide up again. "Let's get you something to eat."

"No," I snap, shrugging his hands away. "I need to go back to the hotel. Now, please."

He comes around to look at me, holding my face in his hands. I want him to hold on to me but for all the wrong reasons. I'm tired of falling for the wrong guy. I'm tired of being alone. Fifteen minutes ago, he was my guy.

He made me smile when I thought my face was paralyzed.

He brought in sun when all I saw was clouds.

Now, I just feel unsteady.

He leans in, his forehead resting against mine. Closing my eyes, I try to forget everything else. I try to pretend that everything is okay, but I've never been good at pretending. "What's the matter, Lila?" he whispers, gently brushing his lips against mine while his hands circle my hips.

"I saw him."

"Who?" he asks quietly, forehead still pressed to mine.

My heart stops, just for a second. I'm going to say his name, and it will be real. And Pierce will know it's real. "Blake."

His body stiffens. His fingers dig into my skin. "Where?"

"He was here, but I think he left. I only talked to him for a minute."

His hands slide up to my stomach, holding me tighter. "What did he say?"

Those damn tears are threatening. "He asked me if I'm happy. That was it … he just wanted to know if I was happy."

He inhales.

My heart aches no matter how much I tell myself everything is okay—that nothing has changed. It's taken me so long to get to where I am, and now, I'm lost again. Torn between two worlds … new and old, perfect and damaged. That line between right and wrong faded a few minutes ago. I thought I knew what I wanted; confusion is a nagging little bitch.

LISA DE JONG

"What did you tell him?" he finally asks, drawing me away from the internal battle that's raging. I just want it to go away.

"You know you make me happy," I whisper, thinking of last night ... the last few days. For at least a few seconds, the thought of him on me—inside of me—erases everything else.

It's just temporary then the fleeting, contradictory feelings return, dragging my heart to my knees.

"Let's get out of here," he says, cradling my elbow to pull me through the crowd. My eyes are locked on the fancy travertine floors. I don't want to see or hear anything; I just want out.

Before long, I'm tucked into the backseat of a waiting car. Pierce's strong arms wrap around me, pulling my head to his chest. Gripping the lapels of his jacket, I hold him as close as I can, breathing in the subtle cologne he wears. He reminds me of the warm fleece blanket I carried around as a kid; it fixed everything.

"I knew he was going to be there tonight," I finally acknowledge. My voice is purposefully quiet.

His fingertips that had been tracing small circles on my back still. "What did you just say?"

"Mallory warned me before we left the hotel. He's working on the project, Pierce. Wade hired him on to complete the artwork."

Silence follows. Too much silence.

"I should have told you," I add. "I just didn't want to believe it ... I didn't believe it."

"I'm going to kill that asshole. It's not a coincidence that he ended up on this project." His hands leave me, and without looking, I know he's combing his fingers through his hair. It's what he does when he's thinking. "We can leave in the morning if you'd like. I'll tell Wade he needs to find someone else to design the project. That'll through a fucking curveball at his timeline."

I shoot up, looking at Pierce's angry expression under the faint glow of the streetlights. "No," I answer, shaking my head.

He holds my cheeks in his hands. "I would never ask you to do this ... to work with him after what he did to you." He pauses, brushing his thumbs along my cheekbones. "You just

59

found your way back, and I'm not going to lose you again. I won't let him —"

"Pierce," I interrupt. "I've worked so hard on this. For months, it was my everything, and I'm not going to let Wade or Blake take it away from me."

"Then I'll ask Wade to pull him from the project."

"No."

Taken aback, he loosens his grip on me. "I don't know if I can do this. I don't want him looking at you, talking to you … you're mine now. I don't share. After last night, there's no way I'm ever going to let you go."

"Nothing's going to happen. We just need to be professional about this."

"It's not us I'm worried about," he snaps. "Can you tell me something?"

I stare at him. I'll tell Pierce anything he asks, and he knows it.

"Why didn't you tell me, Lila?"

"Because I knew you wouldn't go. Your business means —"

"Cut the bullshit. Why didn't you tell me?"

My heart skips. Like a ton of bricks, it just hits me … the real reason I wanted to go tonight even though I knew Blake would be there. "I needed to see him. Partly, because I wanted to make sure he's all right, and partly because I needed to know how I'd react. Closure I guess."

"And?"

"And what?"

"What did you feel? When you saw him … what did you feel?"

I cross my arms over my chest, forming an even stronger barrier. My heart pounds. My hands tingle. "Do you really want to hear this?"

"Yes."

"A little bit of everything: shock, confusion, anger."

"And?"

"Some of what I didn't want to feel is still there. After everything he did, I can't hate him." My stomach churns, and suddenly, it feels too warm in here. Not enough space … not enough air. "In fact, I felt something for him that was the opposite of hate. A few months and a broken heart didn't change that."

His gaze bounces from me to the window then back to me. He drags his hands through his hair. If looks could scream, I'd be deafened by his alone. "What are you saying?"

I shrug. "I guess I'm saying my wounds aren't as healed as I'd thought. They may never heal."

He reaches toward me, brushing his thumb against my cheek. "Wounds that deep always leave scars."

I nod, knowing that a part of me will always be with Blake, just as a small part of me stayed with Derek. Life is a journey for which we leave little pieces of ourselves behind. We write words in every chapter then leave them to continue to the next. It's our legacy, and if we're lucky enough, we'll meet someone special to take the ride with.

Before I can respond, the car comes to a complete stop, and the driver opens the door giving us a straight shot to our hotel.

"Is there anything else I can do for you this evening, Mr. Stanley?" he asks as Pierce climbs out.

He holds his hand out to me. "No, but be back at eight tomorrow morning. I have a meeting, and then I think Ms. Fields and I may be heading out of town a little early."

"We have the collaboration meeting tomorrow afternoon," I blurt as I stand next to Pierce on the sidewalk.

His arm wraps around my waist, pulling me close to his body. "We'll talk about this later."

Seconds after, he's pulling me through the hotel using his grip on my hand. The elevator door opens before either of us has a chance to push the button. A couple steps out. We step in.

I'm not a stranger to long elevator rides but this one may be the longest of them all. It's a polar shift from last night when everything felt right.

The door opens, and we step out in silence. We walk side-by-side, uncertainty still hanging in the air. As my room comes into view, I pull my key from my clutch, which is not an easy task with shaky hands.

He's not talking.

I'm not going to push.

I swipe my card, wasting no time before turning the knob. I let a bad thing ruin a good thing tonight. For that, I may never forgive myself. I push against the door just enough to slip inside, but before it closes, he pushes it back open, stepping in behind me.

The door clicks. I stand motionless, waiting for whatever will happen next. I've already had all I can take. I have no energy to fight.

His hands settle on my hips then slowly wrap around to my stomach. His body perfectly aligns with my back until all I feel is him ... all I think about is him.

"I'm not going to let him take you from me. Do you understand that?"

He gently brushes my hair away from my neck, kissing the delicate skin below my ear. I melt immediately.

His hands slide up against my ribs then cup my breasts. "I want you so damn bad, Lila. Since you walked out in this dress earlier, I've wanted you so damn bad."

I cover his hands with mine, lying my palm flat against his warm skin.

He groans, kneading my breasts in his hands. "You're mine, and I'm not going to let you forget that. When I'm with you ... when I'm inside you, you only think of me."

I moan, laying my head back against his shoulder. Without warning, he spins me in his arms, pressing my back against the wall. Last night we played nice but tonight, I just need him to help me forget.

His kiss is punishing as his hands work at the bottom of my cocktail dress. I hear a zipper then my lace panties are pushed aside. He lifts me, and on instinct, I wrap my legs tightly around him. Then with one quick thrust, he's in me ... all the way in me. I kiss him once, pulling his lower lip between my teeth. He leans back, giving me a look into his lustful, hooded eyes before burying his face in the crook of my neck. "Mine, Lila."

He pounds into me over and over. He touches me so deeply, it's almost painful, but I welcome it. The pain overrides every other emotion.

"I'm not letting you go," he murmurs against my skin.

I wrap my arms tightly around his neck.

He slips in and out of me, carefully punishing me with every thrust. I close my eyes and let the whole world just be. I live in the moment, not thinking about what happened earlier or what might happen tomorrow.

"Pierce," I moan, feeling myself pulse around him.

"Oh, Lila. I could stay with you like this for the rest of my life and never get bored of you."

He rolls his hips, and I completely fall apart around him. He completely loses himself inside of me.

He holds me close for God knows how long after. I hear him breathing. I feel his heart beating. "I love you, Lila. What ever happens after this, I want you to remember that."

I freeze, unsure of what to say … of what I feel. One thing is for sure: when I feel unsteady, he rights my world again.

"I'm falling for you," I whisper, kissing the base of his neck.

"I can accept that." He carries me to the bed where I stay the rest of the night, wrapped tightly in his arms. Sleep eludes me, but contentment keeps me warm.

WHEN I WAKE UP, the bed is cold and bright sunlight shines through the window blinds. I reach behind me, feeling nothing but an empty bed.

I listen for a sound—water running, footsteps—but I hear nothing. Curious, I rub my eyes then open them slowly to guard them against the morning light. My dress lies against the back of the chair where I left it last night, but all signs of Pierce are gone.

Moving my eyes to the clock, I'm surprised that it's past nine. I throw the covers back and roll out of bed. Pierce is with Wade, probably telling him that we're off the project, and I can't let him do that. We've both worked too hard to get here.

In less than ten minutes, my hair is pulled back, my teeth brushed and a belted royal blue dress covers my skin. Not the way I'd usually approach work when I'm in the middle of a high stakes business deal, but all that time and effort won't mean anything if Pierce gets his way.

I grab my mood board and make my way out to the busy street. With no time to waste, I flag down my own cab, ignoring two bellboys who repeatedly ask if I need help.

I open the door to the first little yellow car that stops and slide onto the torn leather seat. "Where to, miss?"

I ramble off the address, focusing my attention out the window. The morning traffic is easier to navigate now than it would have been an hour ago. If luck is on my side, I'll get there before the damage is done. I changed my life and dreams for a man once, and I promised myself I would never do it again. I want to think I'm stronger than my emotions … that my mind can overwrite anything my heart feels.

My theory is about to be tested.

I see Wade's high-rise up ahead, but traffic has us locked up. "I can walk from here."

"It's not safe to cross in this — " he starts, but I cut him off by handing him a rolled up twenty; double what I owe him.

"Thank you," I mutter, opening the door closest to the sidewalk. Traffic is a mess. Horns honk. Two cab drivers yell at each other out their windows. I carefully weave my way between cars, making sure I'm seen along the way. By the time my heels touch down on the other side of the street, my heart's beating so fast, I feel like I might pass out.

But there's no time for that.

Without pause, I open the door to Wade's building, sprinting past the woman who sits at the front desk, straight to the elevator. The wait for the doors to open is agonizingly long. All I can do is pray that I'm not too late. Pray that Pierce hasn't done something that can't be undone.

The door opens and closes with only me inside. I will it not to stop until we reach the floor with the conference room I've come to know so well.

I run out as soon as the door opens. My heart pounds faster as I cross through the waiting area, and this time, I don't get past the receptionist without her calling for me to come back. I block her out, continuing down the long hall toward the conference room I loathe. Nothing good ever happens in there.

My fingers turn the knob just as I hear the receptionist's heels coming closer. I sprint inside before it's too late. My eyes lock on Pierce first. He looks annoyed, angry even. And Wade just smiles as if he just won the lottery. It's a good thing they're sitting on opposite sides of the table.

"I'm sorry. I tried to stop her!" the receptionist yells as she steps in the room.

Wade lifts his hand. "It's okay. Ms. Fields is welcome to join our little meeting. Isn't that right, Stanley?"

Pierce scowls, but I ignore him, placing my things on the table.

The receptionist retreats, probably just as afraid to be in here as I am. "Okay, let me know if you need anything."

Wade leans forward in his seat. "I was hoping I'd get to see you one more time before you two skip town. It's too bad you're pulling yourselves off the project. I was looking forward to working with you."

His gaze skims my breasts as he talks, but I have more important things to worry about. "Actually, I have no intention of stepping down as the designer for this project. I hope you'll keep me on even if Pierce decides not to continue." I pause, glancing over at Pierce. His jaw ticks back and forth, and there's probably nothing more he'd rather do right now than drag me out of this room and out of this town. "I worked hard on this. It's all I've done the past few months."

Pierce rises from his seat, coming to stand in front of me. His legs are planted wide, arms crossed over his broad chest, blocking Wade out of my view. "It's a done deal. There will be other projects." He runs his fingers through his hair. "I'll build a hotel for you myself if I have to," he whispers.

Seeing the wounded look on his face almost makes me want to give in, but then Blake wins. Wade wins. "I'm in this with or without you."

"We're a package deal, Lila. He's not keeping you if I pull my half of the funding."

"That's not true," Wade interrupts. "Contrary to what you might think, your money didn't buy her a position. Ms. Fields is talent with or without you."

Pierce's hands curl into fists. "I wasn't inferring that I bought her anything Wade. I won't let her stay on this project without me because I don't trust you or that other bastard."

"That's a shame. Aren't new relationships supposed to be based on trust?"

Wade's attitude is almost enough to make me change my mind. But then again, I'm better than that ... than him.

"Our relationship is none of your business." He turns to Wade giving me a second to catch my breath. "Give us a couple minutes, okay? When I'm ready to put up with you again, I'll let you know."

"Have you forgotten you're in my conference room?"

Pierce steps forward. He's got a few inches on Wade, but Wade isn't fazed. "Don't test me any more than you already have this morning. It wouldn't hurt my feelings to rearrange your face, and I happen to know you're quite fond of your face and the ego behind it."

"My ego doesn't give a fuck if you stay on this project or not. Remember that." They stare each other down for a few seconds before Wade disappears out the door, slamming it hard enough to shake the artwork.

I stare at Pierce's back, afraid to move, too afraid to speak. I'm being selfish by asking him to stay on this project. We have something so new — so fragile — and all he's trying to do is protect it. I may end up ruining it all just to prove something to myself.

"Pierce," I say quietly, wanting him to come back to me on his own terms.

He stays quiet, slowly tearing my heart in two.

"I can do this. I bet we'll barely see him, and even if we do, I've moved on. He shouldn't matter to you."

He turns back around and grabs my arms, leaning in until we're eye-level. "I saw the look in your eyes last night. He matters to you, Lila. He still matters to you. Damnit," he seethes, gripping my arms a little tighter, not causing me pain but relaying his frustration. I'm choking on my own guilt.

I swallow, uncomfortably, searching for words. He's right, mostly. Blake matters to me — what we had can't be easily forgotten — but the man standing in front of me matters too. How do I get him to see that? "Do you remember what I said last night? That should mean something to you."

His eyes are glued to mine, but he stands speechless.

"And, it wasn't just words. I meant every part of it. I'm falling for you, Pierce."

His hands come up to the base of my neck, thumbs caressing my skin until his palms cover my cheeks. He tilts my head up and presses his lips to mine, punishing and possessive. He's fighting to be with me just as I'm fighting to be with him. We face different obstacles, but as long as we want the same thing, we can do this.

He softens the kiss, skimming his lips over mine twice more before pulling away. His eyes show some of the sparkle they lacked earlier. "I meant what I said, too. Those words held more meaning than they've ever held before."

"So, do you trust me? Can we do this?" I ask, my voice begging.

He closes his eyes and pulls me in for one more kiss. It's answer enough. "I trust you. If you want to continue on this project, you're doing it with me by your side."

"It's a deal."

Wade chooses that moment to walk back in the room. I can tell by the look on his face that he's disappointed to see us locked in an embrace. There's no doubt in my mind he planned all this.

"I see everything is good in paradise now," he jokes. "Where does that leave us?"

Pierce winks at me before turning his attention to Wade. "The project will go on as planned, but you, my *friend*, better watch yourself because this project doesn't mean shit to me." He stops, glancing back at me with a smile. "But it means everything to her, and she means everything to me."

"Someone is getting a little soft in his old age."

"Don't let my kindness fool you, and don't fuck with me again."

Wade's cocky grin falls. Inside, I'm smiling. He deserves every second of it. "I take it you'll be at the planning meeting this afternoon then?"

"We'll be there."

After grabbing some brunch, Pierce and I retreat back to the hotel to regroup before the afternoon meeting. The only thing I want to do is curl up in the comfortable bed and drift off to sleep. This morning was draining, and the thought of having to be in the same room with those two again in a few hours is frightening.

Pierce stands next to me outside my hotel room, smiling. "Can I join you?" he asks.

"Don't your moods ever wear you out?" I ask.

He shrugs. "You're a woman. You should know what it's like."

I sock him in the arm, but it's the truth. My moods change daily like the weather outside. "I guess you can come in, but all I plan on doing is showering and taking a quick nap."

His hands grip my hips, pulling me into his body. "You didn't shower this morning, did you?"

I shake my head.

"You still smell like me," he whispers, lips brushing my cheek.

"I guess I do," I answer back, feeling a tingle between my legs. His whisper sings the song of sex.

"Since you're tired, maybe it would be best if I help you in the shower. It's the least I can do after the morning you had."

My body trembles just thinking about his hands on me ... all over me. "It would make up for the problem you caused. I'm still a little mad that you left me alone in bed. I was cold and lonely."

He grabs the key card from me, opening the door with one hand while keeping his other arm wrapped around me. The door slams shut, and he lifts me in his arms carrying me to the bathroom. He sets me on the edge of the counter then turns the shower on. I'm in awe over the size of his heart. He doesn't just tell me that there is nothing he wouldn't do for me; he shows me every single day.

You can fall in love.

You can be in love.

Or you can simply love.

And, the best type of love is felt before it's spoken. It elevates your soul and fills your heart. I'm falling hard, and it just ... it just feels right.

I watch as he undoes his cuff links and quickly unbuttons his white dress shirt. I ponder reaching over to help him, but instead I enjoy the show. As he slides his shirt off, I look into his eyes. They're glued to me, and I can't help but be stuck on him. I hear his belt hit the floor then his zipper, but my eyes are still on his.

He steps between my legs, running his long fingers up the inside of my thighs until he reaches my panties. His thumbs curl around the edges, carefully pulling them down. The way he does it—slow, methodical, letting his thumbs brush my inner thighs—drives me absolutely crazy.

Next, he pushes my skirt up, leaving me completely exposed. I scoot to the edge of the counter wanting him inside of me so badly, I could almost scream. Instead, he slides me off and pulls my dress over my head, leaving me in nothing but my bra.

"Pierce, I need you to touch me," I beg, wrapping my arms around his neck.

He remains silent, pulling my arms away and pinning them behind my back. He uses his leverage to bend me back enough to give him full access to my covered breasts. Leaning in, he bites my nipple through the fabric. I yelp. He does the same to the other side before carving a path of kisses down the center of my chest. I rub my legs together to relieve the ache, but it's pointless. He's the master of my body; he controls my desire and release.

My bra falls to the ground and I'm lifted into his arms and placed in the oversized, steam-filled shower. Tiny droplets hit my back as I wait for him to join me.

He surprises me, taking a seat on the bench rather than joining me. "I want to watch you," he says, resting his head against the tile.

"I thought you were going to help me," I groan, the ache between my legs building just staring at him naked.

"When the time is right," he answers, a huge grin lighting up his gorgeous face. He hands me a bar of soap, purposefully brushing his fingers against mine. "Soap up, Lila."

I follow his instruction, soaping my arms, back, stomach, and legs. His lips part when I rest one foot on the bench, opening myself up to him. I glide the bar between my legs, back and forth watching him. I brace my hand against the shower wall and close my eyes, rubbing faster—harder. My tongue darts out to lick my lips. I'm so close ... so damn close.

"Stop," he commands, wrapping his hand around my wrist.

"Please," I beg. "I need you inside me. Please."

He stands up, and in one swift move, he has me sitting on the bench staring up at him. He spreads my legs, sitting on his knees between them. Water drips from the ends of his bangs, falling to his lashes and rolling down his cheeks. I couldn't want him any more than I do right now.

He pulls me to the edge of the bench, forcing my back to arch with my head resting against the tile. "I give you pleasure. Only me," he growls, circling his thumb between my legs as he presses his lips to the inside of my thigh. "Your scent is so sweet."

I grip his long hair between my fingers. "Pierce, please," I beg, pulling his hair gently. He buries his head between my legs and works his tongue against my sensitive skin, occasionally tugging to cause the most painful, yet pleasurable experience I've ever felt. I cry out as the first orgasm rocks my body. He pulls me up holding me against the shower wall as he pushes inside of me, feeling the ride he's taken me on.

"You're so fucking perfect," he groans as I come down from sweet bliss. His strong arms hold my legs up as he pumps into me. I fall apart two times before he finds his release.

"I've never been with someone who's so amazing at everything," he breathes as he slowly tries to regain his composure.

I smile, burying my head in the crook of his neck. "Where did you learn to do that?"

He laughs. "Probably not what you want to hear, but I've had experience."

I lift my head. Lila Fields actually feels a hint of jealousy, and she doesn't like it one bit. "And where do I rank?"

He kisses the tip of my nose. "If you have to ask, we may have to do this all over again because I don't think I made it clear enough."

"It was the best," I answer, honestly. Not for one second did I feel used … I just felt love and desire.

"Same for me." I watch the water hit against his back. I think about what it would be like to do this every morning with him. To have a guy who worships me, who understands my tough exterior only hides a damaged soul.

He knows what I need and when I need it.

"I THOUGHT YOU WERE never going to pick up your phone," Mallory says when I call her back after twelve missed attempts on her part.

"I'm on a work trip. It's not like I'm sitting on the beach sipping pina coladas."

"How are things going?" she asks, cutting the meaningless bullshit short.

"Not too bad so far. I mean ... the trip has had a few ups and downs, but nothing I can't handle." I sit up, pulling the sheet up over my breasts. Pierce left a few minutes ago to prepare for the meeting we have this afternoon.

"Have you seen him?" she says, quietly.

"Yes," I answer back, the emotion I felt when I saw Blake creeping up in my voice. "When you said he was here, I didn't want to believe you."

"I wouldn't lie to you about something like that."

I pause, thoughts whirling in my head. The one that's plagued me the most is the one I can't let go of. It's more a question than a thought, and the answer scares me to death. "Why did he take the job?"

"He's been in hiding for months. I think he was just ready to get back to a somewhat normal life. He's been working on himself ... he's been working hard to become the man he used to be before Alyssa."

My heart clenches every time I hear her name. Her end ripped two men apart, and like an earthquake, there are lingering aftershocks. "Did he know I'd be on the project? When he took it, I mean."

She breathes heavily in the phone. "He loves you, Lila. He may not show it. He may not say it. But he loves you, and he wanted to make sure you were okay." She pauses, and I don't know if I want her to continue. She's said enough in the last thirty seconds to complicate my life as it is. "He called me ... last night, and that's how I know he's grown. As much as he wants you, he wants you to be happier even more than that."

"Stop!" I yell, feeling the tears welling in my eyes. "He can't do this to me. I just started to put myself back together, Mal. I ... I can't do it."

"I'm sorry. I'm so sorry. If I'd known before he signed on, I would have talked him out of it. Are you going to stay on the project?"

I wipe the moisture from under my eyes. "Yes, I worked too hard on this to walk away. Pierce tried to put an end to it, but as of right now, we're still on."

"Pierce is a smart guy."

I smile even though a tear slides down my cheek. "He's a really smart guy. I, um, I told him I'm falling for him."

"Holy shit! Are you serious?"

"Yes, and I meant it. You should see the way he is with me. He told me he loved me, but it wasn't necessary. He tells me in everything else he does." Thinking about him momentarily wipes Blake from my mind. Pierce should be the only guy who resides there.

"Wait, did you sleep with him?"

"We slept, we made love, he fucked me. We've done everything, and I still want more."

"So, Blake has no chance?" she asks, voice low.

"He lost his chance months ago. I can't open myself up to that kind of hurt again."

She sighs. "I get it."

Glancing at the clock, I realize I only have twenty minutes before we have to leave for the meeting. I should at least attempt to go in better shape than I did this morning.

"Look, I have to run. We have another meeting this afternoon."

"Call me later if you get a chance."

"It might be tomorrow morning if that's okay. Pierce changed our flight home to tonight. I think he's had enough."

She laughs. "Can't blame the guy. Look at you—smart and sexy."

"Shut up."

"Awe, love you, too. I can't wait to see you in a couple months."

"I already have that night marked off so we can order Chinese and curl up on the couch with a movie."

"Add some wine, and I'm in. Bye, Lila."

"Bye," I answer back before ending the call and throwing the phone onto the center of my bed.

Today is the day I present to the group, and I need to look sure of myself ... sure of my work. I pull on a pair of cropped black pants that hug my curves in all the right places. The waist is higher than I'd usually wear, but they work perfectly with the sleeveless black and white striped blouse I tuck into it. After taking a quick glance in the mirror, I unbutton the top three buttons, leaving just a peek of cleavage. I top it off with the simple diamond pendant necklace my parents bought me for the wedding that never was.

With little time to spare, I use my curling iron to add a few light waves and comb my fingers through it. Some powder, mascara and lip-gloss are all I need to finish the look.

As I am pulling on my black heels, someone knocks on the door. *Pierce and his perfect timing,* I think to myself.

He whistles as soon as the door opens. "Wow. Are you sure you don't want to skip this meeting, fly home early, and spend the rest of the night wrapped in my bed? I think that sounds really good right about now."

I wrap my arms around his neck, kissing him. "Meeting first, wrapping later," I whisper against his lips.

His arms circle around my back, hugging me to his body. "At the rate we're going, we may not even make it home. Thank God for private jets."

At the rate we're going, we'll be lucky if we make it out of this room.

75

I pull back enough to look up into his dark gaze. If there's any question how much he wants me, it's answered in his eyes. "Let's get this meeting over with. The sooner we're done, the sooner you get me alone again."

He squeezes me so tightly that my feet leave the floor. "God, I'm lucky."

He's perfect ... absolutely perfect.

My overactive nerves make the ride go by quicker than I would've liked. I repeat the basis for my design over and over in my head, hoping that when tons of eyes are watching me, my mind won't go blank.

"You ready for this?" Pierce asks as our car pulls in front of Wade's building.

I'm as green as they come, and I'm about to present to a group of professionals who've all been in the business for years. I've never been one for public speaking, but it's not for lack of confidence in what I do—it's the fear that the wrong word is going to spill out. That someone might ask me a question, and I'll freeze up. That even though I love everything about this design, they'll hate it, and my misread will cost Pierce millions.

His hand cradles my cheek, caressing my skin with the pad of his thumb. "It's flawless. Your whole design ... the concept. You wouldn't be here if it wasn't."

Closing my eyes tightly, I lean into his touch. His words, the tone of his voice ... calm me instantly. I open my eyes, finding myself staring right into his. "I've got this," I say with a genuine smile.

He kisses me, letting his lips linger on mine just long enough to slow my racing heart a little more. He's good at that.

When we break apart, he climbs from the car taking the mood board with him. As usual, he holds his hand out to me, but instead of letting it go, he grips it tightly in his as we make our way inside. He doesn't let up in the elevator or on the long walk down the hallway that leads to the conference room.

He lets go to open the door, and I inhale deeply. No going back, now. Like a zombie, I walk across the room. My eyes survey the people crowded around the table, but I'm looking through them, not at them. Pierce pulls a chair out for me, and I take it grateful there's an open one next to it for him.

It's a room of suits — mostly men — and almost every set of eyes is on me. This is what it must be like to be a tiny droplet of water falling on a drought. I definitely prefer being amongst the pouring rain.

"I think it's time for us to get this thing rolling," Wade announces from the head of the table. The mere sound of his voice sends my nerves back into a complete tailspin.

He starts by going around the table to introduce everyone. I listen off and on, remembering some names, not hearing others.

When he's done, his eyes meet mine. He smiles sadistically, almost as if he's predicting my failure. I wonder if that would make him happy? I twist the cap off the bottle in front of me and swallow down as much as I can before he starts up again.

"Lila Fields is working with Stanley Enterprises. I've contracted with them to complete the design on this project. I haven't seen what she's got in store for us yet, so I'm going to let her take the floor."

Pierce squeezes my knee and whispers, "You've got this" before I stand with the mood board, making my way to the easel. Multiple sets of eyes burn holes in my back as I set it up, standing with my back to them a little longer than necessary. It's good; if it weren't mine, I'd say it was brilliant.

After inhaling one last cleansing breath, I plaster a smile on my face and turn to the crowd.

"The goal is to develop a hotel unlike any other in New York," I start, purposefully glancing over everyone's heads at first. "We don't want travelers to simply choose it because it's the newest or the best ... we want them to come to New York just to experience The Hotel on 5th.

The longer I speak, the further down my eyes go. I see some smiles and even a nod, but not everyone is there yet. "Modern, clean lines are in right now, but what if we took that and added some dimension. What if we created something that can easily be converted to modern in any era? I present to you The Hotel on 5th."

I first show the rendering of the front and then move to the lobby. I explain the layout, the colors, the concept, and when I'm done, I see acceptance. Pierce smiles wide, brushing his finger over his lips as he listens.

"Because we want the hotel to be more of an experience than a place to rest your head, it will only have seventy-two rooms, six per floor." Before I can show the group my drawing of how I envision a guest room, the door clicks open. I ignore it until I see the smile drop from Pierce's face.

"You're late," Wade says, gesturing to the last empty seat.

My stomach clenches when I get a glimpse of him. He's impossible to ignore in this group, wearing his signature faded blue jeans and t-shirt. He's impossible for me to ignore. Period.

I look back to Pierce who's trying to kill Wade with the fire in his eyes. I continue, wanting to do whatever I have to in order to get out of here. "Each floor will have a slightly different feel, so you can stay multiple times and feel like you've experienced different parts of New York."

My eyes float again. Words spill from my lips with little effort thanks to many hours of prep, and when I'm done, I breathe a sigh of relief. *I want to be back in Chicago. I want sanity.*

"Does anyone have any questions?" I ask, holding my breath in hope that I'll be out of this room within a couple of minutes.

Wade starts. "I like the idea of having all rooms essentially be suites, but can we cut the top floor from six suites to two penthouses? For celebrities and such."

I look at Pierce, and he nods. His cheeks burn red, and I swear he's going to hurl himself across the table at any minute.

"Yes," I answer. "We can make that happen."

"That's what I like to hear. Before we meet next time, I'd like you to draw up what they may look like."

I nod, rocking back and forth on my heels. Just when I think it's been silent long enough to sit back down, Blake opens his mouth. "And what if the art I have in mind doesn't fit this concept?" he asks.

"Then I suggest you start on some new pieces," I snap back, smiling to hide my contempt.

"Hmm," Blake chides, pulling a folded up piece of paper from his pocket. "My contract states I get a creative opinion. That I'm to work with the designer for the best possible result."

I open my mouth to reply, but Pierce beats me to it. "Wade, we need to talk in your office. Now!"

Wade shrugs, the cocky grin never leaving his face. "Excuse us for a few minutes," he says, slowly rising from his chair.

Pierce walks toward me, the whole time I'm hoping he'll take me by the hand and lead me as far away from here as possible.

He rests his hand on my shoulder. "I'll make this quick. Stay put," he whispers.

I disagree, but I'm not going to argue in front of these people. He knows that. This whole thing was bad fucking idea.

The door shuts behind them. The room is dead silent. I almost wish someone would throw another question at me, but it's not often I get what I wish for.

"I'm going to take a quick break," I announce as I head for the door. As soon as I hear it shut, I feel as if I can breathe again. I take a couple turns, looking for anywhere to hide for a few minutes.

"Lila, wait," Blake says from behind me. I quicken my pace until I see the Ladies' Room door. I open it, but before I can lock it, his strength forces me back. I'm now locked in a small room with the one person I was running away from.

"You need to leave."

"And, how do you plan on making me do that?" he asks, leaning back against the door.

"I don't have to make you. You're good at leaving all on your own," I say, my choice of words a reminder of everything I've been trying to forget.

He steps toward me.

I step back.

We repeat in rhythm until my back hits the wall. "I need you to stay away from me." My voice shakes as my heart beats against its shield.

His right forearm rests against the wall, caging me in. "I didn't have a choice."

"We all have choices."

"You wouldn't be with him right now if I'd stayed. Admit that much."

His body isn't touching mine, but I can feel its warmth. It's driving me insane. "But you didn't stay, and what we had ... it doesn't matter anymore. It's part of the past — a broken past — and you can't fix it."

He stares down at me with the familiar eyes — the ones I fell so hard for. I remember some of the good times, and I begin to melt ... the tears start to form. You don't forget love. You can fall out of it, but you never forget it.

"I don't want to fix it," he finally says, leaning in a little closer. I smell the mint on his breath and have to turn my head to gain back some of my control. "I want to build something new. If I can't have you the way I want to, I'd rather be your friend than nothing at all."

"I can't trust you."

"I can't live without you."

"I'm not yours."

He sighs, using his index finger to turn my face back toward him. "I said friends, Lila. That's all I'm asking for."

"I'm not changing my concept."

He smiles for the first time since I've seen him this week. "See, that's the good part about being friends. Friends compromise."

"But," I say, forming my own smile. "You're the one who needs to gain my trust. I think you need to bend a little more. Show me how serious you are."

He laughs. "There's my Lemon Drop. God, I've missed you."

My smile falters as I slip out of the cage he's had me in. "You can't do that," I say, my hand firmly on the doorknob. "You can't bring up the past. It — "

"Stings. I know, Lila. I fucked up, and there's not a minute that goes by that I don't remember the look on your face when I walked out of the apartment that night. There's not a minute that goes by that I don't wish I'd done everything differently. They always say you don't know what you have until it's gone, but I knew what I had, and I didn't think I deserved it. I'm sorry, Lila. You may not want to believe me, but I'll live with my regret for the rest of my life."

There's so much I want to say, but this isn't the time or the place. "I need to go," I say quietly. "Pierce is probably looking for me."

He doesn't say a word as I open the door and walk out of it. I'm in such a rush to get back to the conference room before Blake catches up to me that I almost don't see Pierce leaning against the wall outside the bathroom. Paralyzed by the look on his face, I can only watch as he slowly walks toward me. Without a word, he grabs my hand and pulls me with him.

We pass the conference room.

We pass the receptionist, only stopping to push the button on the elevator.

My eyes follow the lines that separate the travertine tile, anything to keep them away from his. The tension between us is so thick; as much as I want to get out of here, I'm not necessarily looking forward to being alone with him. There so much we need to talk about.

He uses his grip on my hand to pull me into the elevator behind him. My shoulder brushes his, and I smell his faint cologne.

I'd give anything for him to push me up against the elevator wall and explore every inch of my body until he was all I thought about ... until pleasure trumped my sadness and frustration.

But that's not what's going to happen ... not this time. The elevator door opens, and I'm pulled out of the building and tucked into our waiting car.

I feel him slide in beside me as I stare out the window, holding my eyes open to dry up any remaining sign of tears.

"What happened in there?" he finally asks when the car pulls away from the curb.

"He followed me in. I guess he thought we had some unfinished business that needed to be tended to," I answer without looking in his direction.

"Look at me."

I hesitate for a second then realize no reasonable amount of time is going to wash away my puffy eyes and the grimace that comes with it.

His eyebrows draw together as he looks at me. He takes a deep breath and runs his knuckles up and down my bare arm. "Did he hurt you?"

I shake my head vehemently. "No, he would never hurt me—or anyone—not like that."

"What unfinished business did he feel you had to take care of in the women's bathroom?"

Everything, I think to myself. "He wants to work on the project together, and he didn't want anything from the past to affect that."

His fingers move up, caressing my cheek. "I don't like the thought of you alone with him."

"I can handle him."

He wraps his arm around my shoulders, pulling me into his body. "We can quit the project. I don't need it."

"No, I've worked hard on it, and I want to do it."

"Then, I'll just make sure I'm with you."

"But you hate him."

"I guess I love you more than I hate him."

"I love you, too," I say, some of the fog finally lifting. My love for Pierce is the only thing keeping me from making what would be the second worst decision in my life. The first was letting myself fall for Blake in the first place.

I FIDGET WITH MY PURSE straps as Pierce pulls in front of my apartment building. Between the meeting and the flight home and all the drama in between, I'd rather not have company tonight.

"I'll walk you up," he says, unbuckling my seatbelt.

I smile, thinking of all the things this man does right. "Where did you learn to be such a gentleman?"

"I guess you could say my mother taught me well. Although, I don't think I was such a gentleman on the flight home. The stars heard you screaming my name."

He carries my bag on the way up to my apartment and waits patiently as I fiddle with the lock. With any luck, I'll be able to throw come pajamas on and curl up under my covers with my own thoughts within the next few minutes.

"So I guess I'll see you at the office tomorrow?" I ask, slipping my heels off.

He grips my hips. "Are you sure you don't want me to stay?"

"Not tonight," I reply, wrapping my arms around his neck. "I need some time to clear my mind, and I'm sure your bed is much more comfortable than mine."

"Do you want to find out tomorrow? I'll cook you dinner."

"Are you sure you're real?"

"The way my heart is beating right now, I'd say I am."

It's not easy to let him go, but we've spent almost every minute together the last few days and I need to catch my breath.

"Night, Pierce."

"Night. Call me if you need anything or if you just want to talk or if you want me to come over." He smirks.

I return his smile, standing on my toes to kiss his lips one last time before he disappears down the hallway.

Sleep comes easier than I thought it would. I guess that's what happens when you ride the emotional roller coaster for three straight days.

The smell of bacon hits me before my eyes open to the morning sun showing through my curtains. Mallory hates bacon, and she's still in Europe supposedly.

Curious, I crawl out of bed and make my way to the kitchen. The scene reminds me of a morning six months ago except this time, a shirtless Blake reminds me of lemon drops and paint and heartbreak.

He turns toward me, and he's not like the man who I met months ago. There's no cocky smile or hungry stare, just a man biting the inside of his cheek studying me, wondering if I'm going to run or stay. I wonder the same thing.

"How did you get in?" I ask, breaking the spell.

He pulls a set of keys from his jeans pocket, dangling them in the air. "I'm moving back into town and need a place to stay for a couple days until I get one of my own."

"What's wrong with your studio?"

"It's fine for sleeping, but it doesn't have fun stuff like a refrigerator or stove. I'm partial to food."

I expect him to turn around, but he stares instead, his eyes slowly traveling the length of my body. "I like your new pajamas. They're very *telling*."

When I got home last night, I was so tired, I'd just thrown on a long white t-shirt. I didn't realize the material was so thin. Crossing my arms over my chest, I step back into the doorway of my room. "I think you should leave."

He turns his attention back to the stove. "You could at least let me eat first."

"I'm going to get ready for work, and I want you out of here by the time I'm done. This isn't going to work for me."

"We'll see," is all he says before I lock myself in the bathroom and turn the shower on as hot as my skin can bare. I go through the motions slower than usual, giving him time to disappear from my apartment.

It's quiet when I step back into my bedroom, and as I open the door, I can see why. Blake sits at the table with a plate full of eggs, bacon and toast reading a page in the newspaper. "I thought I told you to leave."

"You should know by now that I'm not good at following directions," he replies without looking up.

"Fine then. Forget looking for an apartment. I'd rather you stay here and make my life hell." I throw a few things in my bag before heading to the kitchen to find something to eat on the way to work. The pans he used for breakfast are wiped clean. "If you're going to come into my apartment to make yourself breakfast, you could at least make enough for both of us."

"Lila."

"What?" I shout, realizing he used the last of the milk.

"Come here. I want to show you something."

I do as he asks not out of obedience but because I'm ready to unload on him. "You're such an asshole, Blake! Why don't you go into somebody else's apartment and eat all their damn food." I'm about to unleash more fury on him when I spot the second plate sitting across from him. "Is that for me?" I ask, timidly.

"Yeah. I probably would have told you a while ago, but you were too busy making assumptions."

I feel like a hypocrite sitting across from him, but my stomach aches from skipping dinner last night. "I guess I should say thank you."

"That would be nice."

"What are you doing back in Chicago anyway?"

He looks up, holding my eyes for a few seconds before answering. "We have a project to work on. I thought it would be easier if I were here, especially since we have a babysitter now."

"What are you talking about?" I ask, between bites of delicious buttery scrambled eggs.

"Oh, your boyfriend didn't tell you? He threatened to pull funding for the project if I stayed on. Wade talked him into letting me complete my contract, but we're not allowed to meet unless Pierce is present. Sounds like you've got yourself a relationship built on trust." He sips his milk, waiting for me to react. Inside I'm boiling, but I'm not going to let him see that. It's exactly what he wants.

"Why do you hate Pierce so much?" I ask. While I don't agree with how Pierce feels about Blake, I don't get Blake's hatred. It's puzzled me for months.

"He's never liked me. Even when Alyssa was still here, he hated me. He thought she could do so much better. I think when she died it validated everything he'd already assumed." I still hear the sadness in his voice when he talks about her. It lessens my anger. It reminds me that for weeks after he left, I was ready to forgive him for leaving if he would just give me the chance.

"Where have you been all this time?"

"Trying to forgive myself."

"And?" I ask.

He sets his fork down on his empty plate, leaning back in his chair. "I don't know if it matters because she's not my only regret. I have a lifetime of mistakes to work through."

I stand from the table. "I have to get to work."

He steps behind me as I rinse my plate in the sink, caging me in with his arms. "Tell me I still have a chance with you. That's all I want ... a chance."

"Do you want me to lie to you?"

He comes even closer, his body aligned with mine. "I see it in your eyes. I've always been able to read your eyes."

"Sometimes hurt is too much. You left a scar, Blake. There's no getting over that."

"I can't make you forget, but I can fix it. That's the difference, Lila. Some of my mistakes can't be fixed, but if you'd let me, you wouldn't regret it." His warm breath tickles my neck. If he kissed me there, I don't know that I could stop him.

Then I think of Pierce, and I can't do this to him. There's something real there I can't ignore, and even if I could, I'm not the type of girl who holds two men on a string at once.

"He told me he loves me," I whisper, feeling his body stiffen against mine. "And, I told him I love him, too. I love him, Blake."

He steps back, giving me space to breathe. I walk away without looking back. The thing is, I love Blake too—enough that I can't chance seeing the pain on his face. I grab my keys and bag and make a hasty retreat out the door.

I don't know how much more of this I can handle.

I SKIP MY USUAL MORNING office routine, electing to visit Reece before finding my own desk. "Hey," she says, standing to hug me. "How was your trip?"

I throw my bag on one chair and slide down into the other. "A mess," I say simply.

"Oh, no! What happened? Did they not like your designs?"

Shaking my head, I say, "No, that part went better than expected, but guess who else signed onto the project?"

She stares at me blankly.

"Blake," I answer for her, rubbing my fingertips against my temples.

"I thought he'd disappeared. I mean, I didn't think anyone knew where he was."

"I guess Wade is better at hide and seek than the rest of us. Damnit, Reece. Every time I think I have my life together, something or someone has to come in and mess with it. Sometimes I feel like I'm a player in the game of chess, but someone else is moving the pieces."

She moves my purse, taking the chair next to me. "But you've been pining over him for months. Aren't you at least happy that he's okay?"

"Of course, I'm happy that he's back with the living, but he's everywhere I go. He was even in my apartment this morning making breakfast."

Her eyes narrow on me. "Let me get this straight; a guy who you've been missing finally came back into your life and he won't leave you alone and this is making you angry because…"

I throw my hands up in the air. "Because I'm falling in love with someone else. He's too late."

Her mouth falls open. "Who? Who are you falling in love with?"

"Pierce," I whisper, careful not to let anyone in surrounding offices hear.

"Shut up!"

I shake my head. "He's been there for me, and somewhere along the way, things changed. I trust him more than I've ever trusted anyone. After everything I've been through the last year, that means the world to me."

"How does Pierce feel?"

"He told me he loves me. He made love to me. I don't question his motivations or intentions. He's real, and that's exactly what I needed. I'm done being with guys who make me question where I stand every other day."

"He's the right choice for you. It may be hard to see now, but he's the forever type guy. Blake isn't that guy for you. This project will end, and he'll leave." She pauses. "I think we both know that."

I nod. She couldn't be more right. "Thank you for listening to me whine. I think you need some man drama so we can be even."

"I don't foresee ever having this much drama, but if I do, you'll be the first one to know."

"I'm pathetic."

She laughs. "I think you're kind of lucky. I can't find a man and you have two who would give an arm to be with you."

"Well, I'm about to go rip the arm off of one because he thinks I need a babysitter."

"I'm going to stay out of that one," she says, going to sit back at her desk.

I finally make it to my desk twenty minutes after I'm supposed to be there. It's no surprise that Pierce is standing there with his arms folded over his chest. His brows burrow at the sight of me. "I was starting to worry about you."

"I was catching up with Reece."

"I tried calling you. A few times actually."

After throwing my purse on my desk, I look back up, my hands firmly planted on my hips. "Look, I'm sorry I'm late. I had a surprise visitor this morning, and he threw my whole routine off."

"Who?" he asks, stepping closer.

My chest rises and falls. This is going to go over like a nun having sex in the cathedral. "Blake."

He runs his thick fingers through his hair. It looks like he's done that a few times already this morning. "I'm going to my office. I want to see you there within the next five minutes."

Before I can reply, he disappears around the corner. There's nowhere to hide. Once Pierce Stanley has something stuck in his head, there's nothing I can do about it. I take my time, filling up my coffee cup before slowly making my way down the narrow hall that leads to his suite. The door is open just enough for me to see him standing with his back to me, staring out the floor to ceiling window.

I quietly slip inside, closing the door behind me.

"I was starting to think you weren't coming."

Looking down at my watch, I say, "Five minutes on the dot. Doesn't seem like you had anything to worry about."

He turns, eyes narrowed in on me. If he thinks he's the only one who has something to be pissed about, he's about to learn a hard lesson. "Why was Blake in your apartment this morning?"

"It's a funny story, but I shouldn't really have to tell it to you. You wrote a part in it."

He takes two steps toward me. "What the hell are you talking about?"

"He wouldn't be in Chicago if it weren't for you and your demand to babysit us while we work on the project," I reply, holding my ground.

"You would do the same thing if you were me," he seethes, hands forming into fists at his sides.

"No, I wouldn't, Pierce," I say, lifting a finger to emphasize my stance. "I trust you."

His expression softens just a bit. "Why was he in your apartment? I don't like that. I don't like that at all."

"It's Mallory's apartment. I guess he needs a place to stay for a couple days until he finds a place of his own."

"Jesus."

"I asked him to be out by the time I get home." I pause, a hurtful pain still searing inside my chest. Not only has the shield cracked, it's disappeared. "Why don't you trust me? You know me, Pierce. You know what he did to me. Besides, was everything we did in New York meaningless?"

He closes the remaining distance between us while I speak. His jaw ticks, but his eyes don't hold the same anger they held earlier. "You said you trust me, but how would you feel if I suddenly had an ex-girlfriend working with me. Better yet, how would you feel if she was alone with me in my apartment?"

His words draw a red line through my whole argument. If Pierce had an ex hanging around, it wouldn't be him I'd be worried about as much as her. If she were anything like Blake, I'd be a mess—a complete, scrambled, twisted mess. "Point taken, but I still don't think a babysitter is necessary. I can handle him."

"Like hell you can. He's your Achilles heal." He stops suddenly, eyes dancing between mine as he grips my elbows to keep me close. "I know without a doubt that if he'd never left you, I wouldn't have a chance. I live with that every time I look at you, but I love you enough to try and forget it." He closes his eyes tightly. "It's not easy when I know your heart is constantly reminded when you see him and don't tell me it's not."

"What was she like?"

"Who?"

"Alyssa ... was she anything like me?"

He swallows, briefly looking over my head before his eyes meet mine again. "In some ways. She always pretended to be happy, but you have more visible ups and downs. I always wondered what she was thinking, but I don't wonder when I'm with you. The words are written all over your face."

"If that's the case, what am I thinking right now?"

Our emotions run parallel. We're not at the same point at the same exact time.

I need us to intersect. I need to understand what he's feeling ... I need him to understand what I'm feeling.

His fingertip traces a line on my forehead, pushing a loose hair away from my eyes. "You're scared."

"Scared of what?"

"Scared of making a decision you'll regret for the rest of your life. I don't want you to make the wrong choice."

"I've already made my choice."

He shakes his head. "No you haven't. You still think about him—more than I'm comfortable with. I think we should cancel our date for tonight so you can decide what you really want to do. I can't get any deeper in this until you're sure."

"Does being done with him mean I'm done with the project, too?"

"No," he says. "But you have to agree to my terms. He already ruined one woman I loved; I can't let him do it again."

My anger boils up again. "Since you brought it up, and I've been waiting a long time to hear this. How did he ruin her? He obviously believes it himself, or he wouldn't be in the position he's in."

"He didn't protect her."

"And you did?" I ask, feeling his grip on me loosen.

His arms fall to his sides. He stares like a stone statue—empty and emotionless. "Get out of my office."

I lift my hands, but he backs away. "Maybe if you knew how to forgive, you could both move forward. It should never have gotten to this."

"Leave."

Without a moment's hesitation, I do. The rest of the day I spend every single second thinking about Pierce and every single minute trying to avoid him.

THE APARTMENT IS NOT HOW it was supposed to be when I got home. The light in Mallory's room shines underneath the door; it's not a scene I'm unfamiliar with.

I knock on the door.

"Come in!" he yells over the faint music.

Without hesitation, I step inside. I gasp as my eyes catch the single piece sitting on an easel in the corner. It's serene with a certain beauty I'm not used to in his work.

"What is this?" I ask. "It's beautiful."

I pull my eyes away from the canvas and look into his swollen, red eyes. He's staring back at me, but he might as well be hundreds of feet away. An ache begins in my throat; after everything he's put me through, my heart is still tied to his. His sadness is mine. I feel every ounce of his pain.

And he feels it. His eyes well up with tears. He knows my heart hasn't completely detached. As much as I don't want it to, it's always going to be hanging by an unbreakable string.

The only sound in the room is "Litost" by X Ambassadors. The melody only intensifies the hurt. I listen to the words—actually listen—realizing it could be our anthem. Our love is like a hole, and I don't know if I will ever fully recover … ever climb out.

The art, though, the art isn't about me. It's too beautiful, too peaceful, too innocent. It reminds me of when I was a little girl, when the whole world was perfect through my eyes. It's the opposite of anything I've ever seen Blake paint.

I see a tear spill down his cheek when I glance back over at him. I can't take it—watching his pain—so I do what my heart tells me. Closing the gap between us, I wrap my arms tightly around him. He nestles his head in the crook of my neck, soaking my shirt with his sorrow. "Today was supposed to be her birthday," he finally chokes, whimpering. "I just wish I could hold her."

"I'm sorry," I whisper, running my fingertips along his spine as my own tears fall. "It's not your fault, Blake. You need to forgive yourself. She wouldn't want you to hold this on your shoulders."

"I would have done anything for her. I thought I'd done everything."

"I know."

We cling to each other like it's somehow necessary for our survival. It may just be for his. After what could have been seconds, minutes, hours, I step back, holding his face in my hands. "You need to talk to someone. Do it for yourself. Do it for your future."

"I have been," he whispers, looking me straight in the eye. "This is the part I don't like—I have to feel worse before I can feel better."

I close my eyes, praying I'll never regret the words that slip from my lips next. "I'm here for you. We'll never be what we were, but I want to be here for you."

He lowers his eyes and nods. "Can I have one thing?"

"What's that?" I ask, biting down on my lower lip.

"Kiss me."

"What?"

"Kiss me. I want to remember the taste of your lips. I want to—"

I shake my head. "I can't. I—"

"Please," he whispers, brushing his thumb along my lower lip. "Just kiss me."

One more look at him and my resolve falls like the Berlin Wall. Wrapping my arms tightly around his neck, I press my lips to his. Neither of us pushes it further. It's a transfer of emotion — maybe forgiveness, or goodbye. Maybe it's comfort. Whatever it is, I'm selfish; I wanted this just as much as he did, but not for a second did I think about the ramifications it would have with him ... or Pierce. To love one man complicates the heart, but two ... there are no words for that.

Pierce. My chest tightens. Even after everything that happened earlier, I can't do this to him. It's innocent enough, but he wouldn't see it that way.

I break away, moving back a few steps. "I can't do this," I cry.

"I'm sorry," he says, staring up at the stark white ceiling.

"Don't be," I whisper, shaking my head. "In some way, we both needed that."

He's about to say something else when there's a knock at the door. I start toward it; Blake is in no shape to deal with company.

Pierce stands on the other end of the peephole, staring down at the ground. The thought of not answering crosses my mind, but I've already done him wrong a time or two today.

"Hey," I say, opening the door to him with a forced smile on my face. I didn't expect to see him this weekend after how we left things earlier.

He holds up a bouquet of flowers. "I think I owe you an apology."

I take them from his hands, bringing the fragrant red roses to my nose. "For what?"

"For blaming you for my problems — for his problems. I know you would never do anything to break my trust, and I need to stop treating you otherwise."

There's a pain in the back of my throat. In a way, I just proved him wrong, but I did it with the best intentions. "Pierce, he's here. He's staying in Mallory's room for a couple of days."

He looks over my shoulder, but the door is closed. Light still shines under it, and I wonder what he's doing in there. Is he painting? Is he standing where I left him, staring at a blank wall? "Stay with me for the weekend. I can't stand you being here alone with him."

That's when the real struggle begins. The one between doing what I should and doing what I want. I should stay here—make sure that Blake is okay, but I want to disappear with Pierce.

"Can you wait outside?" I ask, looking over my shoulder.

He groans, eyes burning a hole through Mallory's closed door.

"I don't want any drama tonight. Please ... just wait downstairs. I'll pack a bag and be right out."

He hesitates. I know this isn't easy for him, and it's not a picnic for me either. He nods. "Okay. I'll give you five minutes, but then I'm coming back up."

"Nice compromise, Stanley."

He smiles. "I'm working on it."

As soon as he's gone, I throw a few things in a bag and slip on a pair of shoes. I'm about to leave when I hear a crash in Mallory's bedroom.

I open the door to find Blake curled in a ball on the center of the bed. I want to run to him—hold him—but I need to draw the line.

"I'm leaving for the weekend," I announce from the doorway.

"He deserves you."

"What do you mean?"

"As much as I hate him, he's a good guy. He'll protect you in ways I'll never be able to."

Before I close the door, I say, "I am still here for you if you need anything."

As the door closes, I swear I hear him say *"All I need is you"* but I block it out, convincing myself that it was just my imagination playing tricks.

Pierce is leaning against a gray sports car when I step outside. He grins, and I can't help but return it. When we are close enough to touch, he wraps his arms tightly around me, forcing me to drop my bag. He pulls me into a kiss making my whole body melt into him. He teases—licking then tugging, pulling me even closer. My arms curl around his neck as he leans me back to blaze a trail of kisses along my throat.

"We should go," I pant, the warmth between my legs almost unbearable.

He reaches back, opening the passenger door for me without breaking the mood. He turns us around, slowly letting me go so I can sink into the seat.

His small car moves quickly down the barren streets, his hand resting on my upper thigh through every turn. I want so badly for him to curl his fingers between my legs, to make everything better.

The car whizzes into a packed parking garage, winding up to the third floor before pulling into a spot next to the elevator. "We're home," he announces, opening his door. Mine is open before I even get a chance to find the knob. He grabs my hand in his while holding my bag in the other.

The elevator closes, and he pulls me in for a kiss.

Then another when we exit in the hallway outside his door.

And again after placing his key in the lock.

As soon as we're safely inside, my back is against the wall, my legs wrapped around his waist as his lips caress from my collarbone to the exposed skin above my breasts.

"Pierce, please," I beg, kissing no longer enough to satisfy my desires.

"Tell me exactly what you want. I need to hear you say it." He pins my arms above my head, taking away all my control.

"I need you, Pierce. I need to know that everything is okay. I need to know we're okay."

He moves both my wrists to one hand, using the other to push my skirt up to my waist. I hear his zipper then seconds later, he's inside me, filling me until it hurts.

His lips capture mine, and I give him everything — my heart, my mind, my soul. When we're like this, he's all I think about ... he's all I want.

He thrusts.

I whimper.

He swallows my screams. He finally releases my arms, and I hold on to him for dear life as I clench around him. "Oh God, Pierce. That feels so good." My body trembles as I come down from the high.

Holding me tightly, he whispers, "I love you." Over and over again.

"I love you, too," I say when I catch my breath.

He carries me through the dark apartment, down a narrow hall that leads to a massive bedroom with windows overlooking the city. It's the kind of view I always had in my city dreams.

Lowering me to my feet, he carefully undresses me, letting my clothes fall onto the plush rug in front of his bed. The city lights are the only things illuminating the room, but I still see the way he looks at me. It's the way I've always wanted a man to look at me; something in his eyes tells me he would give up everything to stay with me, and that's all I've ever wanted.

He makes love to me—slow and tender—and it's not until after, when I'm wrapped in his arms that I wonder if he tasted him on me.

And, it's only then that I think about him again. My life is a merry-go-round; I'm not sure which direction I'll be looking when it finally stops.

As I drift off, the spinning slows, and all I see is that painting.

A WEEKEND TUCKED AWAY in Pierce's apartment was just what I needed, and as we pull up in front of my apartment on Sunday night, I'm not ready for it to be over.

I learned that he cooks just as well as he makes love. He likes staying in and cuddling on the couch with a movie. He literally checks off every box I had and some I didn't know I had.

Friday may not have been a good day for us, but I look at it as another sign this is all going to work out. We can fight then make up, and then the next day it's like it never even happened.

"So, I guess I'll see you in the morning?"

I lean in to kiss him. "Of course."

"Don't ever think about taking another job," he whispers against my lips.

"Don't ever think about taking another girlfriend," I chide back.

He presses his lips to mine. "Never."

Our relationship skipped the pace of a freight train and went straight for jet speed. It should scare me, but we sat side by side for months before the key was even put in the ignition.

"See you tomorrow, Stanley."

"Are you ever going to stop calling me that?"

I pucker my lips as if I'm deep in thought. "Hmm, probably not. I like having a man whose last name could be his first."

"Stanley makes me sound less than—"

"Sexy?"

He laughs. "I think that's what I was trying to say." As I climb out of his car, he does the same, grabbing my bag from the trunk. "Do you want me to walk you in?"

"It would probably be better if you didn't."

"I still don't like him being here," he says, running his long fingers through his hair.

Wrapping my arms tightly around his waist, I stare up into his eyes. "The other night, before you came to the apartment, we talked. He said you're a good guy ... that you deserve me."

"What?" he asks, narrowing his eyes.

"He let me go."

His gaze wanders left to right, studying the few people who walk along the sidewalk. "Don't be so sure. You're not an easy woman to let go."

"But you trust me?"

He looks back down at me. "Yes."

"Then, you have nothing to worry about."

After one last kiss, he watches me walk away and disappear inside the apartment building.

I've been honest with both men; my heart lies open on my sleeve now. It's clear where I need to be even if it's not always easy.

When I open the apartment door, Blake sits on the couch with a beer in his hand. It's a familiar sight. "What did you do all weekend?" I ask, setting my bag on one of the dining room chairs.

"You're looking at it," he replies, his attention fixed on a basketball game.

"Have you eaten?"

He gestures toward the kitchen. "There's leftover pizza and Chinese in the fridge. I went all out this weekend."

I want to ask so badly how he's doing, but I hold back. It goes over the line I'm trying not to cross.

"What are you doing tonight?" he asks, bringing his beer bottle to his lips.

I shrug. "I think I'm just going to read a book Reece gave me. It's been a long week, and I just need to unwind."

After a few seconds of silence, I walk away, bringing my overnight bag in the bedroom and changing into a pair of leggings and a t-shirt. I wash my face and put my glasses on, ready for a night of books, tea, and quiet. It really doesn't get any better than that.

I'm six pages in when there's a soft knock on my door; he doesn't wait for me to answer before walking in. "What are you doing?" he asks. He walks toward me in gray athletic shorts and a white tank; it's distracting, especially when you know what's under them.

I glance at the cover of the book then look back up. "It looks like I'm reading."

"Can we talk?" he asks, rubbing the back of his neck.

"About?"

He laughs nervously. "I just need to talk ... to take my mind off the path it's currently on."

I breathe a sigh of relief. I can't go anywhere too deep tonight, still feeling emotionally drained from the last week. Then an idea hits, and I smile. "Do you remember when we played Truth?"

He nods, a smile pulling at his lips. *Those damn lips.*

"Why don't we play that?"

"I'll grab the tequila."

Before I can argue that tomorrow is a workday, he's gone. I kind of forgot about the tequila part. He returns with a bottle of Jose, a shot glass and a bowl of lime slices. *I'm screwed.*

"Who gets to go first?" he asks, sitting on the other side of the bed.

"Me," I answer. I have so many questions.

He nods, pouring the first shot of tequila.

"Where have you been the last few months?"

"I went to Europe like I said I was going to, but that only lasted a couple weeks. I was such a mess, so I ended up checking into a facility in California. I was there until just a few weeks ago."

My gaze falls to the liquor bottle.

"My treatment had nothing to do with addiction," he answers, running his finger across my white comforter. "I checked in for depression. It was ruining me." He pauses, looking over at me with dark intensity in his eyes. "I realized I was losing everything good in my life—the things that still existed because I couldn't let go of the things that didn't."

There he goes making me feel guilty about moving on again. I couldn't wait forever, not when someone so perfect had waited long enough. "I'm happy for you ... that you decided to get help, but I hope you did it for yourself, too."

He smiles sadly. "After everything I've done, some days I'm all I have."

"That's not true," I whisper.

He ignores it. "My turn. How did you come up with the design for the hotel? It's fucking brilliant."

Shit. This one won't give me the opportunity to drink. *I need a drink.* "I worked on it day and night. It was all I felt like I had left for a while."

"When did you and Pierce start fucking?"

"Don't call it that, Blake, and you already used your question, so let's move on."

"I'll drink, then you answer." He squeezes the lime between his teeth then takes the shot.

This is going to go down worse than the tequila. "The night I saw you in New York."

His face falls, but I try to ignore it. Sex isn't something I take lightly. It's not something I do for the sake of loneliness. There's a reason I crossed that line with Pierce, and after I did, he meant even more to me. Blake was just a few hours too late.

"My turn," I say, trying to get my head back in the game. "Did you know I was going to be on this project before you signed on?"

"It's the only reason I took it. Wade's an asshole." Now, that's a truth.

"Did you think ... I mean, were you hoping there would still be a chance for us when you took it?" My voice shakes. The answer is written all over his face, but I want to hear it. I want to hear that he came back for me so I know everything I went through the last few months wasn't for nothing.

"Drink," he says. "That's two questions."

I skip the lime, letting the tequila burn a trail down my throat.

"Yes, and at the very least, I needed to find you and let you know how sorry I was. I never meant to hurt you, Lila. Ever."

"I know. After thinking about it, I get why you did it. You can't move forward with your life when the past still has you chained down. I've been there ... not nearly as bad as you, but I've been there."

He stares up at the ceiling for a few seconds before turning his attention back to me. "My turn. Do you think you'll stay in Chicago or have you ever thought about going back home?"

"Why are you asking that?"

"It's my turn to ask a question. That's my question."

"The thought crossed my mind, but I like my job and the friends I have here. It feels kind of like home, but it didn't always feel that way." I reflect on Charlie's and the people I met there all the way to where I am today. There's been days filled with regret, but overall, I'm happy to be here.

"You going to ask me a question, or do I have to drink another shot just to break the rules again?"

I slide down into the bed, pulling the blanket over my shoulder. "The painting you did the other day ... what was it?"

He pours the tequila then glances over at me, downing it in one gulp. "There are some truths I can't tell. You should know by now my truths are better categorized as secrets."

"But it had something to do with her?"

He points to the bottle. I pour and drink.

"Yes," he answers. "Months of intensive counseling wasn't even enough to sort through all my shit, but at least I'm not ignoring it."

I wish there were a star I could wish on to make his pain go away. Not even a wish on the largest constellation in the night sky could cure his heartache.

"If I had come home sooner, would I have had a chance?" he asks, sinking down in the bed until we're eye to eye. He knows he's making it impossible for me to skirt around the truth.

Eyes don't easily lie to eyes.

"Yes," I whisper. "I waited for you. Until New York, it would have been you."

His fingers come up, gently brushing a piece of hair from my forehead. "I really fucked up with you, didn't I?"

"Neither of us was in the right place. It wasn't our time."

He moves closer, brushing his thumb against my cheek. My conscience whispers but the tequila screams. "When will it be our time?"

I think about Pierce. This weekend. Everything. "It may never come, or maybe, it's already passed."

"I'm going to fight for you," he declares, propping himself up on his elbow to look down at me. "I thought I could let you go if I knew it would make you happy, but after sitting alone in this apartment all weekend while you were with him, I don't think I can do that."

I swallow hard. "And, if you don't win?"

"I've already lost, so what do I have left to lose?"

And, he's right. He's already lost so much that the risk is minimal.

"Pierce trusts me," I blurt, my palms sweating against the sheets.

He leans in, kissing my cheek. "He shouldn't trust me, not when he has the one thing I want."

"Blake?"

He slips out of my bed without looking back, carefully closing the bedroom door behind him. He wanted the last word, and he got it.

NOT SURPRISINGLY, I OVERSLEEP. The alcohol should have made falling asleep easy last night, but instead I was left playing Blake's words over and over.

Just when you think things are good, you find out they're not.

I've already offered him more than I can give yet he wants more.

I've asked him to leave, but then let him stay.

I've tried to keep him at arms' length but yet he keeps getting closer.

Unless I get some sort of control, this is just going to keep getting harder.

The thoughts keep coming as I ride to work. Every time things feel like they are falling into place, they unravel again. All I ever wanted was to be happy.

Maybe happiness only exists in fairytales.

I finally walk in the office two minutes after eight. I'm late for the first time in six months, and I don't even care. Sometimes when life weighs you down, you simply stop caring.

The elevator opens to my floor, and I step out in somewhat of a trance—a mix of tired, hung-over, and confused. Monday feels like Friday, and that's never a good sign.

A strong arm wraps around me from behind, pulling me back into a dark room. I'm ready to fight back, but his familiar scent tickles my nose, and I relax.

"You're late." His breath hits the back of my neck.

"I overslept. It won't happen again."

His fingers curl against the fabric of my navy blue shift dress. "Does your new perfume have a hint of tequila in it?" he asks.

"You don't like it?" I ask, hiding from the truth.

"Don't fuck with me, Ms. Fields. Who did you drink with last night because it wasn't me?"

"Why do you have to be so smart?"

"Lila."

I close my eyes tightly, praying for forgiveness in advance. "I may have had a few shots last night before bed."

He spins me around in his arms, and it's only then that I realize he pulled us into a small conference room. He has me pressed against the wall, his arms framing my face. "I've never known a person to do shots alone."

Even with only the dim light showing through the partially open door, I can see his eyes. "I wasn't alone."

He pushes against the door until it closes then frames me in again. There's nowhere to run. No lies to tell. "I don't want him there alone with you. Just thinking about it is making me sick."

I swallow my regret. I can't do anything about what's already been done.

"Move in with me," he says, his lips a whisper above mine. I answer the only way I can, standing on my tiptoes to press my lips on his. I want him to forget just as much as I need to stop thinking.

He grips the back of my neck, deepening the kiss by pressing his tongue between my lips. I'm lost in him—swept away by the waves he creates from head to toe. I splay my hands on his stomach, feeling his taut muscles through his crisp dress shirt. I slide them up until my fingers meet behind his neck, curling into his hair.

"I'm not a jealous man," he breathes as his mouth trails a path down my throat.

"Okay," I say softly, my body aching for his.

"But you make me jealous."

I wrap my arms tightly around his neck. "I love you," I whisper into his ear.

He groans, lifting me until my legs are wrapped around his hips. My dress is short ... it wouldn't take much.

The door clicks, but his lips stay on me. I open my mouth, but the light comes on, warning him before I can. He looks up but doesn't move to put me down. My cheeks burn red when I see who's standing there.

"Sorry, Mr. Stanley," Jane, the receptionist says, her own face turning a deep shade of red. "You asked me to bring Mr. Stone in here. I didn't — "

"It's okay, Jane. I've got it from here," Pierce interrupts. She wastes no time before disappearing around the corner. Not that I blame her.

My face only burns hotter when I see Blake standing where she'd been. He's not looking at Pierce ... just me. The color drains from his face as he steps back, lowering his wounded eyes. I don't want to watch, but I also can't look away.

My chest tightens as I loosen my grip on Pierce and fight to stand on my own two feet again. He lets me, but his body is still flush with mine.

"Let me go," I say, trying my best to make it so Blake doesn't hear.

He does, slowly, adjusting my skirt along the way. "Now he knows," he whispers against my ear before pulling away.

My eyes widen as I watch him take a seat at the conference room table. He looks back at me before turning his attention to Blake. There's nothing I'd like to do more than disappear from this room, but I fear for each of their safety if I do.

"Are you going to come sit down, Blake, or are we holding this meeting in the hallway?" Pierce asks, leaning back in his chair. For a second, he reminds me of Wade; I hate comparing the two.

I glance over at Blake. He's pondering, hands fisted at his side, eyes narrowed in on the man I was entangled with just minutes ago. A still frame of it could definitely go next to uncomfortable in the dictionary. "Did you call me here for a meeting, Stanley, or did you call me here to prove that you have bigger balls?"

Pierce has a smug look on his face, but as he looks over at me, his expression softens instantly. If he thought this was going to be okay—that I was somehow going to not see through him—he was wrong. He didn't just hurt Blake; he hurt me.

His eyes shift back to Blake. "A meeting, of course. We just lost track of time."

Blake steps into the room, walking right past me to the side the table opposite Pierce. I watch—panicked—as he leans over the table. "I swear to God … if you are using her to get back at me, I will fucking kill you. She's not a prize. She's not a way to punish me, and so help me God, if you hurt her—"

Pierce stands swiftly, leaning in until their faces are only about a foot apart. "I would never hurt her because I love her. Do you know what love is because I seriously doubt it." My heart races, and I have no idea what to do to make this all stop. "And while we're having our man to man, I'm going to warn you once to stay the fuck away from her outside of work. I was the one who picked up the pieces you left behind, and I'm not going to sit here and let you hurt her again."

"I was protecting her," Blake says through gritted teeth.

Pierce tilts his head, the look on his face absolutely murderous. "I forgot how good you are at protecting women."

Blake reaches across the table, grabbing Pierce's collar, and I can't take it anymore. "Stop! Just stop it right now, or I'm going to walk out of this room … out of this damn building. I've had it." Tears threaten to spill. I feel weak … I hate feeling weak.

Without another word, I walk straight out of the room, disappearing around the corner to the nearest restroom. It's only when I'm there that I let the tears fall. I'm tired of everything. You think you have everything figured out, but you never really do.

I pull a paper towel from the dispenser, letting all the scenarios play over in my head. The two of them could be engaged in an unsanctioned UFC fight for all I know. God knows neither one of them can stay quiet for too long.

Pierce needs to realize Blake isn't the reason she's gone. I think he knows it deep down inside, but it's easier for him to deal with if he has someone to blame.

And Blake … he needs to come to grips with my relationship with Pierce. I wasn't going to sit around and mourn the loss of what we had forever.

I wipe the black streaks from my cheeks and run my fingers under my eyes before gathering the nerve to walk back into the conference room. I'm really starting to despise conference rooms.

To my surprise, Pierce is the only one in the room. He sits with his back to me, head in his hands.

As I walk up behind him, I let my heels click on the floor as to not scare him. I place my hand on his shoulder, squeezing gently because at the end of the day, I know his actions are sparked by his pain. "Pierce."

He looks up, eyes red and puffy. "I fucked up," he says. "I won't do it again."

I hold his face in my hands, rubbing my thumbs against his light stubble. "You'll fuck up again because no one is perfect. Just don't fuck up like that. Don't you ever do that to me again."

He rests his forehead against my stomach. "I need you."

"You have me," I say, running my fingers through his hair.

"Only because he left."

I step back, taking away his veil. He looks up, and I swear he just ran through hell and back. He's not the same man I met on the airplane months ago. "I'm with you because I want to be with you."

"Then move in with me."

Shaking my head, I say, "It's too soon. We just started this, and I don't want to ruin it by jumping in headfirst. It doesn't mean I'm not committed to us."

He nods, pulling me back to him so he can rest his cheek against my stomach. "I'm an asshole."

I curl his hair around my fingers. "I thought we already defined that, and you didn't fit into the category."

"There are many definitions. We're all assholes from time to time."

"Believe it or not, I already figured that out."

He laughs. "There you go showing your brilliance again."

For a couple minutes, we stay just like that. Me wrapping his hair around my fingers. Him holding me as close as he can without hurting me. I wouldn't accept his apology if I couldn't feel it; it's engraved deep in the center of my heart.

"Where did Blake go?" I ask, breaking through the quietness that was mending us back together.

"Home. You two can meet here whenever you need to, and I promise I'll stay out of it. We both decided today isn't the best day to start."

My fingers halt for a second then start again. "What made you decide to change your mind?"

"This project is important to you, and you've worked hard on it. It's obvious that having Blake and I in the same room isn't going to move it along," he starts. "And, I trust you. If this is what I have to do to prove that to you, I'll do it."

I kneel in front of him, looking into his eyes. "Thank you."

He kisses me much the same way he had this morning, but this time, it's just us. Our relationship has cracks, but it's nothing a little effort can't fix.

When I can no longer feel my lips, he pulls away. "I'm giving you the rest of the day off."

"What?"

"And I'm taking the rest of the day off, too."

I smile, thinking of all the possibilities. "What did you have in mind?"

He grins like a child standing in front of an ice cream truck. "You'll see."

Ten minutes later, we're in the back of a black limo with heavily tinted windows. Not Pierce's usual style, especially mid-day. "Where are we going?" I ask as soon as we pull away from the curb.

He slips off our seat, kneeling in front of me. "When we were in New York, the car ride wasn't quite long enough." He spreads my legs then runs his fingers up my thighs, taking my dress with them. "I want to do everything with you."

His thumbs brush against my core as I slowly slide toward the end of the seat—closer to him. He's becoming really good at erasing my anger ... erasing some of the fragments of bad memories. I feel my panties being pulled off my legs and close my eyes, letting him take me wherever he wants to go.

He pulls my legs further apart. "Relax," he instructs before burying his face between them. His tongue laps my sensitive skin, heating my entire body. It's not even noon, and I'm having sex in the back of a limo; Chicago has definitely changed me.

I breathe heavily, climbing higher with every stroke. I could fall apart now, but I don't let myself, not yet. What he's doing feels too good. I wish these moments lasted forever.

With no more control left, I fall apart, quietly saying his name over and over. He doesn't stop until I've said it more times in six minutes than I have in six months.

"How do you feel now?" he asks, laying his head on my thigh.

"Like nothing else matters."

He kisses the inside of my thigh. "And you forgive me?"

"I did that before we even left the building. It's hard to stay mad at you, Pierce Stanley."

He looks up. "And you're not running this time. That's another memory I can replace."

New York.

"How much time do we have left in here?" I ask, biting down hard on my lower lip.

"As long as we want."

"Kiss me."

And he does without hesitation, giving me a taste of where he'd been. I make quick work of his belt and zipper, slipping his pants and briefs down until he's exposed. He's more than ready.

I scoot to the very end of the seat and pull his hips to mine, letting him slowly sink into me. *He's exactly what I need*, I think to myself as he pushes into me over and over.

If this is Pierce and Lila, I want to be them for the rest of my life.

IT'S HALF PAST FOUR when the limo finally drops me off at my apartment. Sex was followed by a late lunch, which was followed by another round of sex. I guess we had a lot to make up for.

The apartment is quiet when I step inside. It's a relief because I look like a woman who spent her day having sex, which is exactly what Blake doesn't want to see.

I shower, wrapping myself in my favorite blue robe. My phone buzzes just as I begin looking for something comfortable to wear to bed.

REECE: Where were you today?

ME: Long story…

REECE: Do you want to meet for a couple drinks?

I ponder her invitation carefully, deciding it's better than sticking around here alone all night.

ME: Where and what time?

She immediately begins typing.

REECE: Charlie's at 7:00? Dana will be working…

ME: Sounds like a plan. I'll meet you there.

If I woke up tomorrow morning and didn't have a man in my life, I'd still have my girls. It's important to remember that.

I slip on a simple white tank and skinny jeans, letting my hair dry naturally to show off my natural wave. The humidity is getting more and more suffocating with each passing day; it's my hair's worst nightmare.

After debating whether I should call a cab, I settle on walking. It's still light outside after all, and it's only a few blocks. The journey brings back memories of who I was when I first arrived in Chicago, highlighting how far I've come from the naïve, weakened girl who landed months ago.

Walking in, I spot the familiar Monday crowd sitting at the bar. Reece stands out from the rest of the crowd in her quirky business wear. She smiles slowly when she spots me coming toward her, a wave of relief showing on her face. By now, she should know Charlie's isn't a place you want to get to early. It's definitely not the type of place you have to run to in order to beat the crowds.

"What took you so long?" she asks as I slide onto the barstool next to her.

I glance down at my watch. "It's 7:03."

"Seriously?" she says, wrinkling her nose. "It feels like I've been here for at least an hour."

I laugh. "Charlie's will do that to you. Is Dana working?"

"Charlie said she's on break."

Speaking of Charlie, he's making his way to this end of the bar with a big grin on his face.

"Are you looking for a job?" he teases. It's his first question every single time.

"No, Charlie, but I will take a drink."

He shakes his head. "Can't hurt to ask. The usual?"

"Yes, and if you want to save yourself time, bring me two."

He shoots me a look, and I shoot one right back to let him know just how serious I am. He retreats.

Lila Fields really has come a long way.

"Spill," Reece says as soon as Charlie is out of earshot.

"What do you want to know first?" I ask, grabbing a handful of salty peanuts from the bowl on the bar top.

"Where the heck were you all day? I went to your desk at least ten times, and you weren't there."

"I had a meeting this morning, and then Pierce decided to give us both the rest of the day off."

"That doesn't sound fair," she scoffs, taking a sip of her martini. She's the only person who drinks Charlie's martinis.

"He messed up, and I think he knew he had to fix it."

Charlie puts my drinks down in front of me. I waste no time downing a few sips of the ice-cold liquid.

I continue, "Somewhere in his head, he thought it would be a good idea to pull me into the conference room when he knew Blake would be arriving at any time for a meeting. I didn't know he was coming, or I wouldn't have ... you know."

"What exactly were you doing in the conference room?"

Closing my eyes, the vision of what Blake must have seen flashes, but I quickly blink it away. "He had me pinned against the wall, kissing me. I guess he wanted to mark his territory."

Her eyes widen. "That's not cool at all. What happened?"

I sigh, massaging my fingertips over my temples. "Blake ... and Jane saw everything. I was so upset because I don't feel like Pierce trusts me. If he did, he wouldn't do that. And, if he's trying to hurt Blake, it doesn't have to tear me down in the process. I left for a few minutes, and when I came back, Blake was gone. I let Pierce have it, and we spent the rest of the afternoon making up."

"That's it? You just forgave him?"

Love makes forgiveness easy. Love is overwhelming — anger doesn't stand up well against it.

"I love him."

"And, Blake?" she asks.

"What about him?"

I finish what's left of my first drink. "How did he handle this?"

"He was gone when I got back to the room."

There's a rare silence between us. I remember when I was young, my mom used to give me the silent treatment when she was angry with me. She'd wait until she didn't want to yell before addressing whatever she needed to. Reece is doing that to me now. She has to be because she doesn't do silence well.

"Do you remember after Blake left? Do you remember what you told me?"

I nod. My heart was torn in a million little pieces, and I had to talk to someone.

"And you know how I feel about Pierce?"

I nod again.

"Blake doesn't deserve any of this from him. I can't imagine what it's like to be stuck between the two of them, but this isn't right."

"What do you suggest I do then? Break things off with Pierce? Cut ties with Blake completely? What is it that you'd like me to do?" This last week has been so frustrating; it's finally boiling over.

"I just don't want you to be stuck between them," she says quietly. "It won't end well ... not for anyone."

She makes sense. She always makes sense. "I'll figure it out. I just need to wrap up this project first."

An arm wraps around my neck. "Hey, what are you two doing here on a Monday?"

"Charlie is being extra generous with his breaks these days," I tease. When I look back, I see Dana's other arm wrapped around Reece. The three complete opposites reunited again.

"It's slow, and I had some homework to do."

"I'm softening in my old age," Charlie chimes in. I hadn't noticed him standing in front of us.

I laugh. "You better watch it, Charlie, or you're going to end up with a girlfriend or something crazy like that."

He smirks. "Whatever. That wouldn't be crazy ... it would be fucking insane. I'm going to leave the hen party before I start growing breasts. Anything I can get you girls right now?"

Looking down at my full glass, I shake my head. Reece gestures that she's done.

"Lightweights," he mumbles.

"See, he hasn't changed that much," Dana says as he walks away. "So back to my original question ... what brings the two of you in? It's like reunion night in here."

"We have a case of the Mondays," I answer. "A bad case that only alcohol can cure."

"Is the design business a little rough these days?"

Reece snorts. "It's the men in the design business that are a little too complicated these days."

"If it makes you feel any better, Blake just left an hour ago. I think he cleaned us all out of Jack Daniel's."

My heart drops. Pierce may as well have poured a bottle down his throat. I didn't help. "Did he say where he was going?" I ask.

"Charlie called him a cab. Maybe he knows."

"I need to check on him," I say, throwing a few bills on the bar. I turn to Reece. "I hate to cut this short."

She waves me off. "I understand. Go."

"I'll get the address from Charlie," Dana pipes in. She knows some of what went down between Blake and I—how it ended—but I haven't told her everything.

I can't stand the thought of Blake alone, especially when I know what he's been through. Especially when I have no idea what Pierce said before he left earlier or what was going through his head.

"Here's the address," she says, handing me a piece of paper. "Good luck."

After saying a quick goodbye, I grab a cab and read off the address I recognize as Blake's studio. It's not far from here, but it feels like forever before we pull into the rundown warehouse district. It's excruciating—not knowing what I'm going to find when I get there or knowing if he'll even be there.

When we pull up in front of Blake's building, light shines through a single window. I pay the driver and step outside, my nerves on end as I walk up the metal stairs. I debate whether I should knock or just walk in; the second option wins only because my patience is worn so thin. I just need to know he's okay.

The door opens much to my relief, a faint light shining in the room that's very familiar to me—the one where he cemented himself deeper in my heart. Just placing my hand on the knob brings some of those old feelings back up.

I'm not sure what I expected when I opened the door, but this isn't it. The protective covering that used to be on the walls is gone, replaced by splatters of paint.

Blake stands against one wall, paint covering his clothes and face. He looks as if he just completed a full twenty-six miles. His eyes lock on mine, and all I read is misery.

Agony.

Grief.

Torment.

There's a reason he's a brilliant artist.

"What are you doing here?" he asks, sounding out of breath.

"Dana said you'd been at the bar this afternoon. I wanted to make sure you're okay."

He takes a few steps toward me. I shift my gaze from him to the walls, needing to break the intensity. He's too much.

"Do you really care, Lila, or are you playing the game right along with him?"

"I'm not playing any games," I answer, not bothering to address Pierce. His agenda is a little different than mine. "I didn't know you were coming this morning. I never would have ... I never would have done that to you."

His chest brushes mine, and I close my eyes. My knees tremble. My cheeks flush. I should never have come here, but deep down inside, I wanted to. "I don't know what to believe anymore. I don't know who to trust."

"You can trust me," I say faintly, not bothering to open my eyes.

His breath hits my lips. "And how do I know that?"

I finally open my eyes looking right into his. "You should know by now that I can't look into your eyes and lie to you. You can trust me. Your secrets are still mine."

His forearm rests above my head, leaving even less space between us. I smell the whiskey. Some of the wet paint soaks my tank. "Can I show you something?"

"What?" I ask, heart pounding against his.

"This." His lips crash into mine. At first, I fight it—with little effort, I try to push him back—but my body remembers him and curves into his.

The moon is always there. It changes shape, and sometimes you can't see it at all, but it's always there. It's a lot like love.

It changes.

It fades.

But it's still there.

When Blake's lips touch mine, it's a full moon. No one has ever made me feel the way he does. I can try to convince myself otherwise, but he's the one that shines brighter than all others—past and present.

He cups my face in his hands, tugging my lower lip between his, then kissing each corner of my mouth the way he used to. His lips press harder into mine. I get the familiar smoky taste of whiskey. He traces the tip of his tongue along my lips, quietly begging for entrance. With no sense of control, I let him in.

He tastes.

The moon beams at me.

His tongue tangles with mine.

And, I want to cry.

This is what he wanted to show me. No love I've ever felt is more intense than this. No one else makes me feel the way he does.

He's the full moon. Everyone else is simply a crescent.

I wrap my arms around his neck, my body melting into his.

He kisses me breathless.

He kisses me to clarity.

He kisses me until all I want to do for the rest of my life is be with him just like this.

My lips tingle as time passes, and it doesn't even matter that I can't feel them. He's imbedded deep down—a place that only he can get to. He slowly pulls away only to brush feather light kisses along my jawline.

I want to hold him close and never let him go.

"Do you see it now?" he whispers against my lips.

I shake my head, and he immediately lowers his eyes. "Look at me."

He won't look, and I know exactly what he's thinking.

"Blake, please look at me."

He backs away, arms hanging at his side. It takes a few seconds, but he finally glances back up.

Without hesitation, I move closer, grabbing one of his hands between mine. "I didn't see it, but I felt it." Lifting his hand to my chest, I let him feel how quickly my heart beats. "I felt it right here."

I can't lie to him. I can't lie to myself.

Tears fill his eyes before he wraps me tightly in his arms, spreading kisses along my neck. "Does that mean I have a chance?" he asks, hesitantly.

"I don't know, Blake. So much has happened between us — so many things I can't just forget."

He pulls away, cradling my cheeks in his hands. "Since I left, has there ever been a day you didn't think of me?"

A single tear slips from my eye. "Not a single hour has gone by that I didn't think of you."

"Even when you're with him?"

"Even then," I answer honestly. Blake has been in the back of my mind since he left. I compare the things Pierce does to the way Blake did them, but when I'm with Blake, my only thought of Pierce is the guilt I feel for being with Blake. The obvious answer to where my heart lies shows in my thoughts.

His thumbs caress my cheekbones. "I can't stand to watch you with him. When we're all in the same room ... when I watch the way he looks at you or how he touches you. I can't do it knowing that you were mine ... knowing what it feels like to be him. My fingers ache to feel your skin. My heart bleeds slowly every second you're not with me, and I don't know how much more I can take before there's nothing left of me. I miss you so fucking much that there aren't enough words to even say it."

"What are you saying?" I cry.

"I'm saying that I made the biggest fucking mistake of my life letting you go, and I want you back. I'd do anything you ask me to, Lila. Anything. But, if I can't have you, I need to move on ... out of this city. The constant reminders of us are killing me."

The guy who always seemed so sure of himself doesn't seem so sure anymore.

"Make a choice," he begs. "And when you do, listen to your heart. That's how I found my way back to you."

Thoughts flash through my head like a fireworks display ... some louder than others ... some leaving more of an impact. My love for Blake is different than what I feel for Pierce, and there's only one I can't live without. Deep down, I've known it all along.

"You have to promise me something."

"Anything," he murmurs, kissing my lips.

It's hard to think when he's doing that. "Actually there are two things."

He slips the strap of my top off my shoulder, kissing from there to my collarbone. "I'm waiting."

"Would you still want me back if I wasn't with him?"

"Hell yes. I came back before I even knew."

I nod. He moves to the other shoulder.

"And, I need you to stay. No matter how hard things get—what demons invade—I need to know you'll let me help you through it. That you'll help me through mine."

Finally, he looks back into my eyes. "I can't promise that I won't need a break, but I promise that I'll always come back. Every day, I work through it, and every day, it gets a little better. We both just need a little patience."

I nod again. I can live with that.

He untucks my shirt, running his fingers along my bare stomach. I grip his wrist before he can go any further. "There's one more piece." My heart aches just thinking about it. "I need to talk to him first. I never wanted to be this girl, and if I don't stop this now before I have a chance to talk to him, the guilt is going to follow me."

"I want to come with you."

"This is something I just need to do."

"I don't like it."

"You don't have to," I admit.

His hands fall away from me. "When?"

"Tomorrow."

He scrubs his hands over his chiseled jaw, and I imagine them all over me ... where they should have been all along. "I'm going to stay here tonight."

"Why?"

"Because I can't stand the thought of going back to that apartment and not having you in my bed."

I'm at a loss for words. I can't imagine what it will be like to be with him again. It's surreal.

The only sound is a train close by. I came here tonight for one purpose, and it turned into something else. How do I walk away from this?

"It's getting late. I should probably be going."

"Let me change, and I'll give you a ride."

"Thank you."

His hand rests against my cheek as he presses his lips to mine one last time. "I'm the one who should be thanking you."

After he slips away, I wander around the warehouse. The painting he did the other night is perched against the wall. Even in the dark, its beauty is evident.

I wonder if the picture of me still hangs after everything we went through. With bated breath, I walk to the corner where it was hanging the last time I was here.

Arms wrap around me from behind. "That one was never going anywhere."

"It's beautiful."

"It shows exactly what I see when I look at you."

His words are making it harder to be here with him like this without going further. "Should we go?" I ask, consciously breaking the perfect moment.

"Yeah, it's getting late."

Our fingers entwine as he leads me out to his old Trans Am. It just brings back more memories. "I almost forgot about Frank," I remark as he holds the passenger door open for me.

He leans over, smiling. I missed that smile. "How can you forget Frank? He's me with wheels."

I laugh as he shuts my door and runs along the front of the car to jump in the driver's seat. "I missed that laugh," he says before putting the key in the ignition.

"I missed your smile."

"I missed having something to smile about," he adds before taking off down the dark street. The car purrs the same way I remember it, filling the silence between us. I'm still not completely sure how we got here, but it feels real.

I hope it's still real when I wake up in the morning.

THINGS DON'T ALWAYS GO as planned. I should know that better than anyone.

Pierce's car waits in front of the building as the Trans Am pulls up. If a million scenarios flashed through my mind for how this would all end, it wouldn't be like this. This is not how I wanted him to find out. It's all happening too fast.

Blake grabs my arm as I reach for the handle. "I'm coming with you. There's no way I'm leaving you here alone with him."

"No. I need to do this … I owe it to him."

He doesn't let go, and I spot Pierce walking toward the car out of the corner of my eye. Tiny little spots impede my vision. My hands go numb.

"Please, Blake. I'll call you after he leaves," I promise. Blake is fuel. Pierce is a match. I'm not letting myself get caught in the fire.

"I don't trust him."

"You don't have to. Just trust me."

I practically see the wheels turning in his head before he loosens his grip. "If I don't hear from you in the next hour, I'm coming back."

Without another word, I step out onto the curb just as Pierce reaches the car. Blake revs the engine, speeding down the street before he can witness anything that follows. This is the most awkward place to be. I kind of understand why some choose to just run. It's the coward's way out, but it's so much easier.

One look at me—the paint that covers my clothes—and the look on Pierce's face tells me he knows something isn't right. I've never ended things with anyone before, and I'm going to start with a man who didn't even do me wrong.

A man who helped me out of some of my darkest times.

A man I love.

"We need to talk." My voice shakes as the words tumble out.

He glances up at the night's sky then back to me. "Where?"

"Not here. Let's go upstairs."

He follows me in silence, his shoes hitting the steps in the same rhythm as mine. The hallway seems too short, and my hand shakes uncontrollably as I attempt to unlock the door.

"Here," he says, taking the key from between my fingers.

It opens too easily. I walk in first, setting my bag on the counter and slipping my sandals off. I do everything possible to give myself an excuse not to look back. He has to have an idea of what's to come; the air around us has completely changed from what it was earlier today.

My mind is so foggy that scripting what I want to say is impossible. Predicting how he might react is even harder. *If I could just have one more night,* I think to myself.

"Are you going to start talking?"

I turn to him, my lips part, but nothing works its way out. There's no way to do this without hurting him. The last thing I want to do is hurt him.

"Lila," he begs, shaking my shoulders. "You're scaring the hell out of me. Say something."

"It's him," I whisper, my eyes misting over.

"What did he do?"

I shake my head, the first tear carving a path down my cheek. Knowing what my heart wants doesn't make this any easier. "I love him. I tried to convince myself I'd fallen out of it, but he's the one."

He steps back, hands falling away from me. "What are you saying?"

"Do you really want to hear it?"

"Do I have a choice?"

"I love you, but I love him more. I love him differently."

His fingers tug at his hair as I watch his face turn red. "He left you."

"And he came back."

He lowers his head, rubbing his hand along the back of his neck. "He'll do it again. You don't know him like I do."

"That's the thing, Pierce. I know he could leave again tomorrow or the next day, and I'm willing to take that chance. And you don't know him like I do."

He's silent, and there's not much more I can say.

"Have you thought this through?" he asks. "Because it didn't seem to be on your mind this afternoon."

There's the proverbial knife to my heart.

Pierce became my everything because I convinced myself for a few short months that Blake wasn't. There are a bunch of what ifs. What if I'd never moved to Chicago? What if Blake had never left? What if he'd never come back? What if he hadn't forced me to see him the way he sees me?

That's all life is—a series of what ifs. There's not a fork in the road ... there's a whole freaking maze of silverware.

With two steps, he is standing right in front of me lifting my chin until our eyes are level. "Did you sleep with him?"

I shake my head vehemently until his hand falls away. "No, I'd never do that to you. We kissed, but that was as far as I let it go. I was going to talk to you tomorrow. I—"

He interrupts. "Think about it overnight. Don't do anything you're going to regret when you wake up in the morning."

"That's the thing, Pierce. My thoughts may change, but my feelings won't. You deserve someone who can give all of herself to you ... someone who'll love only you."

Walking past me, he peers out the window, hands tucked deep in his suit pockets. "This is partially my fault."

"Why do you say that?" I ask, staring at his back. I wonder if he can see my reflection in the window ... the tears rolling down my cheeks.

"I knew you weren't ready, but I pushed you anyway. You can't blame a guy for wanting a chance."

I cautiously walk toward him. "I didn't do anything I didn't want to," I answer, hoping it'll erase his guilt. I couldn't have predicted things would work out the way they did. I didn't even love Derek the way I love Blake.

"What about work?" he asks.

"I hadn't even thought about it. I'll put my resignation on your desk tomorrow if you'd prefer it."

He finally turns back around. "That's not what I want."

"Are you sure?" I ask, nervously rubbing my fingers together.

He nods, closing the distance between us. "Yeah, I'm going to be out of town the rest of the week, so that will give us both time to adjust. We're scheduled back in New York in a few weeks, and I need you there for that."

"I just want you to be okay," I whisper, doing everything I can to hold myself together. He's too good of a man to have ever gotten mixed up with me.

His hands cradle my face as he leans in to kiss my forehead. I close my eyes as his lips linger there, tears streaming. "Loss isn't something that's new to me. It may not be tomorrow, but I'll be okay."

"I'm sorry," I repeat over and over again.

"I should have asked you to dinner the night we met."

The knife he'd already lodged twists. I'm not the only one with what ifs. Something tells me I'll always be one of his.

"I should get going so you can get some rest. I have an early flight to catch in the morning."

I nod, wondering if the trip was planned before he got here, or if it's just his way of running away.

He starts toward the door.

"Hey," I say, pulling his attention back to me. "Why did you stop by tonight?"

"It doesn't matter anymore," he says reaching for the door.

"I was just curious."

There's a pause. I practically hear him thinking from across the room. Then, in a moment I'll never forget, he pulls a little black box from his pocket holding it in the air without looking back. "You're my Blake."

Disbelief and sadness render me speechless as I watch him walk out my door for what will probably be the last time.

Falling to the floor, I fold my arms over my legs, resting my forehead on my knees. If I didn't get this one right, I'll regret it every second for the rest of my life. Every. Last. Second.

Time passes as I let the tears fall. I relive the memories. I thought having Blake back would make it a little easier, but it doesn't. I hurt someone I love, and what's to come after doesn't matter so much right now.

When I'm too tired to cry, I finally pull my phone from my purse.

Lila: Come home, please.

Ten seconds later, I have a reply.

Blake: Open the door.

I climb to my feet, practically running for the door. He's standing on the other side of the threshold, staring down at me. The color drains from his face then he pulls me into his arms, letting me soak his t-shirt in tears. "I hate that I put you through that," he murmurs against my hair.

"You didn't make me do anything," I cry.

"If I'd never left, you wouldn't have been with him to begin with."

There's truth to that, but I made my own choices. "How did you get here so fast?"

He walks us slowly back into the apartment, shutting the door behind us. "I've been standing outside the door for twenty minutes waiting for you to tell me you're ready."

"Can you just hold me tonight?" I ask trying to see him the best I can with swollen eyes.

"I'll do whatever you need me to do."

I FELL ASLEEP LAST NIGHT knowing my old idea of perfect walked out the door, but that my new ideal was curled up next to me.

I woke up this morning only regretting that someone had to be hurt in the process. I don't regret my choice or how quickly I made it. Blake is still worth risking everything for.

You fall, and you get back up, but it shouldn't be enough to just walk. Floating is better. Seeing the world from another angle. And when you decide to walk again, you should control where you land.

He kisses my shoulder then brushes my hair away to place another on the back of my neck. He held me until I fell asleep, and every time I shifted during the night, he reined me back. Blake isn't the safe choice, but he makes me feel protected. The rest doesn't really matter.

"Did you sleep okay?" he asks, his lips blazing a path to the other shoulder.

"Once I fell asleep, I did. You?" It's hard to talk when he's touching me.

"I kept waking up to make sure you were still here ... making sure my dream didn't turn into a nightmare."

I open my eyes, too scared to admit I fear the same thing. Since I was young, I swear that every spoken fear that slips from my lips comes true. Some things are better left unspoken.

"You can catch up on your sleep while I'm at work," I mumble, closing my eyes and sinking further into him.

His lips still against my skin. "I don't want you working with him anymore."

"I need to work, Blake. Besides, we're in the middle of the hotel project, and I can't just walk away from that."

"Work with me."

I laugh, nervously. "I'm not a painter."

"I'll teach you."

"It's not good for us to spend all our time together. The nights will be better if you haven't seen me all day."

He sits up, looking over me. "My days will be agony knowing you're with him."

"He's gone the rest of this week, and it's not like my desk is in his office."

"Have you ever thought about moving away from here? Starting somewhere new." He grabs my hand in his, his gaze bouncing from my face to the bed then back to me.

I shift, sitting up next to him. "I've done that before. It doesn't work."

"Is Chicago where you always want to be?"

Leaning in, I press my lips to his. "I want to be where you are," I whisper.

He smiles. I smile. Everything else just melts away.

"What if we compromise? I'll finish up this project, and then I'll look for something else. We'll be working together anyway."

"I trust you," he says, lifting my hand to his lips.

"Thank you."

We sit side by side, hand in hand until time leaves me no choice than to get out of bed. "I need to get ready for work."

"Can't you call in?" he asks, wrapping his arms tightly around me.

"No. I have to work on those penthouses Wade wants before I go back to New York."

"But you're all mine tonight, right?"

I nod, leaning over to kiss his cheek. "All yours."

"I like the sound of that."

"I do to," I admit.

130

As I get dressed, I realize that Blake hasn't actually said he loves me since that night he left so many months ago. Deep down, I know this isn't a game to him, but those three words would mean so much. It would solidify my belief that I made the right decision … that they weren't just spoken in a moment when he thought he'd never see me again.

I slip my heels on with only a few minutes to spare before I have to be at the train stop. God only knows where my mind will venture to on today's ride.

Blake stands in the kitchen making breakfast like he always does. I wrap my arms around his bare stomach, resting my cheek against his back. "I hope you're only cooking for one. I have to get going."

"You need to start eating better," he remarks, covering my hand with his.

"I'll grab something on the way in."

"Here," he says, handing me a smoothie. "Start with this."

I take a slow sip. It's my favorite—strawberry banana. "That's just what I needed."

"I know." He grins, a single dimple forming.

"I need to go," I say, looking at the clock on the microwave. After picking up my bag from the chair, I kiss him one last time before heading out the door.

Love is complicated, and in its best form, it's unspoken. It shows in the things we do, not what we say.

Blake may not say he loves me, but his gestures tell me everything I need to know.

Not surprisingly, Reece is waiting at my desk when I get to the office.

"You couldn't wait, could you?" I say, setting my things on my desk.

"My life is boring."

"Find yourself a boyfriend."

She sighs. "I've tried, but no one compares to my book boyfriends so I'm just going to stick with them for a while."

"There are certain things book boyfriends can't do for you." Kissing. Sex. Orgasms. Conversation ... I guess that's important, too.

"I know," she groans. "It's just my excuse until I find a guy."

I can't help but smile as I take in her bright green shift dress with white polka dots. Her thick-rimmed black glasses top it off perfectly. Somewhere in this office is a guy who thinks about her late at night when he lies in his empty bed.

"You'll find him."

"So, back to the whole reason I walked all the way over here ... what happened after you left Charlie's last night?"

I give her the short, condensed version, leaving out the part about the little black box. Her mouth gapes. Mine probably would, too.

Her expression is pained as I finish. "Are you sure you made the right decision?"

"Yes," I answer with no hesitation.

"I can't keep up. Your life is like a tennis match, I swear."

"The game is over now." I smile, feeling in a better place than I have been in months.

She backs away a couple steps. "Is it too early to ask if your leftovers are off limits?"

"Reece!"

Raising her hands, she says, "You can't blame a girl for asking. Not that I'm his type."

"Give yourself some credit."

She walks away in a huff. "I'll work on it while I continue to live vicariously."

I shake my head, quickly getting lost in the re-dos for the hotel project. For whatever reason, what has happened over the past few days has shown me that I have the strength to get through anything.

This project is mine to either exceed or fail in. I'm not going to let myself fail.

The train ride home seems like an eternity. My eyes were glued to the clock all afternoon, waiting for the time when I could make my way back home to Blake. There's still so much we haven't worked through.

It's no surprise, but I didn't hear a word from Pierce all day. It's not surprising that he needs his space, but I still want to know that he's doing okay. I know how it feels to be on that end of things, and I wouldn't wish it on anyone ... especially him.

My phone vibrates.

Mallory: Can you talk?

Lila: You're still up?????

Mallory: Obviously. Can you talk or not?

Lila: Y

My phone rings five seconds later. I accept, not bothering to even see who it is first.

"Hey," she says, sounding slightly panicked.

"What's up? You should be in bed."

"I talked to my brother earlier. He was chipper."

My lips curl, thinking about the way he was this morning.

"What happened?" she asks when there's nothing but silence on my end.

"I realized that no matter how much better for me Pierce may be, I'd always love Blake. Always be in love with Blake."

She sighs heavily. I picture what she must look like—hair pulled up, glasses on, frustrated as hell. "He hasn't worked through all his crap yet, Lila, and I don't want to see you get hurt. He deserves someone like you after everything he's been through, but I don't think this is the right time. Go slow and tread carefully."

"I understand him better now, and I'm not going to let him push me away. I want to help him because that's what you do when you love someone."

"What about Pierce?"

"I was never going to be able to give my whole heart to him. Blake's hold on it is too strong, and he wasn't ever going to let it go."

"I hope this works for both of you. I really do," she says, her voice fading away.

"There's no other option for me." I pause, staring out my window as the train comes to a stop in my neighborhood. "You sound tired. Why don't you get some sleep, and I'll give you a call in a couple days to give you an update. In the meantime, don't worry. If we both try, even just a little bit — everything will be okay."

"Okay, I'm not going to worry about it, but you better call if you need anything. I mean it."

"You're almost as bossy as your brother."

She laughs. "That's not possible, and you know it."

"Okay, you're right. My train just stopped so I'm going to let you go."

"I'm about to drift off anyway."

"Night, Mallory."

"Good luck."

THE WALK TO MY APARTMENT doesn't take long, and when I stand in front of my door realizing it's locked, my heart sinks into my stomach. He said he'd be here when I got home.

I dig my key from my purse, unlocking the door quickly. The scene before me takes my breath away. Candles line the kitchen counter and the center of the kitchen table. Rose petals create a path from the doorway to my bedroom. I follow the path of white petals all the way to my bathroom where I hear water running. Blake sits on the edge of the claw foot tub, his fingers testing the water.

A few steps, and I'm standing in front of him, my fingers brushing through his hair. "What's all this for?"

His chin rests against my chest, his deep eyes staring up at me. "Just proving to you that you made the right choice."

"I didn't know you were such a romantic."

"I'm not. This is just something a guy should do when he has some making up to do."

"Thank you."

"Why don't you get in? I'm going to cook you dinner."

Those three words we have yet to say want to slip from my lips, but I hold them back. He's not ready to hear them.

Bending down, I kiss his lips before he has a chance to walk away. When he's gone, I quickly undress and slip into the water, soaking in the smell of lavender while being covered in rose petals. The only thing that would make this better is a glass of wine.

I sink in further until the water covers my shoulders. The door creaks open, and Blake walks in with a glass of red. Maybe our souls are so connected he can read my mind. "How did you know I wanted this?"

He shrugs. "I know you well enough, I guess. Dinner will be done in about fifteen minutes."

"Are you sure you don't want to climb in here with me?"

"It's tempting, but our dinner would burn, and I need you to eat so you have energy for what I have planned for you."

I rub my legs together at the thought. Blake is no angel; his plans don't involve dinner and a movie. It's perfectly okay with me because I want it just as much as he does.

Before he walks back out, he leans over me, tenderly kissing my forehead. "Just put your robe on," he says. "You won't be wearing it long."

It's like the first time. He's a different person. I'm not the woman he first walked in on in this apartment all those months ago. I let my skin soak in the relaxing water for a few more minutes, enjoying the rest of my wine before stepping into my robe.

The kitchen smells amazing—a hint of sautéed peppers and garlic fills the air. "What did you make? It smells delicious."

He startles, spinning to face me with a spatula in one hand. "A chicken pasta dish. I didn't follow a recipe, but my taste buds are impressed."

I grin, taking a seat at the candle-lit table. I have no idea where this Blake came from, but I like him.

"Would you like another glass of wine?" he asks, setting two plates of pasta on the table.

"I should probably eat something before I have any more of that. I'd hate to fall asleep on you."

"You're always welcome to fall asleep on me," he says as he takes the seat across from me.

"You didn't have to do all this."

He shrugs. "I wanted to."

My taste buds do a happy dance after I take my first bite. I don't think I cooked an actual meal the whole time he was gone. I either ate snacks here and there or take-out. "Where did you learn to cook?"

He stops chewing, looking straight into my eyes. "I was married once."

Honesty ... I like that.

"Did you do all the cooking?"

"Most of the time, if I wanted to eat, I had to," he says sadly, picking his fork back up.

"I can cook," I offer. I don't, but I can. I am a small town Mid-western girl after all.

"Does it always come in a Styrofoam container?" he asks, doing his best not to laugh.

"For a minute, I was thinking that a few months away made you nicer."

"Somewhere under the asshole is a layer of nice. It's hard to get to, but it's possible ... especially for you."

I'll keep peeling those layers away then.

We eat in silence mostly, stealing glances across the table from time to time. When his eyes catch mine, he does this little thing with his lips where one side curls up. It takes every ounce of strength I have to not go over and kiss him; I know where that would lead.

My plate is almost clear when I push it away. As good as it was, my stomach can't hold anymore. "Done?" Blake asks, reaching across the table for my plate.

"I can't eat anymore."

He clears the table, rinsing the plates in the sink. I can only stare. Perfection comes in faded blue jeans and a fitted white t-shirt.

"Did you save room for dessert?" he asks, coming around the counter.

I shake my head. There's no way in hell anything else is going to fit in this belly.

"I think you did." His voice is lower. I feel him everywhere, and he isn't even touching me.

He shifts my chair, so I'm facing him, and kneels in front of me. Closing my eyes, I wait for what he does next. I trust him wholeheartedly with my desires ... he's never let me down there. His fingers work the tie on my robe. Once it's loose, he pulls the sides back, completely exposing me.

The old memories flood back.

The way he touched every inch of my body.

The way he slowly made his way into my heart.

"You define sexy," he says softly, circling his palms against my nipples. I hold his head in my hands, allowing his mouth to worship my breasts. He's the master. I'm the puppet. There's not much he couldn't get me to do.

I ache for him ... not having him inside me is misery. Lowering my hands to the back of his shirt, I attempt to pull it over his head. He grips my arms, putting them back at my side. "I control this tonight. I want to make you feel like you've never felt before ... to erase every memory of him."

His lips appreciate the skin around my belly button before slipping down further. He's so close to where I've craved his touch. So close. Before the craving is satisfied, his cheek comes to rest on my thigh, his sapphire eyes finding mine. "I want to do even better than erase. I want to remind you why I'm the best you ever had even if you can't forget him."

I realized that when he kissed me last night. What he's going to make my body feel tonight will just etch it in stone.

He drags his lower lip between the inside of my thigh. His calloused hands grip my knees, spreading my legs to give him better access. He kisses my core then pulls back to look at me.

Standing, he holds his hand out. "Up."

There's this glimmer in his eyes—bright and playful. He's enjoying the slow burn. Maybe I'll come to appreciate it, too, but right now, I just want him to dull the ache—relieve the pressure I feel.

When I'm on my feet, he turns me until my back is flush with his body, hugging me around the waist as he walks us to his bedroom. He buries his nose in my hair. "You smell exactly like I remember. You don't know how hard I tried to forget, but I can't forget the unforgettable."

The door opens to more candles and rose petals. I have to look back just to verify this is really my Blake. "Just because I've never done this before doesn't mean I don't know how," he says, kissing my cheek.

"I can't believe you did all this for me."

His palms trail back up over my breasts circling once then settling on my shoulders. With each caress he ignites something in me. Then, he's standing in front of me, not touching, just exploring with his eyes. I wouldn't have been okay with this before Blake — being unclothed while someone examines every inch of me.

He peels his shirt off then unfastens his jeans, stripping himself bare in front of me. His skin doesn't graze mine, but yet I sense him everywhere.

"Does it hurt when I'm not touching you?" he asks, his voice shows heartbreaking emotion.

"Yes," I breathe.

"Where?"

Reaching for his hand, I place it at the center of my chest. That's where it aches the most.

"Where do you want me first, Lemon Drop?"

"Kiss me."

His lips mark mine slowly, his forehead pressing to mine. "Now it's my turn," he says, lifting me in his arms. I bury my face in the crook of his neck, letting the journey take me.

My back falls on the bed of rose petals. Blake stretches out over me, propping his head up with his elbow. "I hope you weren't planning on sleeping tonight."

This is worth twelve cups of coffee in the morning, I think to myself.

His touch is agile at first — subtle kisses, soft caresses, and appreciative glances. My love for him only amplifies, but the words still remain unsaid.

I want him to ravish me.

I want him to push me to the edge.

I want his rebellious love.

Minutes pass, or maybe hours. I'm gasping for air when he finally pulls his mouth away.

I feel him at my entrance, lifting my hips to beg for more ... to beg for everything he can give me. I accept him slowly, enjoying the fullness as he goes deeper.

"You feel so fucking good wrapped around me. This was made for me ... only me," he groans, reaching his fingers between my legs. His fingertips circle my skin, and with all the teasing he's already put my body through, I'm only seconds away from pulsing around him.

Then he pulls his hand away, punishing me once more. "Blake, I need to come. Please."

He presses his hips to mine, slowly rocking back and forth. The friction he creates is perfection. The tension builds as he works his way in and out. I moan, digging my nails into his back. His pace quickens as he burrows even deeper. He's carnal, biting down on my collarbone as the first wave of fireworks sweep through my body.

It's ecstasy.

A bolt of lightning.

The pinnacle.

"That's my girl," he whispers against my lips. "If I died now, I'd die knowing you were the best part of my life."

I shake my head. "Don't talk like that."

He continues to sink into me, over and over. "You were the first to believe in me. I'll spend my life showing you how much that means to me … worshipping you."

He penetrates deeper.

I scream.

He sits back on his knees, not breaking rhythm. "On your hands and knees."

With the little energy I have left, I comply. He holds my hips, pounding in then slowly pulling back out. In. Out. Deeper. Harder. I've never experienced sex like this before. Love, lust and affection … it's all there.

He fists my hair, wrapping it around his hand. The sensation sends shockwaves between my legs. It's not long before my body is squeezing around his again. This time, he follows my lead, pulsing inside me as his fingers dig into my hips.

"So good. So fucking good," he moans, a faint comparison to the screams I can't control.

I fall onto my stomach, my knees too weak to hold me up. His body covers mine. Our heavy breaths mix, saying everything we can't. Sweat drenches our skin, gluing us together. Even with the exhaustion, I'd do it all over again. It's worth it. He's worth it.

"How was that?" he asks, kissing the center of my back.

"I loved every second of it," I say honestly. I can't say those three words, but I can hint at them. "I don't know if it beats lemon drops and paint, though."

"I need to be your only one."

"You are," I promise, finding his hand beside me to kiss his knuckles.

He slips out of me, lying at my side. He's the only person I look at and see sorrow and satisfaction at the same time.

"But he's still in your heart. The heart doesn't forget so easily; I know that much."

"Our hearts weren't made to hold one person. They were made to love many with a special place for the one we love the most."

Silence falls between us. The L word seems to do that. "I can't say it," he finally admits. "The night I left—when I said it—I mean it, but I've only spoken those words to one other person and she's gone now. I don't want to lose you too."

"Love isn't a curse."

"It's a superstition."

I run my fingers along his spine as my eyes fill with tears I refuse to shed. Sadness overtakes me because of everything this man has gone through. Anger spills over because that everything may keep us from being *us*. I want to heal him until he believes in happiness again ... until love isn't a curse or superstition.

"She didn't do what she did because she thought you didn't love her enough. Sometimes, our demons are too powerful. They speak louder than the deepest of loves can cure. There wasn't anything you could have done to defeat them."

He smiles sadly. "My therapist tells me that all the time, but you have a better way of saying it."

"What's it going to take before you believe it?"

"Time."

I press my lips to his. I can deal with that as long as time doesn't turn into forever. Our future depends on it.

He combs his fingers through my hair, letting it fall back on his sheets. My eyelids are heavy, slowly drifting shut.

"You're special," he whispers. "You're the first one who's made me want to try. For the first time in years, I'm thinking of what I have instead of what's already gone."

Those are the words I fall asleep to.

THINGS ARE GOOD FOR THE next week. We fall into this pattern. I work. He cooks. We make love. The last part differs; he's had me against the wall before dinner, on the counter after, the shower, the couch, my bed, his. The apartment has been thoroughly christened.

Today is the start of a new week. Pierce is back in town, and I only have a couple weeks left before the new mood board is due to Wade.

Last week was a game of pretend, but this is reality.

Taking a deep breath, I step off the elevator, smoothing my blouse to make sure it's still tucked in. This is one of those days I hope Reece is at my desk waiting for me so Pierce has reason not to be.

A pit forms in my stomach when she's not. I set my stuff down and begin putting the final touches on my board. Seeing his apartment when we were in New York gave me a better idea of what he would favor if he booked a penthouse suite; they always say you should please your audience.

"Wow. That looks great."

I glance up from my desk to see Reece, staring down at me wearing a white blouse with black printed skunks. I've really seen it all now. "My fingers are going to bleed I've been coloring so much."

She lifts a brow. "You know they have computer programs for that these days."

"That's no fun."

"I saw Pierce this morning. The coffee pot was empty, so he took the whole damn thing and threw it in the trash. A perfectly good coffee pot."

Grabbing a pencil off my desk, I focus back on my drawing. "Doesn't Jane get his coffee?" I didn't even think he knew where the break room was.

"I have no idea, but she was in the file room crying this morning."

Her words crush my conscience. Pierce is as even tempered as they come. He keeps control by showing all of us that forward is the only way to go. That keeping our emotion out of our work is the only way to succeed. You can't dwell over failures, or hold onto wins.

"Maybe you should go check on him," she says when I don't ask any more.

I throw the pencil down. "I can't, Reece. Am I the reason for his bad mood? Probably. Is it going to get any better if I go waltzing into his office? Probably not."

"You're stubborn."

Glaring up at her, I say, "I'm sane."

"Do you have lunch plans today?" she asks, ignoring the fact that I'm annoyed.

"Blake is going to be in the area, so he's taking me out."

Her mouth forms an "O". "So," she drags the word out like it actually means something. "The first day your ex comes back to the office, your current squeeze is coming to take you to lunch. Not so much of a coincidence if you ask me."

"It is a coincidence."

She turns to walk away. "Whatever you say. By the way, when you get a minute, come find me. I want to show you someone in IT."

I shake my head. I can't imagine what her latest prospect looks like.

Focusing on my drawing, I try to finish the last bits and pieces. A dark cloud blocks my creativity because all I can think about is Pierce. What's going through his head after we spent several days apart? I want to think it's a failed business deal that put him in this mood, but I know better than that.

In the span of an hour, I shade in one tiny section only to erase it. I stare at it, but my focus is elsewhere.

After two hours of nothing, I pick the board up from my desk and head down the hallway. Jane isn't at her desk, so I keep walking, taking my chances that Pierce isn't in a meeting or on a call.

I tap on his closed door twice, waiting for an answer. When one doesn't come, I try once more.

"Come in," he says in an annoyed tone.

I turn the knob slowly, making sure the door closes behind me. His eyes are locked on his computer, but I'd be surprised if he doesn't sense that it's me. I know Pierce Stanley.

"What can I do for you, Ms. Fields?" He still hasn't looked up.

"I wanted to show you the progress I made last week. See if you had any ideas on how to finish the top floor."

"Schedule something with Jane, and we'll talk about it later this week."

My frustration grows with every second he won't look at me. "She's not at her desk."

"Send her an email. You know how to use it, right?"

I bite down on my lower lip to keep myself from breaking down in tears. He was the first person I met in Chicago. He helped me through some of the worst times. And, I repaid him by letting him down in the worst possible way.

Unable to form words, I leave him alone, walking past Jane's empty desk again back to my cubicle. He'd said we could still work together, but I'm starting to doubt that.

While I wait for lunch to roll around, I attempt to work through a few more aspects of the design, but I hate everything.

I even venture down to Reece's floor to scope out the newest guy in IT. It might be my mood, but he was about as interesting as the pencil holder on my desk and looked like the guy who wears the Dickie on *The Big Bang Theory*.

As I ride back up to my floor, I feel little hope for the rest of my day. I might as well go home sick, hit restart, and pray that tomorrow has a better outcome. The whole idea goes out the window when I see Pierce standing by my desk. His expression hasn't changed much from earlier which leads me to expect an empty cardboard box and a security escort.

"Where have you been?" he asks when I'm within earshot. He leans against the cubicle wall, his tie slightly loosened.

"I had to run down to IT for a minute." I rub my palms against my black trousers, nerves so high it almost feels as if I'm meeting Pierce for the first time. It's weird how quickly we've gone from lovers to strangers.

"Problems with your computer?"

"Something like that."

"Look," he starts, "I just wanted to come over and tell you that I'm sorry for blowing you off earlier. You don't have to make an appointment to discuss projects with me."

I let out a breath I didn't realize I'd been holding. "I shouldn't have barged into your office like that. To be honest, someone told me you were out of sorts this morning, and I just wanted to make sure you were okay."

He laughs. I'm not sure what to think. "The building won't crumble if a guy has one bad day in ten years."

"Where did you go last week?"

"I have a house in Michigan. I go there when I need to think."

I nod, not wanting to delve any deeper. "Did you come to look at my board or do you want to talk about it later?"

"Let's see what you got."

My stomach ties in knots as I flip the board over. Pierce has been critical but helpful. Hopefully, the change in the way he sees me doesn't change how he views my work.

He leans over my chair to get a better look. "I like where you're going, but why so modern?"

The knot gets a little tighter. "I paid attention when we were in Wade's apartment a couple weeks ago, and I tried to create somewhere he would like to stay."

"Okay," he says, tracing his finger along the drawn penthouse walls.

"You don't like it?"

"It's not that I don't like it." He pauses, studying it for a few more seconds. "Think about the rest of the hotel design. If you walked in front of the building or into the lobby, is this what you'd expect?"

That's why he's had the success he has. He thinks from every angle. "This is why you were hired for the project."

"If the client wanted to use his style, he wouldn't have a need for us. Our job is to hear his vision and insert our expertise. That's what we've done with every room in that hotel."

I nod, letting it all sink in. Making notes on what is salvageable and what needs to change.

"You've been back for a few hours, and you're already moving in on her."

We look up in unison, to see Blake standing there, a tight expression on his face. This morning has been so screwed up, I almost forgot about lunch. From the look of it, I'm probably going to regret it.

"Lila is my employee, and the last time I checked, working on a project together isn't equivalent to rolling around in bed," Pierce snaps back.

"It's happened once," Blake shoots back.

"She was just as much a part of it as I was."

Blake lurches forward, but I stop him, curling my fingers around his collar. "Don't."

Our eyes connect, and his whole expression softens.

"Let's go to lunch. Pierce and I can wrap this up later."

Out of the corner of my eye, I watch Pierce walk away. This is one of those forks where the path is easy. I've already made my choice. One man's heart is mine. One man holds my happiness in his hands. Even if I'm worried about the other, this is where I belong.

I loosen my grip on Blake and grab my things off my desk. Without a word, I lead us through the maze of cubicles not oblivious to all the stares. I'm the wrong type of fish to be stuck in this fish bowl.

Just before we reach the elevator, his arm wraps around my waist, pulling me into a dark room. The door closes. The lock clicks. My back is against the wall, his breath against my ear.

"I can't do this. I can't stand knowing that you're going to work every day side by side with a man who had what should have always been mine."

"You left," I remind him. "Just because you decided our life was over doesn't mean mine stopped."

"I hate him."

"I know," I whisper, wrapping my arms around him. "Were you with anyone else? While you were gone." I don't want to know. I need to.

"I didn't touch another woman. I couldn't because all I ever thought about was you. I left hoping that some day I would learn how to be with you."

"You already know."

His fingers deftly work the buttons of my blouse until the tops of my breasts are exposed. His hot mouth covers me as he unbuttons my pants and slips them down over my hips, falling at my ankles.

He places his hands under my thighs to free my legs. With one arm wrapped around me, he uses the other to free himself from his jeans.

I've heard that having sex in public heightens arousal ten-fold, and I was never a believer.

Now, I am.

A worshipper in the religion of it, actually.

Blake spins us around, carefully laying me back against a hard, cold surface. My legs are spread wide as he impales me over and over again. There's no lovemaking, kissing or sweet words. Every time he penetrates, he's reminding me who he is ... who he owns. He damaged me for anyone else the first time we were together; it just took him coming back for me to realize it.

Some people try to tell me he's no good, but what's good for them might not be good for me. This is for him. No matter how much I tell him, this is how he solidifies his place.

If only he knew how he commands my heart.

How he hugs it.

He's my anchor. Where he goes, I go. What he feels, I feel.

I lift my hands to his sweat-soaked t-shirt, yearning to feel something more as I lose all control. His hand covers my mouth. I bite down hard on his finger to muffle my screams. He's not far behind, grunting as he explodes into me.

He tugs my arms, folding them around his waist. His heart pounds against my cheek as I work to calm my trembling body.

"There's no one I want if I can't have you." His voice is horse, his breathing heavy.

"You have me, Blake. I don't know what else I can do to prove that to you," I say softly, tracing circles on his stomach.

"Don't spend your days with him."

"We talked about this."

"That doesn't mean I accept it."

For a few minutes, we hold each other, climbing off the high. It's only then I realize we're in the same conference room where he walked in on me with Pierce. My life has come full-circle.

I rest my chin on his chest, looking up into his eyes. "We missed lunch."

He smooths my hair and runs his thumbs under my eyes to help mask the after-effects of sex. "I'll run and get you a sandwich since it's my fault we didn't make it out of the building."

"Don't worry about it. I'll grab a bar from my desk."

"The hell you will. You need to eat, Lila. Take care of yourself."

"You're pretty bossy for someone who just got his way."

He kisses my forehead. "Maybe someday you'll learn, Lemon Drop."

IT HAS HAPPENED ONE other time. Four days before my high school graduation to be exact. I drove thirty minutes to another small town to buy a test where no one would know me. I'd stopped at our crumby little gas station—the type where you still have to go inside to ask for the key.

I remember my hands shaking so badly I almost didn't get the package open before I peed my pants. I held it under me, praying to God that there would only be one line showing in five minutes.

As I held the test in my hand, I stared at the stained white walls processing what my future would hold if I didn't get the result I was praying for. There would have been no college, at least not in the dorms. Derek would've had to make a choice between a life with me, and the life he had planned. I was pretty sure he would choose me, and maybe we would get married, and it would all work out. And then I thought about how I would tell my parents. That would've been the worst part.

And tonight as I look down at the test, the result is different than it was all those years ago.

A prayer didn't save me this time. I bite down on my lower lip, trying to process it all. This time, it's not the future that scares me, or making the phone call to my mother to let her know I'm taking life's steps a little backwards. It's telling someone he's going to be a father.

Someone I've only known for less than a year. Someone who I've never discussed marriage or kids with. Someone who can't even say I love you because he's too afraid of losing me over it. Someone I've only been back together with for four weeks.

"Lila, are you still in here? I'm ready to get something to eat."

I stand, straightening the skirt of my dress and open the door. Reece peers in. "Why are you crying?" she asks.

I hold the white plastic stick up. Her eyes widen as she comes closer. "Oh. My. God."

"What am I going to do?" I ask, shifting back and forth on my heels.

She looks around to make sure no one else is inside. "Who's is it?"

"It's mine," I say, visibly shaking.

"I know that, but whose baby is it?"

My lips tremble. I never thought the day would come when someone would have to ask me whose baby I'm carrying. "It has to be Blake's. I used condoms with Pierce as far as I can remember, but Blake and I haven't been." I pause, glancing down at the two pink lines again. I keep thinking this is a dream I'll wake up from, but it isn't.

"Aren't you on the pill?"

I shake my head. "I've been taking the shots instead. I did the math, and the last one expired a couple months ago."

"You need to tell him. You can't do this by yourself."

"I'll tell him tonight. I just don't know how he's going to take it," I admit.

"He loves you."

I shrug. I hope he does.

"Maybe you should take the rest of the day off and process this," she suggests as the tears continue to roll down my cheeks.

She's right. There's no chance in hell my mind is going to be able to focus on anything else. "Can I get a rain check for lunch? I'm going to let Pierce know I'm leaving and try to catch the 1:00 train."

"Of course, and you better call me if you need anything. I'd be more than happy to bring a pint of ice cream over."

I tuck the test into a plastic bag and toss it in my purse. I have no idea what I'm going to do with it, but I'm not ready to let it go just yet.

She hugs me and waits while I wash my hands, passing me a paper towel. I wish I could rewind a few weeks and do things all over again, but this is one thing I'm just going to have to live with.

I walk quickly back to my desk, noticing I have twenty minutes until the next train leaves. Too blotchy from crying, I pick up the phone, hoping Pierce will answer.

He does on the third ring. "I was just about to call you."

"Is there something I can help with?" I ask, throwing some work into my bag.

"Are you okay?"

"Yes. Why?"

"You sound as if you've been crying. If he hurt you, I'll—"

"He didn't do anything. I'm just not feeling well. I was calling to tell you I'm taking the afternoon off," I say, keeping my voice as steady as possible.

"Our trip to New York got moved up to tomorrow instead of Wednesday," he announces.

Pressing my fingertips to my temples, I massage slowly. "What time?"

"Eight. My car will pick you up at 7:30."

"Okay. If you need anything this afternoon, don't be afraid to call," I add, feeling terrible about bailing before a big meeting.

"Hope you feel better."

"Thank you."

I haven't said anything to Pierce yet about leaving after the hotel project is complete, but I've hinted at it. He sees the writing on the wall.

With only minutes left before the train stops, I pull my purse over my shoulder and scurry to the elevator. Once inside, I watch the numbers go down hoping the elevator doesn't stop as each one passes. With three minutes to spare, my heels click across the lobby floor. I run as fast as I can, hopping on the train right before it roars down the tracks.

The ride is just long enough to sort out my thoughts and worries. It's already done—there's a baby growing inside of me—and whether he decides to stick by me isn't up to me.

He could walk, but all I really want him to do is hold me and tell me everything will be okay. I need a partner in this. I need my lover.

As I climb the stairs, I'm undecided as to whether I want him to be home or if I'd rather have time alone with my secret.

I'm relieved when the door is locked. I slip my key in and step into the quiet apartment, setting my stuff down on one of the dining room chairs.

There's one place in this small apartment that relaxes me. I turn on the bath water, pouring in the rest of the lavender Blake bought me several weeks ago. The sweet fragrance fills the air as I undress, tossing my work clothes haphazardly across the floor.

The scent alone brings back memories of that night, the night we may have created this baby. After testing the temperature with my toe, I sink deep into the water letting it flow over my shoulders.

With no distractions, I let my mind wander off. I envision a little girl dressed in one of the frilly little outfits my mom always put me in. She'd have my red hair and curls, with any luck. I see her giggling, and I wonder what I would name her. Something pretty, yet simple. Something that would match the strength I'd hope she'd have.

Then I picture a little boy with Blake's dimple and light, sandy hair. I picture him in Blake's studio covered in paint, smiling at me with the same mischievous grin Blake often wears. He'd be a heartbreaker … that's for sure.

"There you are," Blake says, scaring me enough that water splashes from the tub.

I cover my chest, attempting to catch my breath. "I didn't hear you come in."

He sits on the edge of the tub. "I wasn't expecting you to be home."

"I wasn't feeling very well, so I decided to take the afternoon off."

Leaning in, he rubs the backs of his fingers across my cheek. "Can I get you anything?"

I shake my head.

"Is there anything I can do to make it better?"

"You could get in here with me."

He smirks, staring down at my bare breasts. "Nothing would make me happier," he remarks, pulling his shirt over his head. His movements put me in a deep trance — quietly studying the ridges of his stomach as he unbuttons his jeans letting them fall next to my clothes.

He slides in across from me, his eyes glued to mine. He pulls my legs between his. "Are you going to tell me what's wrong?"

There are times in life when words just aren't enough. Or when words are too much. I stand on my knees and straddle his lap as my lips crash into his. I push until my teeth hurt because that's how much I love him ... I love him so much it hurts.

His hands slowly inch up my back, holding me close to his chest. I could stay trapped in his love forever.

Desire sweeps through my body. I pull back just enough to gaze into his sapphire eyes. This man loves me. He may not want to say it, but he does.

Reaching between our bodies, I grab hold of him and sink down. His mouth falls open, his hands grip my hips as I come up a few inches then fill myself with him again.

"Jesus, Lemon Drop, did you come home early because you missed me?"

His fingers travel up my sides, his thumbs brushing against my breasts. Our breaths echo in the small, enclosed room.

I speed my pace, enjoying the friction. Enjoying the feeling that comes before I lose control.

"That's it, let go, Lila. I'll catch you ... I'll always catch you."

Tears prick my eyes as I reach my peak, screaming his name over and over. He's my harbor from the storm. My safeguard. My shelter. That's what I still want him to be after I break the news.

I nestle against his chest, enjoying the feel of his strong arms wrapped around me. I cry silently, my tears falling into the water. I just got him back, and I don't want anything to change us. We're not perfect, but I still like us.

"Hey," he says, putting space between us. "Are you crying?"

"Yes."

"Why?"

"Because I love you, Blake."

He looks away. He can't say he loves me, how is he going to accept a baby? First comes love they always say.

"You can't say it. I get it." Standing, I pull my robe from the hook and wrap it around my body. "I need to go lay down. My head is killing me."

Anger fills my heart as I lie on my pillow and stare out the window. The sun from earlier has disappeared. Dark clouds cover the sky, rain falling steadily against the windowpane.

All I've ever wanted was to be happy. Why is that so hard? I see flashes of bliss, but just as quickly as they appears they're gone again.

The side of my bed dips. If he only knew the power he holds over me. How I ride the ups and downs with him.

He wraps his arm around me. "I'm sorry. You mean so much to me. I just ... I can't."

"Do you want children?" I ask. It just comes out.

His arm loosens. No response comes. That pretty much answers the whole question.

"I'm pregnant, Blake."

He's speechless, body suddenly rigid behind mine. This little voice echoes in my ear, telling me over and over I'm going to be in this alone. Blake's a drifter—in and out of my life ... my heart. Babies ground you. They give you a purpose outside of yourself—something beautifully unselfish.

Unable to stand the silence any longer, I turn to face him. He squeezes his eyes shut. My heart absolutely shatters.

"Who?" he asks, voice shaking.

"Who what?"

"Who's the father, Lila? Is it me or is it *him*?"

I verge on tears. What's going through his head right now is ten times worse than what's going through mine.

I reach up to stroke his cheek but think better of it when he rolls onto his back, staring up at the stark white ceiling.

"It's our baby. I was never with him without protection. Never."

He hops up from the bed, staring down at me completely naked. "You're hitting me with a lot right now, Lila. I honestly don't know if I can do this. Babies deserve nurture and love; I'd be a shitty parent."

"We're in this together," I answer back, attempting to hold him with my eyes. I've seen this Blake before; he's ready to run. It's easier for him to run.

"I need to think for a while," he says staring at the open door.

"You said you wouldn't leave," I whisper as he starts walking away.

He does anyway. I hear him rummaging in his room then the door slams leaving my heart broken. I laid it all on the line, and now that it's all said and done, I have nothing left but the baby that's growing inside me.

BLAKE DIDN'T COME HOME last night. After what happened in the past, it's something I should have come to expect.

Things got hard.

He ran.

This is all of my worst nightmares coming true at once. Alone. Pregnant. Lost. Unloved.

Life more than sucks sometimes.

A knock sounds at my door causing me to jump up from the kitchen table. I grab my purse and luggage, heading to the door in my carefully chosen silver flats. I'm exhausted. My breasts feel like they're going to either explode or start on fire. Sore feet don't need to be added to the mix.

I open the door, and Pierce immediately reaches for my luggage. "I can get that for you."

"Thanks," I say, trying my best not to cry over his simple, kind gesture. My hormones are already making me crazy.

After locking the door, I follow him down the steps, through the door, and into the waiting car. It's just enough time to pull myself together. A Starbucks cup waits, and for just a moment, I smile. My whole world hasn't completely gone to crap yet.

"Where's Blake this morning?" he asks as the car speeds down the city streets.

"I don't know," I reply honestly. I never even got a chance to tell him I was leaving today instead of tomorrow.

"That didn't take long."

"What do you mean?" I ask, spinning the coffee cup over and over in my cup holder.

"For him to walk out again."

"He just had some things to do. He'll be back."

Pierce laughs sadistically. "Everything is a competition to him, Lila. He only wanted you because I had you. You can sell his sincerity to yourself a hundred different ways but none are worth buying."

"You don't know us, Pierce."

"No, but I know him, and I know you. I was rather good at addition back in school. This is simple math."

I slouch down in my seat, unwilling to listen to anything else he has to say. Pierce shouldn't enter judgment when there's so much he doesn't know.

The silence continues as we board the plane and wait for the pilot to get the all-clear. Pierce overstepped his bounds, but I can't decide if I'm upset about that or the fact that he's right about some of it.

I couldn't imagine leaving someone after they just told me they were carrying my child.

I also can't imagine losing someone I loved for years the way he did.

Maybe Blake and I are like a complex math problem, but there are factors Pierce doesn't know. Factors I don't know.

Pierce holds a glass of champagne out to me. "This will make it better."

But it won't because I can't drink it. "No thanks. I'm not feeling very well this morning."

"I know it's him,' he says. "I'd say I told you so, but I know my voice doesn't speak louder than your heart."

"Can you just leave it?"

"I'm sorry. We should probably be preparing for the meeting and not this."

The plane takes off. We sit quietly, staring out our windows. I try to think about work, but it's a blip compared to everything else going on in my life. Not having alcohol for the next nine months might kill me.

"Why aren't you married?" I ask out of the blue. I've wondered that for a while—why a woman wouldn't have snatched up Pierce Stanley by now.

"I've had a few serious relationships, but none of them have lasted long enough to get to that point."

"Why not?"

"You tell me, Lila."

I lift a brow, sipping from a bottle of cold water. "How would I know?"

"You're one of the few."

If that doesn't make your heart sink, I don't know what will. I've been with him twice. I've left him twice. Maybe it wouldn't be so bad, but I've never met a man more deserving of a true love.

"It wasn't you," I finally answer. "I think love has a lot to do with the order in which people walk into it. We all have many people we could love—who we could fall in love with—but it all comes down to who we find first. I'm guessing some of the women you met just weren't the right match or weren't deserving of the type of love you give. Blake wove himself into my heart first. Once that happens, it's hard to get untangled. Not impossible, but difficult."

Pierce throws back the rest of his champagne, quickly pouring another glass. "Are you sure you don't want some of this?"

Waving him off, I say, "I'm fine."

Another long pause. "There's never going to be a morning I wake up and don't regret not doing more on that flight from Omaha to Chicago. Or wish I didn't call you sooner," he says sadly.

Tears well. I want to hide them, but it's impossible. "A time may come where I wake up every morning wishing you had, too."

The rest of the ride is quiet. I sip slowly on water while Pierce downs almost a whole bottle of champagne. If it has any effect on his abilities, he doesn't show it as he helps me out of the plane and into the waiting car.

This is the first time I've ever flown somewhere for just a few hours. We'll meet with Wade then hop right back on this plane.

"Is he going to like the penthouses?" I ask, needing something to break through the silence.

"I love the penthouses."

"That's not what I asked."

"Who gives a fuck about Wade's opinion?"

I sigh, staring down at my watch. "You're drunk. We should get something to eat quick before we head off to the meeting."

He laughs loudly. "I'm not that drunk, but if you're inviting me to lunch I won't refuse."

I'd yell at him, but this is my fault, too. I ask the driver to drop us off at a sandwich shop near Wade's office. Maybe if I can just get a little food in him and buy some time, we'll get through this. If I put an inebriated Pierce anywhere near Wade, one of them is bound to die from manual strangulation.

"The Carnegie Deli for lunch?" he asks, shaking his head. "This might be the only meal we get while we're in town."

"It's the only thing we have time for. The meeting starts in less than an hour."

"It's okay to be late to a meeting every once in a while, Ms. Fields."

I snort. "Yes, I'm sure that will make him appreciate my penthouse designs even more."

After picking up two sandwiches and water, we find a place to sit.

"There's something different about you today," Pierce remarks as he takes his seat. "Did you color your hair or something?"

I shake my head, taking a careful bite of my sandwich. Plain turkey shouldn't upset my stomach too much. Pierce is too freaking smart even when he's had too much to drink. My hair hasn't changed, but my breasts are swelling more and more every hour.

His eyes slant. Sooner or later, he's going to figure it out. Lila likes to drink. She likes to wear pencil skirts that hug her tight from her stomach to her knees. Pregnant Lila isn't going to be able to hide for long.

"How's your sandwich?" I ask, just pulling pieces of bread from mine. The meat is not sitting well.

"It's sobering me up if that's what you were trying to do." He grins, but the cocky look quickly disappears.

My skin clams up as my stomach goes from mildly nauseated to a full turn. Without a word, I run to the bathroom, barely finding an open stall before losing the little bit of food I ate. Sweat rolls down my forehead. I rip a handful of toilet paper to wipe it away, making sure the nausea settles down before I stand back up.

After fixing my make-up and quickly brushing my teeth, I rejoin Pierce who eyes me cautiously from across the table. "Are you going to tell me what's wrong?" he asks after a seconds long staring contest.

"I'm just nervous about my presentation this afternoon," I lie.

"He's going to eat it up." The way he looks at me tells me he isn't sold. He's never an easy sell.

I nod, doing my best to look anywhere but at the uneaten food on the table. "Should we get going?"

"We can walk if that's okay with you. He's only a couple blocks from here."

"Some fresh air would probably be good … as fresh as you can get in New York, anyway."

Pierce picks up my portfolio and tucks it under his arm. He's defined asshole, but he's also defined gentleman.

"Are you sure you don't want to talk about him?" Pierce asks, tucking his free hand in his pocket.

"That would be a little weird, don't you think?"

"I just don't like seeing you like this again."

"Thank you for caring, but we need to draw a line somewhere in our friendship. He's off limits."

We step into the elevator. Just the two of us. Instead of standing beside me, he stands in front of me, swiping his thumb under my eye. "You missed some mascara."

"You don't have to be so nice to me," I say, trying to avoid looking right at him. Two minutes before a meeting is not a good time to cry.

"I don't know any other way to be with you."

The elevator door opens before I can say anything more.

We quietly walk down the hall and into the empty conference room. I take a seat and pull my phone out, partly to avoid talking to Pierce, but mainly to see if Blake has been trying to get ahold of me.

Nothing, so I take the initiative.

Lila: I'm in NYC. Didn't get a chance to tell you.

It shows as read right away, but he doesn't type a response. Maybe he's relieved to have me gone. Tonight, I'll go home to an empty apartment, and we'll start our old cycle all over again. Only this time, I'm not going to let him spin me in circles. This isn't a game; this is life ... my life.

Wade walks in, all smiles. "Good to see the two of you again."

"I'm hoping it will be the last time for a while," Pierce chides, unbuttoning his suit jacket. He sobers up well.

"I guess that depends what you have for me."

I clear my throat and stand, making my way to the revised board. My stomach churns, but it's hard to say whether it's nerves or hormones. "I redid the penthouses ... a few times actually. I think what I've come up with will appeal to most wealthy travelers while still keeping a sense of fun."

I pause unintentionally, my whole mind freezing up. There's too many personal things weighing on it for me to even pretend that this matters to me today. "I gave the rooms a rustic-modern feel. Rustic furniture with clean lines as well as all the modern amenities people have come to expect."

I step to the side to give him a better look. He takes in every detail, face expressionless. My whole future hangs in the balance.

"Explain to me why we'd have wood planks around the fireplace instead of tile or rock."

I swallow hard. "It fits into the lobby and gives the room a rustic feel. I even thought it would be great if we did wood-burning fireplaces instead of gas. Room attendants could help when a guest wants a fire."

"We're not putting together a proposal for Vail or Aspen, Ms. Fields."

LISA DE JONG

My eyes well with tears. Hurt feelings and hormones are not a good combo. My stomach churns like it did earlier in the plane. "Excuse me," I say, running out of the room, disappearing into the same bathroom I sought refuge in last time we were here.

This time, I lock the door to ensure no one visits unexpectedly. It's only then that I take a few deep breaths. The same thoughts repeat over and over in my head: *Wade hates my designs. I'm going to be a mom. Wade hates my designs. I'm going to be a mom.*

My phone dings in my purse.

Blake: When will you be back?

I debate if I should answer him or just leave him wondering. He leaves me wondering a lot, but I still want him. We tend to always crave what's worst for us.

Lila: Late tonight.

Several seconds pass.

Blake: We need to talk.

Lila: I tried to last night.

I picture him sighing, running his long fingers through his hair while pacing whatever room he's in.

Blake: Tell me again. Give me another chance.

Before I can think of a reply, there's a heavy knock on the door. "Lila, are you in there?"

I wipe my eyes, inhaling a deep breath. "Yeah, just give me a couple minutes."

Stepping out of the stall, I check my make-up, patting my forehead with a paper towel. I would give anything to not have to step back in that conference room again. But the reason people make money in business is because it isn't easy.

When I open the door, Pierce is standing on the other side, hands in his pockets, forehead wrinkled. "I'd ask if you're okay, but I already know the answer to that."

"I'm not in the mood to be picked apart," I say, studying the pads on my fingers.

His arms wrap around me, pulling me into his chest. "I'm sorry you had to deal with that, but we need to go back in for a few minutes to wrap up. I told him if he screws with you like that again, I'm going to take him for everything he's worth. Can't promise it will help, but I'm not beyond knocking his teeth out."

"I'm going to need some chocolate after this," I mumble against his dress shirt.

He laughs, running his hands up and down my spine. "I know just the thing that will make you feel better."

"Is your mind in the right place, Stanley?" I tease, needing to lift about 100 pounds of pressure off my back.

"My mind is exactly where you want it to be," he answers back.

Without another word, he loosens his grip on me and holds my hand in his to walk back to the conference room. Wade chats away on his cell phone, only looking back up for a brief moment when we walk in.

Ignoring the aura he gives off, I stand next to the mood board waiting for the meeting to resume. It gives me a couple minutes to decide what I want to say. Pierce walks the room, glancing at the art pieces Wade has displayed. As soon as Wade says goodbye, Pierce takes his seat, smiling at me to loosen my nerves even more.

"I'm glad you decided to rejoin us," Wade says with a smile only the devil could match.

"Where did we leave off?" I ask, deciding I want to avoid the fight he wants to start.

He rests his forearms on the table. "I was picturing your design in Colorado."

"Oh yes, you were being a jerk. Not sure how I forgot that," I hit back.

Pierce raises his hand. "Let's move on. Ms. Fields and I have a plane to catch soon."

"Fine, Stanley, I'll cut the bullshit. I like the design, and I think with a few tweaks to the furniture proposal and colors, it would work."

I lift my brow in surprise. "So, you're okay with the wood?"

He regains his signature cocky grin. "I love the wood."

There are so many choice words that would like to fall from my lips, but I hold them back. Pierce has less than five minutes to get us out of here before I completely lose it.

"Lila can make a few tweaks and send it back by the end of next week. I don't think this requires another meeting."

"As much as I live for these moments," Wade responds. "That'll work."

"Are we done here?" Pierce's words are tight. We're both ready to kill him.

"We have clear direction now. Let's see what you can do with it."

Our goodbyes are always short, but this one breaks a new record as we exit less than two minutes later, hopping into a waiting car.

"There aren't many people I don't like," I admit as we start down the street. "But I really hate him."

"You're part of a large club." He glances out the window as we speed down 5th Avenue. "Are you ready for chocolate?"

"As much as you can get me."

The car pulls in front of Magnolia Bakery. "Sit tight. I'll be right back."

I've heard of Magnolia before and always wondered if the cupcakes taste as good as people say. Another signature piece of New York I'm going to try.

He emerges a few minutes later with a box and two bottles of water in his hand. "If these don't make you feel better, I don't know what will."

I open the box to six different flavors. "Oh my. What kinds are these?"

He points to one in the center with light brown frosting. "Knowing you, I'd start with that one. It's a chocolate cupcake with peanut butter buttercream."

"I'm sold." I pick it up, carefully pulling back the paper. After taking my first bite, I close my eyes, letting the flavors marry on my tongue. "This is so damn good."

When I look to Pierce, he's finishing off the last of a red velvet cupcake. "What?" He shrugs. "Did you think I was going to let you eat the whole box?"

"Have at it. I'm getting full already."

I polish off the cupcake then stare out the window as we pass stores, restaurants, and people. My mind has time to wander again. In a few short hours, we'll be back in Chicago, and I have no idea what awaits me there. I need space, time … actually, I don't know what I need.

I'm not ready to face him—he's either going to make it better or break us apart forever. Sometimes, I forget to put myself first. Sometimes, I jump into things without clarity. There's only one thing I can do to get me there.

"I need to go home," I announce.

"That's where we're heading."

"No, I mean Nebraska. I need to go home."

I am met with silence. Long and awkward.

"Are you going to tell me what's going on?" he asks, his voice softer.

Pierce has been like my journal; he always gets the truth.

"I'm pregnant."

His eyes widen. His mouth opens, but no words come out.

I start crying; that seems to be the only thing I'm good at today. "It's not yours if that's what you're thinking. I've done the math, and you always used condoms didn't you?"

"Yes. I mean, I think I did." His stare is distant … empty as he rubs the heel of his palm against his chest. Any hope he had for us is crushed. I crushed it.

"I don't know what to do," I confess, watching him because I deserve his pain.

"Have you told him?"

"Of course. Why do you think he wasn't at the apartment this morning?'

He shakes his head, baring his teeth. "I never would have left you."

Does he think I don't know that?

"I need to go home for a few days. I need to get away … to clear my head."

"Do you want to go now?" he asks, pulling his phone from his pocket.

My thoughts are all over the place. Blake wants to talk, but I don't know if I want to hear what he has to say. Plus, time may be exactly what we need.

I nod. I have clothes at home. Most everything else I can get somewhere, and it would give me time to see my doctor.

Pierce puts the phone to his ear. "Hey, Mike, can you change our flight plan? We need to make a stop in Omaha before going home." There's a pause. Pierce nods. "Thanks, Mike. I appreciate it."

This is one of those moments where I question my decision. My stupid heart must have something against perfection.

"Thank you." There is nothing else to say.

He wraps his arm around my neck, gently kissing my cheek then lays my head against his chest. "I'd do anything to make you mine, but what I really want is for you to be happy."

"You'll never know how much this means to me ... how much you mean to me."

His fingers brush through my hair. "I do. I just wish you knew how much you mean to me."

If he says anything else, I don't hear it. I drift to sleep on a heart-shaped pillow.

IT'S DARK BY THE TIME the plane lands in Omaha—the city lights the only thing I see. I recognize Woodmen Tower and the new event center.

"Thank you for doing this," I say to Pierce as the plane comes to a stop.

"You don't need to keep saying it. I did it because I wanted to. Don't worry about coming back to the office until Monday. You should have enough sick time built up."

I nod, pulling my purse over my shoulder. "I guess I'll see you Monday morning." I wrap my arms around him in a show of appreciation.

He kisses my forehead. "Call me if you need anything."

Within a few minutes I'm at the counter renting a car to drive back home. While the agent processes my information, I pull my cell phone out, turning it back on. I wait for it to load as she hands me the keys and rattles off several minutes of disclosures.

Three messages pop up.

Reece: Did you talk to Blake? Call me, plz.

Blake: What time will you be back?

Blake: I need to see you.

For now, I tuck it back in my purse and go claim my mid-size Honda from across the street. Blake has left me hanging so many times that it justifies me doing the same just to pay him back. I'm not that person.

Lila: I went back home to see my parents. Back next week.

Before pulling my car from the lot, I call Reece. It rings four times before she picks up.

"It's about time. I've been worried about you."

"Sorry, we were in New York all day and then I decided to come home for a few days."

"Home?"

I start the car, letting the air conditioning kick in. "Pierce dropped me off in Omaha. I need some fresh air for a few days ... some time to think without all the distractions."

She sighs. "I'm going to miss you, but you made a good call. I guess Blake didn't take it too well, huh?"

"He ran the way he usually does. He's been texting me today, but I'm not going to let him take me on the roller coaster with him this time. I have more than just myself to worry about."

"I don't blame you."

"It sucks, though," I admit, tearing up again. "Look, Reece, can I call you back tomorrow? It's been a long day, and I'm really tired."

"Of course. Get a good night's sleep, okay?"

"I will." Before she can hang up, I add, "You're a great friend. I really mean that."

"You are, too," she replies.

I laugh quietly. I don't see how that's possible when I have all the problems. "I try to be. Talk to you later."

"Bye."

As I drive out of Omaha onto the country roads Nebraska is notorious for, I roll down the window and turn up a little Brantley Gilbert. The smell of fresh cut grass and the occasional scent of cattle seep into my car, but they're just more reminders of home.

It's always going to be my safe place.

My nerves don't show until I pull into my small town. In less than a minute, I'll be in my parents' driveway. There won't be any way to explain my visit without telling them everything.

I take one deep breath and put my hand on the door handle.

I take another and actually pull it back.

After three, I'm finally out of the car making my way to the front door. I still have my key, but they'd probably have a heart attack if I just walked in. I knock instead.

While waiting, I peek through the side window, seeing the glow of the TV coming from the living room. Mom comes around the corner cautiously, her robe pulled tightly over her pajamas.

Her mouth hangs open when she sees me standing on the other side of the door. "Lila," she says, folding her arms around me. "What are you doing here?"

"I need you," I cry, burying my face in her hair. She's used the same shampoo since I was a little girl. It reminds me of the hundreds of times she's comforted me over the years.

"Come in. Do you have any bags you need help with?"

"No," I answer stepping inside. "It was a last minute sort of thing."

"James!" Mom yells. "Your daughter is here!"

I wince. I love my daddy, but he'll have ten times more questions than Mom.

"Hey, baby girl." He smiles, coming around the corner. "What are you doing here?"

Folding my arms over my stomach, I say, "I needed a break from the city."

He pulls me in for a hug, kissing my forehead in the same spot Pierce had just over an hour ago. "I'm glad to have you home."

For a while, we stare at each other. I know they know something isn't quite right. They're just waiting for me to say it or thinking of a way to ask me.

"Do you want to come watch some baseball?" Dad asks, motioning toward the living room.

I shake my head. I hate baseball. He knows it. "I was wondering if Mom wanted to sit on the back deck for a while.

I've been stuck on a plane for most of the day and could use some fresh air."

Dad looks relieved. "I wouldn't want to impede on girl time."

"Do you want something to eat before we head out?" Mom asks.

I haven't had anything since the cupcake back in New York. "Peanut butter and jelly," I say, wrinkling my nose.

She pats my back. "I'm glad Chicago hasn't changed you too much."

While she puts together my sandwich, I go out to the deck leaning against the railing. A cool summer breeze blows through my hair as I look out to the mature trees that fill the back yard and listen to the crickets.

I hear the patio door slide and turn around, watching Mom carry a plate and glass of milk to the table. "This should do it."

"Is that your homemade bread?"

"Did you think I was going to make you something on store bought bread? Never."

I kick my heels off and take a seat across from her. The first bite goes down easily and before I know it, it's half gone. It's a good thing my nausea wore off after lunch.

"Are you going to tell me what's going on?" she finally asks after I down my glass of milk.

"You're not going to like it."

"Nothing you can say is going to make me love you any less. Remember that." If I'm half the mom she is, my baby will be lucky.

"I'm pregnant." My hands shake under the table as I wait for her reaction.

Her eyes widen as she takes a visible deep breath. "I guess I didn't realize you had a boyfriend."

This is the part that stings the most. "I don't."

Her elbows hit the table, hands framing her face.

I continue, "I met a guy after I moved there—Mallory's older brother, actually. We've been seeing each other on and off." I purposefully leave out Pierce. She doesn't need to hear all that.

"Where are you now?"

"Off."

"Oh, baby, your dad and I will help you with whatever it is you need. Have you been to the doctor yet?"

Shaking my head, I say, "Not yet. I was hoping I could get in with Dr. Phelps while I'm here."

"We'll give her a call in the morning." She pauses. "Do you want to know a secret?"

"You have a secret?"

She holds up her index finger. "Just one."

"Spill."

"I got pregnant with you before I married your dad. Our parents put together a wedding in two weeks to try to make it look like you were a honeymoon baby."

I'm not sure if she can see my eyes in the darkness, but they have to be at least double in size. "No freaking way."

"Shocking, huh?"

"Maybe it's a good thing I don't have anyone for you to make me marry."

She laughs. "I would never even suggest it. Besides, I love your dad so much, it would have happened at one time or another."

More time passes. I finish the last of my sandwich as I enjoy the quiet serenity.

"Can we wait a couple days to tell Dad? I want to go to the doctor and all that before I tell anyone else."

"What do you want me to tell him?"

I shrug. "Just tell him I needed a break. There's no lie in that."

"True. You look exhausted. Why don't you head to bed, and we can talk more in the morning. I'll even make you waffles with strawberries if you want."

"Let's try dry toast. The last couple mornings have been a little rough."

"I had the same thing with you. It will be over soon, hopefully."

"Thanks, Mom," I say as she picks up my dishes.

"For what?"

"For not making me feel any worse than I already do. Loneliness is the worst feeling, and I was scared how you would react," I admit.

"If there is one thing I never want you to forget, it's that I'll always be there. Always. Don't you ever question that."

I follow her in the kitchen, waiting for her to set the dishes in the sink before wrapping my arms tightly around her. "I love you."

"I love you, too. Now get some sleep."

It's been months since I've been in my old room, and it hasn't changed one bit. It has the same white four-poster bed. Same white comforter and pale yellow walls. After pulling on one of my old sleep shirts, I find a toothbrush and everything else I need in my bathroom. Within minutes, I'm tucked under the covers and drifting off to sleep.

I hear pounding, but ignore it, tossing to my other side. Dad's always had this thing about getting up before the sun rises and tinkering in the garage.

Two more pounds then it stops. I drift off yet again.

A hand rests on my hip, shaking me carefully. "Lila! Lila!" My dad yells—at least it sounds like he's yelling.

I rub my eyes and look to the alarm clock. It's only 4:15. "What is it?"

"There's a guy here to see you. I told him to get his ass out of here, but he won't listen."

"Who?" I ask, sitting up.

"I don't know. Do you want to come down and see or should I tell him to get the hell off my property?" he asks. My dad has always been my shield.

"I'll go, Daddy. Why don't you go back to bed?" It can only be one of two men; I can handle both.

He lifts his finger. I can barely see him in the darkness. "I'm coming with you until I know you're okay. This guy looks a little worse for wear."

Without another word, I follow him down the steps to the foyer. His back is to me, but I know it's him right away. "Blake," I whisper, trying not to make him jump.

He spins around immediately. His hair is mussed. His shirt is wrinkled. And I've seen those circles around his eyes before; he hasn't slept in a couple days.

"You can go to bed now, Daddy."

"You sure?" he whispers near my ear.

I nod, never taking my eyes off Blake.

"If you need anything, come get me," he says before he walks back up the stairs.

Blake walks toward me slowly. His hands come up when he's close enough to touch me, but they fall back down to his sides. "I need to talk to you."

"How did you get here?"

"I drove."

"When was the last time you slept?"

He buries his hands in the pockets of his jeans. "I don't remember."

Even with the anger and frustration I have with him, my heart easily overrides it all … for now anyway. When you know what I know about him — his past and how great he can be — it puts the negatives through a heavy strain. Especially when I see him like this.

I take his hand in mine. He responds, his whole face relaxing. I could throw him a pillow and show him the couch, but I lead him to my room, closing the door tightly behind us.

"Do you need something to sleep in?" I ask, shuffling things around in my drawer. Derek left his things here a time or two.

I look back when he doesn't answer, and he's already stripped down to his boxer briefs. "I'm good."

"There's an extra toothbrush in the bathroom," I say pointing toward it.

He comes to me like a lion on the prowl, holding my face in his hands. "I need to talk to you. Everything else can wait until later."

Closing my eyes, I take a deep breath. "Can we at least lay in the bed? I'm so tired."

His grip on me loosens, and he takes my hand to lead me to the bed. I crawl into one side. He takes the other. I lie on my back. He towers over me, holding his head up. "Why didn't you come home?" he asks.

"I'm tired of you running. I'm not doing this anymore."

"Who ran this time?" he asks.

"It's not running if I don't have anything to run from."

"You have me," he answers, brushing the pad of his thumb across my cheek.

"I've never had you, Blake. You come and go ... you never stay long enough for me to consider you mine." My voice reflects the sadness my heart feels. It's hard when you love someone, but you don't feel it back.

His hand lays flat on my stomach, and my whole body tenses. "When you said you were pregnant the other night, I panicked. I shouldn't have left, but I didn't know what else to do. I'm so used to being alone that sometimes that's the only way I know how to be."

"You can't run out every time things get hard. I know you've had some bad times—really bad times, but that can't be your excuse forever. We all get dealt shit Blake, but that doesn't mean it has to ruin the rest of your life."

"When you get back to Chicago, there's something I want to show you. Something I've never shown anyone."

"What's that?" I ask.

"I'd rather show you."

There's a few seconds of silence. Warm tears roll down my cheeks. "I don't want to do this alone," I admit.

He rolls on top of me, looking straight into my eyes. It's dark, but I see the way they glisten. "I want this baby—our baby. I drove over seven hours just to tell you that."

"And what does that mean for us?" I ask as he wipes away my tears with the pad of his thumb.

He leans down to kiss me, tugging at my lower lip. "I want to be with you. I've wanted you since the first time I kissed you against the wall in our apartment ... probably even before that."

He kisses me again, lingering longer this time. "And every time I kiss you, I fall for you a little more."

Another kiss. "Every time I look at you, I see how good things could be. You're my hope. I've just had a hard time convincing myself I deserve you."

My shirt slides up over my hips, baring my stomach. He stares down into my eyes before moving down, showering my stomach with butterfly kisses.

Last night, I would have said this will never happen again, but he's too good. His words melt me, and I want to believe them. Every. Single. One. Of. Them.

When he pulls my panties down, I don't stop him. He needs me. I need him just as much.

He comes back up, paving a trail from my stomach to my chest then up my throat back to my lips. "I've been wrong about so many things. I've lied to myself, but that stops now."

He's at my entrance, teasing me. "Blake," I beg, ready for him.

"There was one other thing I wanted to tell you." He gives me an inch, but I need so much more.

"Blake."

"I—" Another inch.

"Love—" Just a little more.

"You—" He pushes in, filling me completely.

I wrap my arms around his neck as fresh tears roll down my cheeks. It's a moment I thought would never happen.

"I love you," I cry, wrapping my legs around him. He rocks in and out of me slowly. I've never felt more connected to anyone ... any moment.

The best part is we stay like that—same rhythm—the whole way through. If he said I love you once, he said it ten times. That's how I know this time is different.

I come. He follows, pressing his lips to my neck. The sun peeks through the curtains as he holds me close, letting our hearts return to their normal beat.

"I'm never leaving you again," he whispers in my ear right before I fall back to sleep.

THE SMELL OF BACON AND eggs wakes me up. Blake's arms aren't wrapped around me, and the bed is cold. It reminds me of so many other mornings, yet it's different.

Confidence was built by his words, his actions. He drove all the way from Chicago to tell me he's sorry ... to tell me he loves me. For once, he ran to me when I needed him the most.

I roll out of bed to use the bathroom but end up bent over the toilet dry heaving instead.

"Lila." I hear Blake's voice behind me. He pulls my hair back away from my face, gently running his fingers along my spine. "I'm here, baby."

When my stomach finally settles, I'm drenched in sweat, and my head aches. Blake sits behind me, wrapping his legs and arms around me to support my weight. I don't know what I would do without him. "Do you think you'd feel better if I ran you a bath? You're covered in sweat."

"Yes, just not too hot. My body feels like it just came out of the oven."

As I attempt to stand, he helps by carefully hugging me from behind to pull me up. "I'm going to go downstairs and grab some crackers and water. Maybe that will settle my stomach."

He puts the toilet seat down then practically sits me on it. "Don't even think about moving." He starts the tub, holding his hand under the water until it's the right temp. It's kind of cute how he keeps looking over to make sure I'm following his orders. I can't disobey those sapphire blues. "I'll go talk to your mom about getting you some crackers. Your water should be ready in a few minutes."

My fingers touch my temples, tracing perfect little circles. All of the sudden, I feel dizzy again. "Where were you this morning when I woke up?" I ask, trying not to sound as panicked as I feel.

He smiles sheepishly, rubbing the back of his neck. "I went downstairs to get a drink and ran into your mom. It was a little rough at first, but I ended up making us breakfast."

"You made my mom breakfast?"

"Yes. I mean, she didn't ask me to, but you know how I am with my eggs. They're my coffee, babe."

My fingers move faster, ignoring how adorable he sounds. "What did you talk about?"

The water turns off then he's kneeling in front of me. "Let's get you in the tub. I'll get you something to soothe your stomach, and then we'll talk."

I nod, starting to feel even worse for the wear. He helps me pull my T-shirt over my head then watches like a hawk as I sink into the tub.

"I'll be right back," he says when I'm all the way in.

The water instantly relaxes me. It takes the weight off my body, releasing tension in places I didn't know existed, my mind the only exception. Blake said a lot of things last night, and I believe every single word of it.

But then my mind shifts to what my mom must have been thinking this morning when she saw him, especially after the talk we had last night. What did he tell her? What did she say to him?

The door creaks, and Blake walks in carrying a small plate of saltines and a cup. He sets them on the edge of the tub. "Your mom said to try ginger ale, so I got that instead of water."

"I can safely say this is the first time I've eaten crackers while taking a bath."

He sits beside the tub, resting his arm over the top to use as a pillow. "I wish I could make it better since I'm half the reason you're in this position."

"I should have been more careful. This wasn't planned ... I don't want you to think I was trying to trap you," I acknowledge, nibbling on a cracker.

"Lemon Drop, no one has caught me in their trap yet. I'm with you because I want to be. The news just caught me off guard. That's all."

"What did my mom say to you?" I ask, my patience wearing thin.

"Before or after she threatened me with a steak knife?"

I cover my eyes, thinking of the one time I actually saw my mom do that. My boyfriend at the time had snuck in, not realizing she was such an early riser. "What did you do?"

"I told her I was your baby's daddy."

"Oh my God. Are you serious, Blake?"

He laughs. "It didn't come out quite like that, but it was enough to get her to drop the knife."

"Then what?"

"She sat me down and lectured me for about twenty minutes. I'm not going to lie, she kind of scares me, and that's not an easy thing to do." He hands me the ginger ale, waiting for me to take a sip. "She made you an appointment for 1:15 with Dr. Phelps."

"What time is it now?"

"A little after 11:00."

We sit quietly for a few minutes. I successfully eat eight saltines and drink half the glass of ginger ale before the water starts to turn cold. "I should get out before I shrivel up."

He stands, grabbing a towel from the hook. "Here. Do you want me to grab you some clothes?"

I wince, remembering the things I left behind when I moved to Chicago. "Look in the drawers. I should have a pair of shorts and a T-shirt."

He wraps the towel tightly around me then pulls me into his arms, kissing the tip of my nose. "When I said I loved you last night, I meant it. I love you."

"I love you, too." I press my lips to his cheek before he has a chance to get away.

While he's getting my clothes, I apply some lotion and brush my teeth twice. Crackers and ginger ale may work wonders for my stomach, but they didn't leave the best taste in my mouth.

"Will these work?" Blake asks, holding up an old pair of jean cutoffs and an off-the-shoulder white T-shirt.

I wrinkle my nose at him. "Weren't there any athletic shorts in there? I know I used to have some."

He grins walking toward me. In one quick motion, he undoes the towel leaving me naked in front of the mirror. "Have you looked at yourself lately?" He brushes my hair over my shoulder, kissing the back of my neck. "You've always been beautiful, but there's something even more beautiful about you now that you're carrying my baby. You're glowing."

His hands settle on my hips, sliding up my sides then under my breasts. They're sore, but he's careful with his touches.

"Look at yourself," he whispers against my neck. It's something I've never done when I'm aroused, and I'm definitely there. I blame that on my hormones, too. He can flip me on like a switch.

I lift my lids, adjusting to the light. Blake is right; my stomach is still toned, but my breasts have filled out giving my body more shape. My skin glows. My lips are parted. My eyes glossed over.

"Blake," I moan, wrapping my arm around the back of his neck while his lips caress my shoulders.

"Tell me what you want."

"You. I just want you. I've always wanted you."

He pulls my arm from his neck and spins me around in his arms. Tears fill my eyes as I look into his. "You have me ... all of me. Even when I'm not with you, I'm with you."

He uses his strength to set me on the counter. I stare in his eyes, believing every single word he says. For months, I believed what he said because I wanted to. Now, every word sinks into my heart, my mind, my soul because he's proven there's reason to believe. Nothing seems forced anymore.

Freeing himself from his jeans, he easily enters me. I've been ready for him since the second he made me look at myself in the mirror.

I dig my fingers in his back as he kisses me deeply, burying himself deep inside me over and over.

"Blake," I breathe, wrapping my legs around his waist. My body shakes as the tension builds.

"Do you know when I knew I loved you?" he asks, touching his forehead to mine.

I bite down on my lower lip, so close to orgasm I almost can't take it anymore.

"The night I took you to the studio ... that was the only way I knew to show you without saying it."

He thrusts a few more times, and I'm a goner, pulsing around him repeatedly. He follows, burying his face in my neck to muffle his screams.

I hold him close while we both climb down from the high. Sex has become a truth serum.

"When I walked away from you on Christmas, it just about killed me."

Holding his face in my hands, I say, "But it made us stronger. We've lived through the worst, and neither one of us wants to go back to that."

"You're mine. No one else is ever going to be with you like this again. Just me."

"I'm yours."

His lips press to mine one more time before he lowers me to the ground, using the towel to clean me up. "There's nothing I'd rather do than stay locked in this bathroom with you for the rest of the day making up for all my wrongs, but you need to go check on my baby."

"I'm going to be honest ... I never thought you'd embrace this. This is going to ground you, you know that?"

"I've been waiting for something to ground me for years. I'm happy to be grounded with you." He smiles, throwing me my sports bra.

I laugh for the first time since the situation became real. "Your seed has officially been planted."

"Turn that into a Hallmark card. Daddies across the country will love your little analogy. Maybe add a tree to the front."

"I think it's time for you to give me some space so I can get to the doctor on time. You're distracting me," I say, turning out my lower lip.

He sticks out his lower lip mockingly. He probably looks cuter than I do. "I'll go back down and talk to your mom. I think she's just starting to not hate me."

I open my mouth to object, but he's gone before I get a chance.

After pulling on the clothes he gave me, I tie my hair up in a loose knot and put just enough makeup on to mask the dark circles under my eyes. There's not much to the outfit, but it's acceptable around here this time of year.

I slip on a pair of brown leather flip-flops and make my way downstairs a little before one. My mom is stirring something on the stove while Blake flips through one of her old recipe books. "You two are really freaking me out," I admit without thinking.

"What?" Blake says without looking over. "You know I like to cook."

My mom chuckles. "That's good because it's never been one of her strong points. I tried."

"I'm glad the two of you have made an alliance at my expense, but I need to leave for the doctor, or I'm going to be late."

Mom stops what she's doing, pulling the pot off the burner. "Am I driving or are you?"

Blake doesn't say anything or look back, but the pages stop turning. I can tell by his eyes he's staring, at one point, not actually reading.

"Actually, Mom, I was hoping Blake and I could go together. It's just—"

She holds her hand up to stop me. "I get it. See if you can get me a picture, okay?"

I shake my head, watching Blake stand from the table with an easy smile. "I don't think there's much to see at this point, but I'll see what I can do."

Blake pulls his keys from his pocket. "We can take Frank."

LISA DE JONG

Great. I'm going to pull up at the doctor in an old Trans Am wearing a pair of cut-offs. Better yet, my boyfriend looks like he hasn't touched a comb or a razor in a few days—he definitely doesn't look like he's from here. He's still the sexiest thing I've ever seen, just not what I would have dreamed of a few years ago.

"See you in a little while, Mom. I think I might take Blake out to Grandpa's farm after so I can show him my spot."

"I'll have something ready for dinner when you get home," she replies, waving as we head out the door.

He opens the passenger door for me before going around to his side. The engine roars as I give him directions to the one and only clinic in town, my legs shaking uncontrollably as we get closer.

"Hey," he says, placing his hand over my knee. "It's going to be okay. Besides, I'm here now, and there's nothing we can't get through together."

"I know. I hate going to the doctor in general."

We pull into the parking lot with only a few minutes to spare. "I don't want this to come off wrong," he says. "But, do you have insurance? I can help out if you don't."

"Yeah, I got it through Stanley a few months ago."

He cringes but drops it as we make our way inside. My fingernails tap on the reception desk as I wait for her to get off the phone. "Can I help you?" she asks, staring at my hands.

"Lila Fields for Dr. Phelps."

"Oh, yes, I'm going to need you to fill out a couple forms since it's been a while." She hands me a clipboard and a pen. "Take a seat and bring it back when it's complete."

I take a seat, filling out as much as I can. It's the standard health history and insurance information they get every time I come. After handing it back to her, I sit back down next to Blake, resting my head on his shoulder.

"You feeling okay?" he asks.

"I hate waiting."

His knees bounce up and down. I'm not sure I've ever seen him this nervous. We're quite the pair. "How did you know you were pregnant?"

"Umm, I took a test."

"No, I mean, how did you know that you might be pregnant?"

I think back to the couple of days before I finally bought the test on the way into work. My cycle had been irregular since I got the shot so there was nothing out of the usual there. I felt queasy for two or three straight mornings but had chalked it up as a case of the flu. Then, my breasts started to hurt just from putting my bra on. When the exhaustion hit, I couldn't ignore it any longer. "When you know your body, you can just tell. The test was just confirmation of what I already knew deep inside."

He nods, throwing his arm over my shoulder. "You're going to be a great mom."

I smile, thinking that in a matter of months, I will definitely be someone's mom. It's scary and exciting at the same time. "I have a feeling this baby might love Daddy even more. I don't think he or she will have to work hard to have you wrapped around their finger."

Blake is a little tough—little arrogant—but under it all, he knows how to love better than anyone I've ever met. He shows it differently than most. He doesn't shout it from the rooftops or make grand gestures. Blake loves like only Blake can. It's my favorite love.

"Lila?" the nurse asks, perching the door open with her foot.

I pick up my purse and walk toward her, feeling Blake's hand at the small of my back.

"Good morning," she says as we walk in. "We're going to start by getting your height and weight then I'll need you to use the bathroom before the doctor comes in to see you."

Blake stands by for my weight and height, which doesn't bother me a bit.

She picks my purse up from the floor, handing it to Blake. "I'm going to bring you to room 3 while she goes to give her sample. She'll join you in just a couple minutes."

He squeezes my hand before we go our separate directions. The nurse hands me a cup, and I lock myself in the bathroom, easily filling it and tucking it behind the metal door. I wash my hands and find room 3—my Blake. At times, I still can't believe he's here until I actually see him.

"How'd it go?" he asks, wrapping his arm around my shoulders when I take the seat next to him. His knees still bounce nervously as his fingertips tap along my shoulder.

"Are you okay?"

"Just nervous, you know? I just want everything to be okay." He bites down on his thumb.

"It's—"

There's a quick knock at the door before Dr. Phelps walks in. She's cut her hair, but other than that, she's the exact same as she was a year ago.

"Well, Lila," she announces. "You are definitely pregnant. Congratulations."

My eyes well when I look at Blake whose face has relaxed from just a couple minutes ago. There really is a baby in there.

The doctor takes the stool next to me, typing in the computer. "Do you remember when your last period was?" she asks.

I shake my head. I've never been one to mark it on my calendar and since they are so irregular, it's not like I can just count back.

"What I'd like to do then today is an ultrasound to determine how far along you are. Lay up on the table so I can take a look at your stomach then I'll have the nurse walk you down to radiology."

Blake watches as she positions me, and gently presses against my abdomen. "Do most women know they're pregnant before they take a test?" he asks.

Dr. Phelps smiles down at me. "Of course. That's why most women buy the tests before they even call the doctor. There are very few who I've broken the news to."

"How far along are they when they usually figure it out?"

She looks at me curiously, but answers anyway. "Generally anywhere from four to eight weeks. It all depends on the regularity of their cycles and how their body adjusts to the increased hormones."

I turn my head to look at him; he looks so pale. My mind wanders, and it hits me that if I'm any further than six weeks along, the baby could be Pierce's. If it's going through my head, it must be hammering into his.

"Okay, Lila, let's get you down to radiology." She turns to Blake, holding her hand out. "I'm sorry, but I forgot to ask your name."

"Blake," he says quietly, accepting her hand.

"I'm assuming you're the father. Congratulations," Dr. Phelps says.

He simply nods as he looks past her to me. There's question in his eyes, mixed with a pain I've seen a few times before. It's the look he often has before he runs.

"Follow me," Dr. Phelps instructs, motioning to the door. If she picks up on the tension in the room, she doesn't say it.

I follow the doctor, and Blake stays behind me. His mood changed quickly; I'm used to that, but not here. Not when I need him now more than I ever have, and even if this baby is Pierce's, it wouldn't change how I feel.

Blake is it. He's the one I want to spend forever with.

The doctor hands me a gown. "Take everything off from the waist down. We have to us the transvaginal ultrasound this early to detect the baby."

The door closes, and I quickly undress and pull the gown on oblivious to Blake. My teeth chatter as I lay on the table waiting for the ultrasound. The room isn't cold, but my nerves are getting the best of me. What happens in this room could change everything or nothing at all.

The tech explains the probe then gently inserts it inside me. It feels strange at first, but everything else on my mind makes the sensation easy to ignore. Blake doesn't say a thing as he stands a few feet away, hands tucked in his jean pockets. I know he senses me watching him, but he keeps his eyes on the monitor.

"Is this your first baby?" the tech asks as she watches the screen.

I wait a few seconds to see if Blake will respond, but he doesn't. "Yes," I answer, biting down on my lower lip.

She stops on a black oval shape. "There's your baby," she says pointing to a small, light colored spot within it. It looks like a little white bean.

This is when it first hits me … that I'm going to be a mom. It's one thing to know, but when you actually see it growing inside of you, it's a whole new feeling. Not too long from now, this little baby is going to count on me for everything. No matter where I am or what I'm doing, I'll always be mom to him or her.

Tears fill my eyes as I watch the tech take measurements. My little bean is going to come into the world soon and become the greatest thing I've ever accomplished … greatest things we've ever accomplished.

The door clicks, and I look over noticing the tech and I are the only ones left in the room. I want to yell for him, but what would be the point? He's been running scared since the day I met him. What made me think he would change now?

A few words … a few promises. Maybe they were empty after all.

A single tear rolls down my face as I focus my attention back on the screen, and the dark room provides a good mask.

"The doctor wanted me to measure and see how far along you are; from the measurements I just took, I'd guess you're at five weeks."

A lump forms in my throat. I panic, and the words just come out. "Does that mean the baby was conceived five weeks ago?"

"No, no, it means you more than likely conceived about three weeks ago. It's hard to say at this point, but from looking at the size of the yolk sac, it couldn't have been more than a few days before that. Pregnancies are kind of weird in that way—the weeks start ticking before there's ever a baby. Does that make sense?"

I nod out of relief. I understand the important part—that this is Blake's baby. The rest can wait until later.

She removes the probe and helps me up from the table. "Let me get you some pictures before you leave," she says. She pulls them from the machine and smiles, handing me three. "Hopefully, he'll come around," she says softly, squeezing my shoulder.

If only she knew he comes and goes faster than the seasons change. I change quickly, and as I make my way out the door, my mind wanders to where he might be. What made him leave before he even *knew*? If he left again, I'm not taking him back. This time, he's not going to be the one to take it all away.

Surprisingly, he's standing a few feet from the door with his back against the wall. One glimpse of his red eyes and some of the frustration eases away.

"Is there somewhere we can go to talk?" he asks. He's looking at me but not really. He's here, but yet he's gone. "There's something I need to tell you."

WHEN HE ASKED, I PICKED the farm because it gives me peace. It's where I always used to go when I needed time to think or mend a broken heart. If he's going to hurt me, he might as well do it here.

Not a word was said on the way out to the car or on the ten-minute drive out here besides a few directions from me on where to turn.

He pulls into the drive of my grandparents' old farm. My dad inherited it after grandma passed away a couple years ago but he hasn't gotten up the nerve to sell it, and I don't think he ever will. I hope not anyway. Behind the house is a big red barn and just beyond that is a narrow creek and miles of cornfields. Along the creek is where I like to sit and think. No one bothers me back there.

"Park in front of the barn," I instruct.

He does, and I waste no time jumping out to grab one of grandpa's old horse blankets from the barn.

"Where are you going?" he yells from behind me.

"Meet me behind the barn!" I yell back, not even bothering to look at him. Sometimes, when you feel your heart cracking, you do your best to build a shield around it so the pieces won't fall apart completely. That's what I'm doing—bracing for the worst while also trying to convince myself I can do this on my own. It won't be easy—nothing ever is—but I've proven to myself over the last year that I'm strong. Hopefully, I'm strong enough to get through this.

When I walk out behind the barn, he's standing with his back to me overlooking the water. I would give anything to have a glimpse inside his head ... to get a snapshot of his thoughts.

"Here," I say, throwing the blanket down to clear a spot in the long grass. Dad doesn't get out here to mow often.

"I'm okay," he replies as I sit down, resting back on my elbows. The warm sun beats down on my pale legs, but I can't complain because this is what summer on the farm is all about.

"Blake, I need you to say something. I may not like what you're about to say, but silence is worse," I admit.

"Do you ever wonder if you really control any part of your life?" he asks, throwing a long piece of grass into the creek.

I'm not sure where he's going, but I play anyway. "I think our lives are ours to live. Things we don't plan for are simply obstacles."

"I didn't want to get married at such a young age, but with her I just knew. She made me want to be better without even asking. My job was to protect her—make sure she had everything she needed—but I couldn't even do that. I didn't chose to live without her, and sometimes when things are really bad, I go to the studio and pretend she's still at home waiting for me."

My heart hammers as I wait for him to start talking again. I wonder if he feels it, or if he feels it too much, and that's why he can't look at me. I'm waiting for the part where he tells me he can't do this, and as much as I thought I was prepared for it, it's going to crush me.

"There's something I've never told anyone. It's been slowly eating away at me, and I'm not going to be the father your baby deserves unless I deal with it."

I open my mouth to tell him it's our baby, but he cuts me off. "The day I lost Aly, I lost a baby too. One I didn't even know she was carrying."

My mouth gapes. I never thought ... I never would have thought. "How did you find out?" I whisper, quietly standing behind him. I want so badly to wrap my arms around him.

"The doctor told me after her autopsy. He guessed she was about eight weeks along."

"Why didn't you tell anyone?"

"Do you think she knew?"

I can't take it anymore. I wrap my arms around his waist. I'm not sure where this is going ... where we're going, but he shouldn't go through this alone. "That she was pregnant?"

"Yeah," he whispers.

My cheek rests on his warm T-shirt, feeling how fast his heart beats. "No, I don't think she knew. It's hard to describe, but after only a few days, I already love my little bean. I want to do everything right by him or her. I couldn't imagine ... I couldn't."

He inhales a deep breath. "She used to talk about having kids. I wasn't ready and didn't think it would be good for her. After she died, I thought—" he chokes up, his breaths coming faster.

"It's okay. You don't need to tell me." Tears stream down my cheeks. His pain is mine. It has been since he stole my heart all those months ago.

His hand covers mine. "No, I do. I've kept it in for so long. After she died, I thought she did it because she didn't want to disappoint me. That maybe she knew, and didn't want to tell me. That maybe she thought I'd leave her."

"It's not your fault," I cry, pressing a kiss to his spine. So much of what's happened over the last week makes sense now. He wasn't running from me; he was running from the memories.

"Do you believe in God?" he asks out of the blue.

"Yes. He's given me more than I think I can handle a few times, but I've always gotten through with his help."

"I used to, but after everything that happened with Aly, I couldn't. Why did he let her get to that point? Why would he let an innocent baby die in the process? Why didn't he give me a reason to stay that night?"

"She was sick, Blake. She may not be here anymore, and there may be a baby you never got to meet, but God made them angels. They're watching over you, and they'd want you to be happy. I know she'd want you to be happy."

His whole body shakes. I loosen my grip and move around to face him. I thought my heart broke when Derek ended our relationship. I thought it shattered when Blake left on Christmas Day. Those were merely cracks compared to what I'm feeling now staring up at Blake. I've never seen a person look so defeated—the wet lines down his cheeks, the way his shoulders curl over his chest, clenched jaw, skin bunched around his eyes in a pained stare.

"She left a note." His voice shakes.

My hands move up and down his arms, trying to comfort him, but I can't take my eyes from his face. No matter how much it hurts, I can't.

"She said she thought I'd be better off without her. She said I'd be able to move on with my life without having to worry about her. She said she loved me ... that she'd always love me." He pauses, taking a deep breath. "Maybe she just didn't know how much I loved her. There's nothing I wouldn't have done for her."

Holding his face in my hands, I force him to look at me. "That tells me she knew you loved her so much you'd never give up on her. She was tired, Blake, and she didn't want you to live that way. You were never going to give up on her."

I swipe my thumbs under his eyes, trying to wipe some of the tears away.

"She was pregnant in the picture I painted of her," he says after a couple minutes pass. "She was going to be a mom and didn't even know it."

"You'll have that—the painting and the memory."

He nods against my palms. "I'm starting to believe in God again."

"Yeah?"

His eyes find mine for the first time since we've been out here. "I didn't want to fall in love with you, but you changed that because ... because you're you. I never wanted to come back after I left, but you were all I could think about no matter how much I tried not to. You're stuck in me, or I'm stuck in you. Fate didn't put us in that apartment together; I think God did. He handed me what I needed when he gave me you."

LISA DE JONG

I stand on my tiptoes, kissing his salty lips. "You're my super glue, too, Blake. Until I met you, I was falling apart. Our love isn't easy. We've had to fight for it, but it makes us stronger."

"The night you told me you were pregnant, I left because it brought back too many memories. I needed some time to sort out my feelings, but I want this baby with you. I do, Lila."

Everything makes sense now. He's not running from me. He runs from his memories ... or to them. I guess it depends how you look at it.

His hands circle my neck, his thumbs running along my jawline. "And when I walked out of the room today, it wasn't about you either. I felt like I was losing it. It was selfish, and I'm sorry."

"Do you want to see the pictures?"

"You have pictures?"

I nod, smiling. "Give me your keys."

He does, and I take off running to his car to grab my purse. I pull them out and run back as fast as my feet will let me in the tall grass. "Here," I say, handing them over to him.

His brows furrow as he rotates the pictures around.

"You can't see much yet, but that's our baby right there." I point to the little white dot. "That's why I'm calling him or her bean."

"And everything looks good?" he asks, running his finger along the picture.

"So far, so good. I'm due in April."

He places his finger under my chin to bring my eyes from the picture to his. "Even if bean isn't mine, I'm not going anywhere. I mean what the tech said — "

"It's yours. She put me at five weeks which means the baby was conceived about three weeks ago."

He wraps his arms around me tightly. "Oh, thank God."

I brush my lips against his neck. "It would have been you for me either way, too."

"Are you feeling okay?" he asks, pulling back just a bit.

"Yeah, I just need to sit down. I'm feeling kind of tired ... it's been a long day."

"Give me a second." He sits down on the blanket, patting the space between his legs. "Sit."

And I do, laying my head back on his shoulder. We listen to the sounds of the water running in the creek, and the few cars that drive by in the distance. It's the most at peace I've felt in a long time.

"Have you ever thought about living out here?" he asks after a few minutes.

"A few times. This is my place I come to when I need to get away from everything else just to think."

"I like it out here," he admits.

I try to imagine Blake on the farm working in nothing but his jeans, sweat drenching his hair and chest. It's not a bad picture.

"When we get back to Chicago, I'm going to tell Pierce that I can't keep working for him. It's not fair to you, and I'm sorry."

"What are you going to tell him?"

I shrug. "He knows about the baby. I think I'm just going to tell him I'm taking some time off to concentrate on me ... us."

His body tenses. "When did you tell him?"

"The day we went to New York. I was sick and could barely function. I needed someone to talk to. He's the one who flew me here."

"I hate that he's always saving you from me. I'm done giving him reasons to save you."

"You don't know how happy I am to hear that. Is there anything else you want to tell me so you don't have a reason to run anymore?"

He groans, wrapping his arms around me. "Pierce was the one who gave me your parents' address. I called him after your text and promised him I was going to do my best by you. Took me almost twenty minutes, but the perfect ass finally gave it to me."

That's one thing to thank Pierce for when I talk to him. "Is there anything else?"

"Just that I love you. I'm all out of secrets."

I push my way out of his arms, and turn around straddling his lap. Folding my arms around his neck, I kiss every inch of his handsome face ending with his lips. We kiss until I'm out of breath and numb.

"Does anyone ever come back here?" he asks between kisses.

"Just me."

His lips brush against my throat, his hand tugging on the neck of my T-shirt to give him access to my chest. "I'm going to spend the rest of my life proving to you how much I love you."

"Just stay," I pant. "That's all I need you to do … stay."

"What else?" he asks, pulling my bra below my breast, sucking on my nipple. They may be a little tender, but he does it gently. My hormones are out of control—I either find myself wanting to cry or have my clothes ripped off. Pregnancy is going to be interesting.

I tug at the bottom of his shirt until he lifts his arms allowing me to take it off. "I need you."

"You don't have to ask twice," he murmurs, his lips still exploring my skin.

Within a few seconds, he has me on my back, tugging my clothes off in record time before working the button of his jeans. He thrusts into me without hesitation keeping his eyes on me the entire time. "Have you ever been out here before like this?" he asks, pushing in then slowly pulling back out.

"No," I answer, struggling to speak.

"I like being your first."

The pressure builds. "You're my first baby daddy, too."

He thrusts all the way in, filling me completely. "I'm your only baby daddy. Now and forever; I promise you that."

The rest is sweet bliss.

A feeling that goes beyond happiness to euphoria.

And ends in ecstasy.

26

WE DROVE FRANK BACK to Chicago yesterday. It wasn't without a few bumps with a bout of morning sickness that slowed us down in the morning, followed by a craving for pancakes — pancakes with Nutella.

Today is different. I'm about to walk into Stanley Enterprises for the last time. And Mallory comes home, that's something to look forward to. I'll need it after a day like today.

The first few minutes are like any other day. I set my stuff on my desk and power on my computer. Reece is leaning against my cubicle with coffee in hand right on cue.

"Hey, stranger. How was your trip home?"

"Crap. I completely forgot to call you. Things got a little hectic."

She raises her brow, shaking her head. "You have to give me more than that."

"Blake drove all the way to Nebraska. We made up, I went to the doctor and confirmed that everything was okay, and then we spent some time with my family."

"Back up," she says, holding her hand up. "You took him back *again*?"

I wrinkle my nose. It's hard to explain without telling her things I can't. "To understand Blake, you have to know him. There are things he told me I can't share that help explain why he runs. You just have to trust me when I say he deserves another chance. Besides that, I love him enough to try again."

"I really want to yell at you right now, but I'd probably do the same thing. In fact, I know I would because I'm even more of a hopeless romantic than you are."

I smile. "Isn't that the truth."

"So where are you guys at now?" she asks, sipping from her cup.

"We're together. I'm his. He's mine."

"I'm happy for you. I really am, but if he leaves again, you better let him go."

"Oh, don't worry. He's already been told. Having a baby is forcing us to at least pretend to be adults."

She's beaming this morning. Something is definitely different about her, but I can't put my finger on it

"What have you been up to this week?"

"I went on a date with the guy from IT. He doesn't look so bad in jeans and a T-shirt."

Now it's my turn to raise my brow. "Big Bang Theory guy?"

"Yes, I actually went on a second one the other night. He gave me the best kiss I've ever had, hands down," she says quietly, glancing around to make sure no one else can hear.

"Does that mean there's going to be a third?"

She grins. I notice she has a new shade of red lipstick to go with her tight red dress. "He's taking me out to dinner tonight. I'm glad I gave him a chance; he's funny and smart. There's never a quiet moment."

"Oh, Reece has herself a boyfriend. I'm happy for you. I can't think of anyone who deserves a little romance in their life more than you."

"Maybe we can double sometime? I don't know how much Blake would have in common with him, but it would be fun."

Sadness rains on my mood. There's something else I need to tell her, but I need to talk to Pierce first. "Yeah, let's do that if tonight goes well and all."

"Oh, I'm hoping it goes really well."

"Reece!"

"What?" she says through gritted teeth. "You aren't one to talk."

"You're right. I'll shut up."

"Yeah, that's right."

I rub my forehead, stressing over everything I have to do today. "Can we catch up later? I have to go talk to Pierce for a few minutes."

"Are you still battling morning sickness? You don't look so good."

"I kissed the toilet twice before I even left for work. It's usually over by lunch, so I have that to look forward to."

"Just let me know if you need anything," she says as she walks away. I almost wish she could stay so I could avoid the inevitable.

After yet another trip to the bathroom, I head to Pierce's office. The door is open a crack so I knock lightly, pushing it open in the process.

He immediately stands from his desk, giving me all his attention. "You're back."

"We drove back yesterday. You can't avoid real life forever."

"It would be nice, wouldn't it?"

I smile, shutting the door behind me. "It would. Look, Pierce, I need to talk to you about something."

"Take a seat."

I do, mostly because my stomach is already turning again. Add some nerves to morning sickness, and it's a whole new ball game. "First, I want to say thank you."

"For what?" He comes around the desk, sitting along the edge with his arms crossed over his chest.

"For helping Blake find me. I know how hard that must have been for you."

He shrugs like it was nothing. "It was the right thing to do."

I nod, leaving it at that. "Today is going to be my last day here. I appreciate everything you've done for me, but it's not fair to Blake. The more I think about it, I'd hate to be in his shoes given everything that you and I've been through."

"I know how he feels, but is there any way I can change your mind? You may be one of my newest designers, but you're also one of the best."

Shaking my head, I say, "No, I think I'm going to start something small from home. Something I can continue after the baby comes."

He smiles sadly. "I'm going to miss you."

"I'll miss you, too," I admit on the verge of losing it. Pierce was the first person I met in Chicago. A lot has happened between us that I'll never forget, but sometimes, you even have to let good people go.

"I told him if he hurts you again, I'm going to kick his ass. Hold him to the promise he made me."

"Trust me, if he leaves again, there won't be any need to. I'll kick his butt first."

I stand, needing to make my escape before I turn into a mess. He surprises me, pulling me in for a hug. "If there's anything you need, don't be afraid to call me. You'll always have a special place in my heart."

"You'll always be in mine. Someday, I hope you find someone who will love you the way you deserve to be loved. You deserve that."

"I thought I had, but I had to let her go."

"There's still someone out there for you. I truly believe that. It wasn't me."

"Only time will tell," he remarks, letting his arms fall away from me.

"Bye, Pierce," I say, putting a couple feet of space between us.

"Bye, Ms. Fields."

When I look up, he has the look of sorrow. This is a forever goodbye, and we both know it.

I hurry out, running back to the same bathroom I'd been in before stepping into Pierce's office. I cry for a few minutes because in some ways I just lost my best friend.

In another time, he could have been the one, but my heart belongs to Blake. It always will.

After straightening myself out, I head to Reece's desk to break the news to her. It's not going to be easy, but I'll still get to see her after I leave here.

She's staring at a drawing on her computer and doesn't see me coming. "Reece." My voice is quiet in an attempt to not scare her.

"Jesus, Lila. I'm supposed to be the one scaring you."

"Sorry, I was wondering if you could come over tonight before your date for a little bit? Mallory will be back, and I'd like you to meet her." *And there's something else I need to tell you,* I think to myself.

"I should be able to. I don't think our dinner reservation is until 7:30. Do you want me to bring anything?"

"No, I'll have a bottle of wine chilled, though."

"Now you're talking. Do you want me to ride home with you?" she asks.

"No. I mean ... I'm going to leave early today because I have a few things I have to take care of."

"You're okay, though, right?"

"More than," I say, smiling. There's a lot to look forward to. "Does six work?"

"Perfect. I'll see you then."

I head to my desk next, throwing the few personal belongings I have into my bag. As I walk away, I glance back at my desk one last time, putting it into memory. I always thought this was my dream, but it wasn't really. My dream was to be happy, and I'm finally there.

I drop an envelope off to Jane with Pierce's name on it that holds my keys and passwords inside. For the last time, I step in the elevator and ride to the lobby. It's just another moment where I hope I'm making the right decision. Another one of those darn forks in the road.

Blake isn't home when I open the door, but Mallory is standing in the kitchen making cupcakes. I feel like we're right back in college again. She drops her mixer and pulls me in for her signature bear hug.

"I haven't done that in over a year."

I laugh. "I hope you didn't break my ribs."

"Are you hungry?"

"What are you making?"

She practically skips back to the kitchen, pouring chocolate chips into her bowl. "Chocolate cupcakes with cream cheese, chocolate chip filling and a ganache on top."

My stomach growls. Nothing has stayed down yet today. "I'll have a few crackers and some ginger ale while they bake. I'll be more than ready by the time they're done."

She grimaces. "Is that a new diet I haven't heard about?"

I clear my throat and take a deep breath. Might as well just get it over with. "No, I'm pregnant."

The spoon literally clanks against the metal bowl as she looks up at me. "What?"

"I'm going to have a baby. I just found out last week."

She grasps the edge of the counter, mouth hanging open. "Who—"

"It's Blake's. I had an ultrasound last week when I went back home. There's no question about that."

"How did he react? You told him, right?" she asks, shoulders falling forward.

I nod. "We're fine. More than fine actually."

"You're talking about Blake Stone, right? My Blake Stone."

"Of course. The jerk I fell in love with because you neglected to tell me I was going to have a roommate when I moved here."

She stirs frantically. "Do you know where he is? I got in a little after noon and haven't seen him."

"He was heading to the studio today to work on a few things. I'm actually going to run over there if you want to join me."

"I'd love to, but I'm so tired of traveling. Besides, I think I need a few minutes to process all this before he comes home. I don't know if I want to hug him or kill him."

I give her my evil eyes. "Don't kill him. He's my baby daddy."

"Gross," she gags, stirring even faster.

"By the way, my friend Reece is coming over at 6:00, and I'm going to call my friend Dana, too. Want to join us for a few minutes? I kind of had something I wanted to tell everyone all at once."

Her eyes widen. "There's more?"

"It's not a big deal … not compared to the other news."

"Do I get my bed tonight?" she asks.

"It's all yours. I'm curling up with Blake."

"You can go now."

"I feel so loved!" I yell as I walk out the door to hail a cab.

I find a ride easily since it's only two o'clock on a Monday afternoon. When I came to Chicago, I was running from my emotions—from the past. I found a new home, but it had nothing to do with where I'm at, but everything to do with the people I met. They could go anywhere with me, and it would be home.

As we continue down the familiar city streets, I call Dana, asking if she can meet us at the apartment tonight. Not much to my surprise, Charlie agrees to give her the night off because it's Monday and all. I mention the baby because I want her to hear it from me before she steps into the apartment tonight. She's surprised, but like everyone else, she's supportive, telling me she'll do whatever I need. Her kindness makes leaving even harder.

After paying the driver, I run up the metal stairs. Blake is standing right in front of me with his arms wide open when I walk in.

"Hey, baby. How did everything go today?"

I bury my nose in his T-shirt, breathing in his familiar scent. *Home.* "It wasn't easy, but I have no regrets."

"Did you tell the girls?" he asks, rubbing his hands up and down my back.

"They're coming over at six. I figured I'd tell Mallory then, too. I told her about the baby."

His hands stall for just a second before they continue massaging my back. "What did she say?"

"She thinks we're nuts."

"We are."

I laugh, standing as tall as I can to kiss him.

I notice his paintings stacked against the wall. "What are you doing with all those?"

"I'm keeping some and putting others in a gallery to sell. We're not going to have room for all of this."

"Which ones are you keeping?" he points to the smaller stack, and I immediately walk to it. The first is the picture of me, then a few I don't recognize, and the last is the one he'd done in the apartment several weeks back. The one that was very unlike his usual work. "Are you going to tell me about this one?"

"The day I painted that was the day she was supposed to be born two years ago," he responds, coming to stand behind me.

"She?"

"Yeah, the blood work determined the baby was a girl. For some reason, it really hit me that day. Finally letting myself mourn Aly while I was gone for all those months let me mourn her. I even gave her a name."

I reach my hand back, tangling my fingers with his. "What is it?"

"Anna. Aly always loved the name Anna."

It's a simple gray tree with no leaves, only branches. To the right sits four little pink birds. What I never noticed before were the letters etched inside each that spell Anna. My eyes well up just thinking about how lucky our baby is going to be to have a dad like him. He's a little hard on the outside, but all kinds of sweet on the inside.

"I'm glad you're keeping it. Where's the one of Alyssa?"

"I'm not selling it. I just haven't decided where I want to put it. Maybe I should give it to Pierce."

"But, it's yours. I don't want you to feel like you have to give it up because of me."

His arms come around me, hands covering my stomach. "It has nothing to do with you. There just comes a point where you have to let go."

"What do you want to do?"

He rests his chin on my shoulder. "I'll always have the photograph and the memory. I think I'd like to give this one to Pierce."

"I think he'd like that." I can only imagine Pierce's face when he sees it. Pierce cleaned up some of the bad blood between them when he helped Blake find me last week. If this doesn't take care of the rest, I'd be surprised.

"Let me get these loaded into Frank and then we'll get you home. I'd like to see Mallory for a few hours before we go," he says, pecking my cheek.

"Do you want some help?"

"Don't even think about it. I'm putting you in bubble wrap until April. By Christmas, you won't even be able to leave the house without me on your tail."

"Blake—"

"Don't argue with me, Lemon Drop. You know you don't have a chance at winning."

He's right so I might as well save my energy. He carries the first two out to the car, only allowing me to unlock the trunk. I hold it open as he carries out the other three then we drive away leaving the warehouse in the rearview.

"How do you feel about all this?" he asks.

"I'm excited and nervous, but that comes with any change," I say honestly.

He grabs my hand. "We'll be fine as long as we're in it together."

"Are you sure you're okay with this?" I ask.

He pulls my hand to his lips, kissing each of my knuckles. "More than okay."

When we walk into the apartment, I stay back waiting to see if Mallory is going to hug or strangle Blake. She pulls him in for a signature hug but says something to him that makes his eyes double in size. She pinches his side, which causes a yelp.

"What was that for?" he asks, rubbing against his ribs.

"For being a jerk to my best friend."

"Jesus, Mal. Stop acting like a thirteen-year-old girl."

"I will when you start acting like a twenty-seven-year-old man," she chides back.

"I'm all man, obviously." He winks at me, and all I can do is roll my eyes.

"Pig," she teases.

"Squirrel!" he yells before he disappears into his bedroom. She told me once that he always called her that when they were kids.

"I can't believe it." Her voice is quiet as she stares at his closed door. "My brother actually looks happy."

I shrug like it's nothing, but inside I'm dancing. Before I have time to respond, there's a knock at the door.

"Do you want me to get it?" Mallory asks.

"No, I've got it," I answer back, opening the door to Dana. She looks cute in a pair of black leggings and an oversized black and white striped tank.

She wraps her arm around my neck. "How are you doing, Mama?"

"As long as we're past noon, I'm good."

"I brought a bottle of sparkling grape juice so we can celebrate." I laugh when I get a glimpse of the brown paper bag it came in. She shrugs. "I don't want anyone to think I can't hold the real stuff."

Mallory comes up behind me. "Hey, I'm Mallory. It's nice to meet you."

"Nice to meet you, too. I've had the female version of Blake on my mind, and you're not it." Mallory is naturally thin with long brown hair; she looks like an angel compared to her brother.

"I'll take that as a compliment." She smiles. "Let me take the bottle from you. I'm guessing this is for her," she says nodding in my direction, "because I have the real stuff for us."

"You're darn right."

Another knock sounds on the door. *Reece.*

"I haven't seen you in forever," I tease when I open the door.

"Eight hours does seem like forever." She sticks out her lower lip.

"Awe, but you have the Big Bang to keep you company."

She wags her eyebrows. "Maybe I'll find out if he lives up to that nickname tonight."

"Reece."

"What?" She throws her arms up. "I've been reading a lot lately, and I have an itch that needs to be scratched, or I'm going to go crazy."

Dana and Mallory both laugh. Reece's face burns red. "Reece, I want you to meet Mallory."

Reece raises her hand slowly to take Mallory's. She has the I-want-to-get-the-fuck-out-of-here-look on her face. "If it makes you feel better, it's been forever for me, too. My electric boyfriend is getting a little tired of me," Mallory admits in an attempt to ease Reece's embarrassment.

"Sounds like Lila is the only one getting any around here," Dana chirps in.

They all start laughing, but I don't really find it funny. Their shoes would be easier to fill—no broken hearts.

We continue small talk as Mallory brings a plate of cupcakes and glasses of wine to the table. I wonder what Blake is doing, but then I hear the shower running.

"So," Dana says, "why did you call this meeting, Lila? We know the *big* news, but there has to be something else. It's too early for a baby shower."

Taking a deep, cleansing breath, I start, "Blake is moving back to Nebraska with me tomorrow. I didn't realize how much I missed it until last week, and Blake fell in love with it. We both agreed it would be the best place to start our family."

"But I just got home," Mallory pouts.

"I know," I say, pouting right along with her. "I don't want to leave any of you. I've never had friends who are more loyal ... who are there when I need them like you all are. You could always move to Nebraska."

All three quickly say no.

"I'll come visit, especially after that little baby is born," Reece says, sipping on her wine.

"This baby is going to have three of the best aunts ever," I add. I never had any sisters, but now I feel like I have three.

Blake comes out of the bedroom in gray workout shorts and a white tank, his hair still wet from the shower. Every time I look at the man, the other crazy pregnancy symptom creeps up. *Maybe he'll take another shower with me later,* I think to myself.

"Blake, you're going to hate Nebraska," Mallory says as soon as she sees him.

"Why do you say that?"

She throws her arms up. "It's nothing but cornfields and grass and people in overalls. What is there to like?"

He looks into my eyes. "The company. The quiet. It's exactly where I want to raise a baby. Lots of babies."

Reece rests her head on her hand. "Swoon."

"Don't egg him on," Mallory snaps.

"I'd go to Nebraska with him," Dana whispers into my ear.

Blake pulls me up from the chair, sitting down on it then setting me on his lap. "You guys are invited for the holidays, and we'll come back here when we can."

He pulls me against his chest, kissing my shoulder. No one can argue with what we have.

"Where are you guys staying?" Mallory asks, crossing her arms over her chest.

"I rented an apartment for now," Blake replies. "I'm hoping we can fix up Lila's grandparents' old farm before the baby comes."

"Farm?" Dana's eyes double in size.

"You'd love it, Dana. There's a creek that runs along the back."

We spend another hour talking about Nebraska and even getting suggestions on what we should name our baby. With every one, Blake whispers no behind me; at least we won't take any of their favorite baby names, should any of them have children.

Reece leaves first, followed by Dana. I'm not going to lie, tears flowed with each one. There won't be any more stops into Charlie's on the way home from work or quick morning chats or lunches with Reece. Those are the things I'm going to miss most.

When they're gone, Mallory stands up and announces she's ready for bed having flown the night before. I hug her, too, knowing we'll probably be gone before she gets up in the morning.

"I just got you back," I whisper in her ear. "Sorry I'm leaving so soon."

"It'll be okay," she says. "I'll be out there in less than a month. I guarantee it."

"Love you," I say before letting her go.

"Love you, too."

We've been crossing paths like this since college. This is nothing new. We move apart, but we always find our way back to each other.

Blake wraps his arms over my shoulders as soon as she's gone. "You look tired."

"I am. It's been a long day."

"Let's get you to bed. I'll wake you up at six, and you can sleep in the car."

"I need a shower before bed then." I bite my lower lip, hoping he takes the bait.

"Maybe you need some help washing a few spots," he offers, kissing the spot below my ear.

"That would be nice."

And he does. For the last time, we make love in this apartment. It's just another fitting goodbye.

"HEY, BABY, WE'RE HERE," Blake announces quietly, shaking my arm. This trip went much like the last, and I finally drifted off after filling my stomach with truck stop pancakes.

I rub my eyes, sneaking a glance out the window. Instead of seeing houses or the small shops that line our small town, I see my grandpa's old farmhouse. "What are we doing here?"

"This is our home, baby. You said you wanted to live here so I made it happen."

"But it needs to be cleaned and fixed up. No one has lived in it for a few years. We can't stay here, Blake."

He covers my lips with his index finger. "I talked to your dad before we left. A cleaning company came out yesterday and got it all ready, and he moved some of the old furnishings out. We still need to renovate, but I thought we could make it ours together."

I freaking hate how easily I cry these days. It's nice to have someone who listens to me—who makes my dreams come true when I least expect it.

"I love you," I say, kissing his finger.

"I love you more," he answers back, running his finger along my lower lip.

I hop out, practically running for the front door.

"Lila!" he yells. "Wait, I need to show you something!"

For once I listen, standing on the front porch waiting for him to catch up with what looks like a picnic basket. "What's in there?"

He flashes his cocky smile. "You'll see. Can you wait out here for two minutes, or do I have to tie you down?"

"Don't tempt me with a good time," I tease.

"I swear to God your sex drive is going to kill me if it doesn't slow down. I didn't think that was possible."

"Challenge accepted."

I sit on the old porch swing while I wait for him. I imagine him setting up a blanket so we can have our first meal together here. Or maybe he's drawing me a bath after the long ride.

The wondering stops when he comes through the door. "Come here," he instructs, holding his hand out to me.

I walk quickly, listening to the old boards creak under my feet. The place smells like lemons as we step inside and looks as clean as grandma used to keep it—shiny hardwood floors, gorgeous woodwork and an array of outdated wallpapers.

He squeezes my hand, leading me to the kitchen. "There are so many things I didn't do right since I met you, and I can't go back and change them, but I want to do what was right all over again. I want a second chance to make everything right."

His fingers find the bottom of my sundress slowly lifting it up over my thighs. His fingertips brush my bare stomach then my breasts. "Arms up, Lemon Drop."

I do as he asks, shifting my feet in anticipation. He unfastens my bra then slides my panties down so I can easily step out of them. Before I know it, he has me sitting on the counter as his warm mouth explores my body.

Reaching between us, I work the button on his pants. It hasn't even been twenty-four hours, but it feels like forever.

"Hey," he groans, gripping my wrist. "There's no rush, Lemon Drop."

My thoughts flash back to the night he had me on the counter, teasing me while explaining the nickname he'd given me.

He talks between kisses. "The first moment I'd want to do again is Truth. That's when I started seeing you differently. Ask me something, baby, and I'll answer it. Anything."

Caught off guard, I think about it. He's told me so much over the last week that there's not much left to know. "Are you happy, or are you just working toward it?"

He stops what he's doing, tipping my chin up to look in his eyes. "If you don't have an answer to that after tonight, then you can ask again."

"My turn," he says, kissing down my stomach. "What was the first thing that went through your head when you found out you were pregnant? Be honest."

"I just hoped you wouldn't leave me."

"Oh, baby. I'm so sorry."

I grip his hair between my fingers. "I know, but we're trying to forget all of that now, right?"

"Good girl." He opens the drawer, pulling out a lemon drop. Just seeing the small yellow candy brings back good memories. He sucks on it first then kisses me, carefully placing it on my tongue, while skimming his fingers along the inside of my thighs. I roll the candy around and pass it back. He runs his candy-coated tongue along down my throat, against each of my nipples then slips down circling my belly button.

He presses one finger into me while working his mouth back up to my breasts. "You're so wet. What do you want first, baby?" He pushes a second finger inside me, and I swear I'm going to lose it. "Fingers or cock?"

"Mouth," I moan, feeling him smile against the crook of my neck.

"Lean back," he instructs, removing his fingers and spreading my legs.

He's everything. I could live the rest of my life alone in this house with him and have everything.

His candy-covered tongue works its way down between my legs. I wrap my legs over his shoulders as his hot mouth works more core.

He sucks.

Then circles.

Then sucks again.

I lose myself, screaming his name over and over as I tug his hair. He waits for me breathing to slow before working his way back up, passing the little bit of candy that's left back to me.

"And that was number one." He throws out a cocky grin, reminding me of that night.

"You think you can make it four this time?" I tease, rolling the little bit of candy that's left around on my tongue. I taste myself as I watch him strip in front of me.

He rests his forearms against the cabinet as he sinks into me slowly. "Baby, I can give you as many as you want. You just need to tell me when to stop." He plunges all the way in, almost daring me to beg for it. "You're still my Lemon Drop."

I moan. It's all I can do. His words used to cause rivers of desire to flow, but they could cause a tidal wave in the ocean now.

"Do you know how many of those I ate in the months we were apart?" he whispers against my lips.

I shake my head slowly waiting for him to kiss me.

"At least ten a day. I couldn't stop because they remind me of you, and you're my addiction."

"Kiss me," I beg, covering his cheeks with my hands.

He pulls my hands away, pinning them up against the cabinet as he continues to push into me over and over. "This is my game tonight, Lemon Drop. I make up the rules."

The way he has me pinned combined with his words has me coming around him within seconds. Something about giving him all control turns me on. It's only then that he kisses me — soft and tender — weakening my cries.

Blake is a protector.

A lover.

A fighter.

He's not always sweet, but that's what I like most about him.

"That's two," he says against my lips.

When my breathing slows, he wipes us both off and leads me to a spare bedroom that's already been setup as a studio of sorts. The walls and floors are covered in a protective white canvas.

He stands me in the middle of the room and tells me to close my eyes. If it were anyone but him it wouldn't feel right, but trust gives a person a license for many things. Besides, I remember this moment like it was yesterday. I'd relive it every day if I could.

"The night in the studio ... I held back on things that I shouldn't have. I was scared of the way you made me feel."

Cool paint touches the space between my breasts. I flinch at first and then just like I did last time, I try to figure out what he's painting. The contrast against my skin, the coolness ... it feels exactly the same. When I remember the first time he did this, it feels like falling in love all over again. The lemon drops were special, but this stole my heart.

"I want you to listen and feel. Nothing else."

He continues to paint down my stomach. My eyes twitch, waiting to open. "Don't open your eyes, baby. I'm almost done."

If he only knew what he does to me. You think you know what love is until you really feel it. You have to truly fall before someone can catch you.

I've definitely fallen.

I hear his bare feet on the canvas-covered floor moving away from me then coming back. His calloused fingertips trace a line from one side of my hips to the other, not cold or wet. My breath hitches when they slip between my legs, two entering at once while his thumb works my clit.

"Still wet," he growls, pulling my lower lip between his teeth. His touch switches between sensual and rough—loving then teasing. His fingers halt, and I want to cry. "Do you remember what I said that night? What my favorite part of your body is?"

How could I forget? "My eyes. You said my eyes."

He inserts his long fingers inside of me continuing what he'd started. Standing in darkness, the only thing I have to do is feel his skin against my swollen flesh.

The friction.

The tension.

Two hearts further melting into one.

The pressure builds, and I come hard around his fingers, digging my nails into his shoulders to hold myself steady. His mouth covers mine, swallowing my screams. He groans, kissing me hard, punctuating it by lightly kissing each corner of my mouth and the tip of my nose like he'd done that night.

I attempt to open my eyes, but he kisses me before I get a glimpse of what he painted. He's good at diversion. He finally steps back, and says, "You can open your eyes now."

As soon as my eyes adjust to the light, I see "I LOVE YOU". The "I" between my breasts "LOVE YOU" on my stomach.

"I should have told you I love you then because that's when I knew."

"I loved you then, too," I admit.

"Think of how many of our problems could have been avoided if those words had been spoken."

"I'll tell you every day," I promise.

"I feel it, baby, and every time you look at me, I feel it."

He's scrapbooking our whole relationship right onto my heart—the one he forever holds in his palms.

He grabs my hand again, leading me up the stairs to the only bathroom in the whole house. It has a white pedestal sink, toilet, and oversized claw foot tub. I used to swim it in as a kid. He lets go of me just long enough to start the water. The picnic basket he carried in earlier is sitting against it. He reaches inside, sprinkling rose petals over the rising water.

"Let me wipe some of the paint off you," he says, wetting an old yellow washcloth. "You're not going to forget it now, are you?"

I shake my head, enjoying the texture of the warm cloth against my skin—the gentle way he moves it over my stomach. "It's written in your eyes, too, Blake. It's written in lots of the things you do for me."

"Don't forget it. There's going to be days when I'm a complete asshole, but even then, I need you to remember I love you. I can't think of a single thing that would change that."

He kisses me, tracing his thumbs over my nipples. I moan against his lips, ready to go at it all over again.

"Let's get in the tub before I end up bringing you to bed instead," he mumbles against my lips walking us back until the backs of my legs hit the porcelain. He helps me in then sits across from me with our legs entwined.

"Remember the night I came home and climbed in the tub with you, and you started to cry after we made love?"

I nod.

"Tell me what you told me before you climbed out," he says.

"Tell you what?" I ask, staring into his deep blue eyes. There are other parts of that night I remember more vividly.

"That you love me. Tell me again."

"I love you, Blake."

"I love you, Lila."

I bend my legs, closing enough space between us that I can easily kiss his lips. He only allows a taste before pulling back. "If I'd said it back then, what would you have said next? How would that night have been different?"

I scoot back to my side of the tub, looking into his eyes. "I'm pregnant, Blake."

He moves toward me like I'd just done to him. "Are you sure?" he asks, placing his hand over my flat stomach.

"I took a test this morning."

His eyes well with tears. "What if I'm a shitty parent?"

I trace my finger in a circle around his heart. "If you care about this baby the way you care for me, it won't want for anything, Blake. The rest we'll learn together."

He kisses me once more. "If I had to do that moment all over again, that's how I'd want it to be. From that second on, I would never have let you out of my sight."

"I've forgiven you for that, too. You weren't running from me. You were running from the past."

"It's not an excuse."

"But I get it."

He smiles big, tapping my nose with his finger. "Can I trust you in here for ten minutes without falling asleep?"

"What are you up to?" I ask narrowing my eyes at him.

"In ten minutes, get dressed and come out the back door. Follow the path."

"The path?"

He climbs from the tub, wrapping one of grandma's towels around himself. It barely wraps around his hips. "You'll see when you get outside."

I do as I'm told, replaying this whole night over in my head. Everything has happened so fast, but when I look back at it, it sums up our relationship. It's rare ... special. There's no one else in the world I could have this with. I wrap a towel around me and let the water out before opening the door to go in search of my clothes. To my surprise, he's left my simple white sundress and flip-flops right outside the bathroom door. I slip them on and head out the door.

It's completely dark now, and I'm stopped instantly by the two-feet wide path that glows from the bottom of the stairs to the side of the barn. They're tiny rocks that shine a light shade of blue.

My heart practically beats out of my chest as I follow them, hearing the sounds of the crickets and katydids. That's another one of my favorite things about the farm—the natural music that plays at night.

As I come around the back of the barn, I see Blake standing on a blanket surrounded by lanterns. The exact expression on his face is hard to see, but he's wearing khaki shorts and a white button-up rolled up to his elbows.

"I was starting to wonder if you were going to show," he jokes.

"You knew I would."

I walk closer, getting a glimpse at his expression. He grins wide. Cocky bastard.

"Out of all the places we've been, this is my favorite. This is why I wanted to move here with you," he says, his expression turning more serious.

I open my mouth to speak, but all my words are flushed away when he takes my hand and gets down on one knee. "I'm not perfect, or even any semblance of it, but when I'm with you, everything feels perfect. When we're apart, I wake up lonely without you by my side. You're the one thing in this world I can't live without and the one thing I want to live for.

"You make me believe in true love—the unconditional kind. You make me believe in God again. You make me want to be better. You make me want to move forward.

"Lila Fields, I promise to give you me so we can be us. I promise to never shut you out or run away. I promise to cover the scars I left on you every single day until you can't see them anymore. Most of all, I promise to be there forever if you'll let me."

He pauses, tears streaming down both our cheeks. This is better than any fairytale I watched as a little girl because it's my fairytale.

"Will you marry me, baby?" His voice shakes.

I cover my mouth as I nod my head saying "yes" over and over again. He slips a ring on my finger with ease just before I wrap my arms around his neck, pressing my lips to his repeatedly until I can't feel them anymore. It's only then that I look over my shoulder at the ring that sparkles in the faint light.

"I designed it myself," he says, taking his turn to kiss me. "It's an antique diamond from Europe with a slight yellow hue. I had the jeweler etch the shoulders of the band with flowers and taper it in. It's unique just like you."

"It's beautiful, but you could have wrapped a string of grass around my finger, and I would have said yes."

"I'll remember that on our anniversary," he teases. There's a pause and he's staring at me like he can't believe this is happening either. "I had "love is enough" etched inside the band. I think I told you once that it wasn't, but it's the reason I came back. It's what I want you to remember when we're apart or when we fight. Love is enough to hold us together through everything if it's strong enough."

"It's also enough to forgive and forget," I add.

"That too."

I look up at the stars then back to Blake. "Do you know something else I've never done out here?"

"What?" he asks, wrapping his arms around my waist.

"Made love under the stars."

He slides one strap from my shoulder, pressing his lips to it. "I'm going to be your first," he whispers against my ear.

"You're going to be my only," I answer back as he lays me down on the blanket.

I want to get married out here.

I want to make babies out here.

I want to do everything with this man right here.

He keeps his promise of four—slow and sweet—making love under the shining stars. And, when I look up, I realize we just made love under a full moon.

I smile as he holds me tightly against his chest. I found my full moon.

EPILOGUE

"BABE, CAN YOU GET me some more milk?"

I roll out of bed, my eyes barely open as I walk down the stairs. Saturday is my day to sleep in, but it rarely works out that way.

Blake gets up when she starts to cry. His big feet creak along the steps. He inevitably drops something on the floor while trying to make a bottle. Then, the stairs creak again. He fumbles with her diaper while she shows off her little lungs.

Then comes the part I like—where he hums the "ABC's" and "Twinkle, Twinkle Little Star." I could listen to him forever. He's the best daddy. I have one lucky little girl. She's quiet for maybe fifteen minutes then she screams again.

"Coming!" I yell back, feeling the cold hardwoods against my feet. The house is still dark, the sky purple with a hint of orange in the horizon.

It's only been three months, but I can make a bottle like it's no one's business. I trudge up to her room, handing it to him quickly before she sees me; it's all over then.

He whispers, "Thank you."

I crawl back into my comfortable bed.

Just as I start to drift off, the bed dips and his strong arm wraps around my waist pulling me close to his bare chest. I pretend to sleep because I want to. I'd do just about anything for six hours of straight sleep.

"You awake?" he says quietly. I think he can tell I'm not by the way I breathe.

"You know I am."

His hand snakes its way under my sleep shirt, the backs of his fingers brushing against my stomach while his lips whisper against the back of my neck. "Lay on your stomach, baby."

I do as he asks, smiling while I think about last Saturday. It went a lot like this and then she woke before I was able to find out how it was all going to end.

My shirt goes all the way up as he straddles my hips.

His fingers run along my spine to my shoulders then down my sides. He does it over and over, and eventually he presses for more, skimming his fingers along the sides of my breasts. He's an expert—he knows just how to get me.

His body covers mines, lips blazing a hot trail from one side to the other. "Did I tell you you're beautiful yet this morning?"

"Not yet," I moan.

"Did I tell you I love you?"

"No."

"Did I tell you I'd be yours forever?"

I shake my head against the pillow, unable to speak.

"I love you forever, beautiful."

His marriage vows—he honors them every single day.

His lips trail down my back.

I remember the crisp fall day three months after he proposed—when I first saw him standing in his suit coat by the creek.

His thumbs slip inside the edge of my panties, pulling them down carefully as he kisses the backs of my thighs.

I remember all the promises he made. The promises I made him.

By the time he reaches my feet, all I remember is the way he kissed me in front of our close friends and family. It was a small wedding, but perfect for us.

He kisses his way back up, subtly slipping his fingers between my legs as he does. He knows exactly what to do, not that he has to try too hard.

"I'll never tire of this body. You're so fucking gorgeous," he says, his lips brushing against my ear. Then, in one quick motion he's inside me. He holds there until I adjust to him.

He pulls out then fills me again.

"Blake," I moan. "Don't stop."

This is the part we didn't get to before Belle woke up last weekend. It's been a few stolen showers here and there, but foreplay has all but become extinct.

"On your knees," he instructs, tugging my hair back. The mix of sensations is all I need before the first orgasm ricochets through my body. He grunts as I pulse around him, but he's not done yet … not even close.

There's no time to come off the high. His thumb moves over the bumps on my spine until there are no more. "Turn around, baby."

I do, laid out naked in front of him, drenched in sex. Desire is wanting a man after only three hours of sleep. I give up sleep for sex … just for him.

He crawls up my body, lapping his tongue around my nipples then up the line of my throat. "How do you want me?"

"I just want you," I answer back with no hesitation. Our relationship is give and take, but mostly, I take what he'll give me.

Without another word, he sinks back into me, burying his head in the crook of my neck. "I love you," he whispers.

"I love you, too," I answer back, struggling to catch my breath.

His pace picks up then slows.

My heart beats rapidly.

He pulls all the way out then thrusts in.

My body is wound. So much tension I can barely stand it, yet it's the moment I love the most. I want to hold on to it, but he knows how to break the euphoric spell.

Two more thrusts, and I'm done. I'm his.

He groans, biting into my collarbone to mask his screams.

"I'll never tire of you," he mumbles, barely able to breathe. His chin rests on my chest, his eyes staring into mine. The sun comes up, shining through our thin white curtains giving me a glimpse of everything I love about this man—his deep blue eyes, sandy blonde hair and that dimple … I freaking love that dimple.

"You better not."

"Every day, I fall more in love with you, so I don't see how it would be possible."

I brush my fingers through his hair. "I like hearing that."

He scoots up, kissing my lips. "I like saying it."

This.

Is.

Bliss.

There's nothing better for our relationship than being alone like this.

Then, just like clockwork, Belle starts to cry. I'm reminded how much our life has changed. We used to hold each other for hours after sex, talking or sleeping. Now, a new kind of bliss is just in the next room.

"I'll get her." He smiles down at me. "Mallory will be here in a couple hours. Why don't you shower, and I'll drive into Omaha to get her."

"Awe, I get to shower today?" I tease. It was a little rough in the beginning but things are falling into place. It's also easier since we both work from home.

"You better. You smell like sex."

"It's become my favorite perfume since I get to wear it less often and all."

He climbs from the bed, throwing on his T-shirt and shorts. "I take that as a challenge, Mrs. Stone. I hope you're not a big fan of sleep because between baby duty and perfume trials, you won't be getting much." His last words trail off as he heads into the bathroom to wash his hands.

"I don't think you have the sales skills to talk me into participating in your trial," I say as he walks back through the bedroom to get Belle from her crib.

LISA DE JONG

I hear him laugh. I am so in trouble; he's not going to let me sleep for a week.

With Blake in the driver's seat, I shower and actually take the time to blow dry my hair. Mallory hasn't been here since right after Belle was born. Most of the weight I gained is gone, but my hair has been in a permanent messy bun, and I couldn't tell you where my make-up bag is.

"Babe, are you about done? I have to leave in ten minutes!" Blake yells from downstairs.

"Coming!" I yell, pulling on a simple blue maxi dress and matching flip-flops.

"Not now, but you will be later!" he hollers back. *I'm definitely going to pay for the perfume comment.*

When I come down the stairs, he's sitting on the couch, knees raised, with Belle perched on his legs. I could honestly watch the two of them together forever and never get bored.

And when Belle sees me, her whole face lights up. No one rocks a toothless smile like our little Isabelle.

I take her from his lap, wrapping her in my arms. "How's Mommy's little girl?"

She coos.

My heart melts.

Blake stands, kissing Belle's cheek then mine. "I better get going."

"Can you pick up Starbucks while you're in town?"

"You don't even have to ask," he says before walking out the door.

If I've learned anything since we've moved here, it's that love has a rhythm. Or, to be more specific, two people in love should live in the same rhythm. You don't have to be alike; I'm a clarinet, he's a drum, but we're playing the same song.

I want a happy marriage — one that others look at from the outside and envy. He grants that dream every day without even trying.

I want Belle to have the best of everything yet still realize that life isn't perfect. He supports that.

He wants to continue his career, which requires traveling from time to time. I want that for him because it's what makes him happy.

He needs to kiss me, or touch me in some way at least ten times a day to make sure I'm still here. I'm more than okay with that, too.

Even now, it's only been a few minutes, and I miss him. When you find something so perfect, you never want to let it go.

I prepare a bottle for Belle and rock her while staring out the living room window. A few vehicles go by, but other than that it's miles of peaceful farmland. Moving here was the best thing we ever did.

My sweet girl falls asleep on my shoulder after her stomach is full. I'm content staying like this, switching between looking out the window and reading the latest news on my phone.

Before long, Frank pulls in the driveway, and it takes everything I have not to jump up from the chair. Even though Mallory and I talk every day, I miss her.

The second the front door creaks open, Belle is awake. I don't get how she does that so quickly.

"How is my girl?" Mallory says, dropping her bag and going right for Belle. That's the other thing about babies—once you have them, you're always in second place.

Blake is beside her making sure she's holding Belle just right. The amount of love he has for our little girl makes my heart explode. "You don't have hold her head like that anymore," he remarks.

Mallory rolls her eyes. "It's not going to hurt her, Blake."

"And she just ate, so she's probably going to poop. Don't know how well that white cashmere sweater of yours is going to hold up," he teases.

"She's worth it," Mallory shoots back.

"Did you happen to get coffee?" I ask Blake, noticing his hands are empty.

"Shit! I knew I was forgetting something."

"Blake Stone, watch your mouth. It won't be long, and this little one will be talking," Mallory says, taking the words right out of my mouth.

"It's not a big deal. I can make some."

Blake cringes. "I used the last of the grounds yesterday. Why don't I run to Starbucks and get you both a latte, and I'll pick up more grounds while I'm at it."

"Yes, please," Mallory says before I get a chance to respond. "Do you know how early I had to get on that plane this morning?"

I want to make a smart comment about how I spent my morning, but I don't. It's a weird line to cross when you're married to your best friend's brother.

He grabs his keys, kissing me yet again. "Be back in a few."

"Love you," I whisper.

"Love you more," he says back, kissing my forehead. I can't help but watch him walk away. He is all kinds of perfect for me.

Mallory doesn't waste a second after the door shuts behind him. "Have you talked to Reece this week?"

I nod. She calls me almost every other day on her lunch break … the time we used to spend together. Not long after Blake and I moved here, Reece became Mallory's new roommate. They're opposites, but it seems to be working out okay.

"Big Bang is practically living with us now. I swear, and they're so freaking cute together. A hundred bucks says they're married by this time next Christmas."

"His name is Dylan," I remind her.

She waves me off. "We call him Big Bang all the time. It's no big deal. Besides, it sure sounds like he lives up to the name."

"She deserves it. Speaking of which, isn't it about time you found a man? You've been back in the states for almost a year."

She smiles shyly, biting her lower lip. "I've been seeing someone actually."

"Did you meet him at work?"

"Umm, no, not really, but it's someone you know."

"Who?"

Words Unspoken, a spinoff novella coming Winter 2016.

Also, keep reading for the first two chapters of **Break Even**, a standalone adult contemporary novel releasing December 2015. It's an atypical love story with a dose of suspense.

BREAK EVEN
Sneak Preview

Chapter 1

"COLE!" I SCREAM, curling my fingers around the edge of the counter. He pulls out slowly then thrusts back inside; there's nothing soft and tender about it.

During the first couple years of our marriage he made love to me. His lips would brush against my skin from head to toe and his hands would caress my inner thighs until I ached for him to be inside of me.

He'd tease.

He had me gasping for breath before he even reached where I needed it the most.

He knew exactly how I liked it; it was insane bliss. It was the reason I sped home from work every night. It was one of the reasons I knew he was the one—our maddening physical connection translated into every aspect of our relationship. Every last inch of me was wrapped around him. Everything.

He pushes in again until it aches, burying his head deep in the crook of my neck.

"Don't stop," I moan, slipping my fingers between us. I need to come so badly. Three weeks and four days… that's how long it's been.

Sex isn't about me lately, and it hasn't been for a while.

His teeth dig into my skin. "I can't stop myself, baby. You feel so good."

"Cole, please," I beg, rubbing my fingers in circles. If he notices, he doesn't acknowledge my need.

He thrusts all the way in. "Christ, Marley," he murmurs against my skin as he releases into me. My heart sinks, but my desire is stuck at an all time high.

My orgasms have become as rare as a full moon. In less than an hour, it will be three weeks and five days since I last felt what it was like to clench around him over and over again.

My breathing is heavy. My fingers still. His head still pressed against my neck as his fingers run gently along my spine.

"Did I hurt you?" he whispers against my skin.

Not the way you're thinking.

"I'm good," I lie, leaning in to kiss his shoulder.

He cups my ass, sliding me off the counter. His hooded eyes stare deep into mine. That look he had on the day we said *I do*...I still see it there. It hasn't disappeared completely, but the way he shows it has. *How do I get that back?*

He leans in, kissing the tip of my nose and each corner of my mouth followed by a simple peck on my lips.

"I love you," he says softly, pulling away.

"I love you more." I've said it for years, but lately I've wondered how much I believe it.

"Not possible."

He slips the strap of my nightie back over my shoulder and adjusts his boxer briefs so we're both covered. "I have to go out of town for a few days. I know I promised no more trips this month, but I — "

"You have a client that needs help on an emergency case," I interrupt, wanting so badly to turn and walk out of the room. It's the same excuse over and over again.

He cups my cheeks in his warm hands. "I'm sorry. I'm really, really sorry."

"But this week — " I hold back the tears.

"I know. I tried to get out of it, but I'm the only one who has direct knowledge of this case." The pads of his thumbs brush the puffy circles under my eyes. He should be the one to take them away since he put them there.

"What day?" he asks when I don't speak up.

"Thursday," I choke, my lower lip quivering. Seven months is a long time to wait to get pregnant, and it doesn't help that my husband never seems to be around when I need him.

"Maybe we'll get lucky and it'll happen after tonight," he says, pulling me in close to his warm body.

Pressing my palms to his chest, I try to put as much distance between us as possible.

"That's three days, Cole. You promised —" He wraps his arms around me tighter, making it impossible to escape.

"I promise," he whispers against my ear. "I promise if it doesn't happen for us this month, I'll be here next month. I know how much this means to you." I choke down the tears that threaten to carve a path down my cheeks.

"Do you?" His grip loosens just enough he can stare down into my eyes.

"I want it to. If you don't believe that then why are we even standing here talking about this?" I shrug in response, unable to find the right words. I don't even know where to start, but this was not the way I pictured our night going.

He leans in to kiss my lips. "I'll think about you every second I'm gone."

I doubt that too.

"Why don't you go get ready for bed? I have a quick phone call to make then I'll join you."

Without another word, I slip out from between him and the counter. After washing my face and brushing my teeth, I curl up on my side of the bed fully aware I'll drift off to sleep before he makes it to bed. To have and to hold doesn't hold much weight for him. Not like it used to.

"You going to miss me?" he asks me the next morning. His arms wrap around me while I pour my first cup of coffee.

"I always do," I reply honestly, resting my hand over his.

"I have a meeting scheduled at the office today that I need you to take care of for me. New client."

"Give me a thirty second brief," I say as his lips press into the curve of my neck.

"I don't know too much about him yet. Beatrice tells me that he's in town trying to close a deal on a vacant building downtown for some new restaurant nightclub venture. She told him I'd be out of town, but that my wife was more than capable of handling it." He pauses and retracts. "Actually, the way she put it was 'even more capable of handling it'. I don't know what kind of bribes you've been throwing her behind my back, but they're clearly working," he teases, as his warm lips begin trailing up my neck.

His hands splay against my flat stomach then slowly skim down, gripping the bottom of my long, white t-shirt. The cotton brushes against my thighs until his hands find my bare ass, kneading it with the palms of his hands. "Maybe we can make a baby right now…before I go," he whispers against my earlobe.

His hands move around to my stomach, traveling up to my exposed breasts. I gasp as he pinches my nipples between his fingers.

"Let go, baby," he demands, pressing me forward until my cheek is pressed against the cold granite. My panties are yanked to my knees when I hear the sound of his zipper. Without hesitation he's inside of me, pumping in and out with caveman-like vigor.

I want to touch him, to kiss him, to make love the way we used to; but this is it. This is how four years of marriage has been defined for us.

"Are you going to miss me, baby?" he asks, pulling on my ponytail. The sensation. The tingle. It's almost enough to send me over the elusive edge.

"Yes!" I scream, barely able to catch my breath. "Touch me, Cole. I need you to touch me."

His warm lips draw an invisible map down my back. "How do you want me to touch you, hmm? Tell me."

"I want to come. Please make me come." He finds the swollen spot between my legs, gently rubbing small circles as the pace of his thrusts quicken. It's become a race of who will get there first. He speeds up once again, and I know he's close.

He thrusts. The pressure inside of me builds.

I close my eyes tightly doing my best to stay in the moment—to think about nothing but the way he fills me. I imagine him shirtless and pinning me against the wall with his strong arms wrapped tightly around my waist. I imagine us in bed; his fully naked body covering mine in a continuous rhythm.

I'm on the verge of ultimate euphoria, but he's so much closer. With one final deep thrust, he let's go grunting behind me as his hand presses into my back. His fingers slip from between my legs and I wince.

Does he know what he's doing to me? Or not doing?

"I better get going," he says as he helps me up from the counter.

"Yeah, you better," I answer, doing everything I can to not look him in the eyes. He'll read me like a simple children's book, and we don't have time to sift through the disaster we've become before he jets off on his next trip. He brushes my hair away from my shoulder and kisses the back of my neck.

"I need to get ready for work," I announce, glancing over at the clock on the microwave.

He spins me in his arms, giving me no choice but to look at him. If he sees sadness in my eyes, he doesn't acknowledge it. He grips my hips, pulling me in for one last lingering kiss. I wish he touched me like this all the time ... with this much emotion.

"See you Thursday, baby." I pull my lips into a smile, albeit forced.

"Behave yourself," I warn him.

"It's not me we have to worry about." He winks, loosening his grip on me.

"Besides wine with the girls tonight, I'll be curled on the couch watching true crime television. I'll then lie in bed with your old wooden bat while I imagine every little sound is a masked intruder that has come to drown me or chop me into tiny little pieces."

He laughs. "Lock the door and set the security system. You'll be fine." He looks down at his watch. "Okay, now I really need to go, or I'm going to miss my flight."

"Be safe," I say, standing on my tiptoes to kiss the tip of his nose.

"Bye, babe."

"Bye, Cole."

I watch his strong suited body retreat and walk out the front door as I fold my arms over my stomach. *Can our marriage even handle a baby right now?*

Chapter 2

"Mrs. Mason, I'm glad you're here," Beatrice announces as I walk past her desk. "River Holtz has called three times already this morning asking what time you can fit him into your schedule."

Beatrice has been part of the firm since we took over after Cole's fathers' retirement a few years ago. In fact, I think she was Robert Mason's secretary for twenty years even before then. She knows what she's doing.

"Who is River Holtz?" I ask, dismissively thumbing through a fresh stack of mail.

"Didn't your husband tell you? He's in town and wants to work with you on an acquisition. A club developer, if I recall."

"Oh yes, he mentioned that. What time does he want to meet?" Her nose wrinkles slightly as she pushes her glasses up.

"That's sort of why I'm glad you're here."

"Spit it out, Beatrice."

She sighs. "He's waiting in your office. And did I mention, he's not very patient?"

"Shit," I mumble under my breath as I smooth out my black sleeveless pencil dress. "Do we have a file on him?"

She hands me the small file. "This is all I could find." She says, staring at me the way my mother used to when I was too quiet at the dinner table or when I came home way earlier than my curfew.

"Are you okay, Mrs. Mason?"

"Why?"

"That's the first time I've heard you swear in all the years I've known you," she responds quietly. She's good at her job—not because she types the fastest or works long hours, but because she studies everything around her. She knows what needs to be done before we even tell her...she more than likely knows us better than we know ourselves.

"I'm just tired," I answer, pushing away the depressive feelings that I thought I'd left at home this morning. Our relationship can be fixed by a BandAid ... it has to be. The seven-year itch probably just hit a couple years too soon.

I start walking toward the heavy mahogany door, which is open just enough to get a good glimpse at my early, unexpected visitor.

"Hey, Marley," Beatrice says quietly from behind me.

I turn around feeling annoyed. Not so much at her but because I have a man in my office who I still don't know shit about and I haven't even had my coffee yet. Cole literally fucked that up this morning. "What is it?"

"He's probably not what you're expecting."

Rolling my eyes, I say, "I wasn't expecting anyone this morning. I have two depositions to work on. He picked the wrong day to just stop in."

She wrinkles her nose again. "That's not quite what I meant."

"Out with it," I say, glancing between her and the door.

"He may have just gotten out of prison from the looks of it." She pauses, smiling just a bit. "He knows how to wear a pair of trousers, though. If you can get a look from the back —"

"Beatrice!" I shout as quietly as I can to still prove my point. She raises her hands in defeat.

Without another word, I take one last look down at my simple black dress and open the door to my corner office. It's easily the best in the whole suite.

My mouth gapes at the sight of the man standing at my window, peering down at the city streets. He's got the ass of a professional soccer player, which is probably why Beatrice noted his trousers. His well-pressed white shirt is rolled up to his elbows showcasing a full sleeve of tattoos that reach his knuckles.

Definitely not my typical client.

I clear my throat, drawing his attention. My eyes widen, but I quickly gain back control. He's got these light blue eyes—almost like glass. "What can I help you with, Mr. Holtz?" I ask, walking around to sit behind my desk. I'm going to need something to ground me.

He puts one hand in his pocket, running the fingers of the other over his perfect pink lips. "I have a deal that I need to close within the next forty-eight hours. I was hoping to work with Cole, but I hear he's conveniently out of town."

He hasn't moved from the window so he's perfectly aligned with my chair; the way his eyes shift from my legs to my eyes while he speaks doesn't escape me.

"Why so quick?" I ask, pulling out a pen to take notes.

"When I want something, I get it. This is a special property, and I know that I'm not the only one who's going to go after it." I point to one the chairs that sit in front of my desk.

"Would you mind taking a seat so we can go over a few details?" He grins, walking towards my desk. His palms lay flat on the edge as he leans in close. His light brown hair falls forward, bringing my attention back to those eyes.

"I don't like being told what to do."

"I asked," I chime back, biting down on the tip of my pen. He sits on the edge of the desk a few feet away from me.

"This is where I want to sit. Now, what do you need to know?"

You have got to be fucking kidding me. I buzz Beatrice.

"Yes, Mrs. Mason?"

"Bring me some coffee. Lots of coffee."

"I'd like one too," River says before Beatrice has a chance to respond.

"I'll be right there," she says before the phone clicks.

"First, give me the address of the property."

He picks up a manila envelope and tosses it across the desk. "It's all in there."

"And the seller?" I ask.

"That's in there, too."

"So, why do you need me? This is what real estate agents are for, no?" My eyes are stuck to the door. If Beatrice doesn't bring my coffee soon, I'm may lose it.

"The property isn't zoned as a nightclub. What I want to do is run a restaurant through the early evening hours then transform it into the hottest night club in town. You're going to be the one to make that happen." The way his thigh muscles pulse through his slacks is distracting.

LISA DE JONG

"Can you please take a chair?" He pulls a pencil from my desk, twirling it between his fingers. Not five seconds later, he snaps it between them.

"I'm fine. Besides, the view is better up here." His eyes trace my legs, stop on my breasts for a split second before finally finding mine.

"I don't know if I have time to take on your case." It's mostly a lie.

"But you will. Cole promised me that he'd get it taken care of and he's not here." I pull my reading glasses on and unclasp the manila envelope.

"Give me a few hours to look through this, and I'll get some documentation ready for the council. Can I call you when I have something?" When he doesn't answer, I look up to see him staring at me, thumb skimming over his lower lip.

"Are you sure you're married to Cole Mason?"

"As far as I know. Do you have a problem with that?" He grins. Cocky ass.

"No. He just seems like he deserves worse...and you deserve better."

"There's this line," I start, motioning my finger between us. "You're not allowed to cross it."

He laughs. "I wasn't hitting on you. I can have any woman I want on any night that I want her. A married lawyer doesn't even rank on that list." I stare back down at the paperwork before he has the chance to see through me. A lawyer must not hit the top of Cole's list lately either.

"You can leave now," I announce, not bothering to look up.

"There's one more thing."

"I'm listening."

"There's a club opening tonight. The guy who runs it went through something similar with the city. Thought it might be good for you two to talk." I look back up, but it doesn't last long. I can't place it but there's something about the way he glares at me.

"Leave me his number, and I'll get permission to talk to his attorney."

"Do you always stare blankly at your desk when you have paying clients in your office?" he asks, voice smokier than it had been.

He dares me.

I accept. For the first time, I stare long enough to actually see the color of his eyes—a blue so pale and vivid they remind me of a laser beam.

"I do when they don't have appointments." Those laser eyes narrow in on me and scan my entire body.

"It's a good thing you're not my type."

"And why's that?" He leans a little closer.

"I won't be tempted to fuck you. I'd hate to have to hire a new attorney."

My mouth gapes. Beatrice picks this exact moment to come in with two piping hot cups of coffee. Her eyes lock on mine. If she doesn't see how badly I want him out of here after all these years of working together, she hasn't paid enough attention.

"Mrs. Mason," she says as she sets the cups down on my desk. "Your 9:30 appointment is waiting."

I smile. She's good. "Thank you. Tell him I'll be done in a couple minutes."

"Will do." Her gaze catches mine one last time just as she walks out the door. She winks. That woman is definitely restricted from retiring. Ever.

My attention shoots straight back to my client. "You're crude."

"See, you already know everything there is to know about me." His pink lips press to the black coffee cup.

"By the way, I'm not leaving you his number. You're coming with me tonight."

Oh, hell no!

"I have plans."

"Cancel them."

I laugh out loud, spinning around in my chair. "My work is done in the office or the court room. Rules are rules, and I'm not bending them for you."

He scoots closer. I back my chair up.

"I'll pay double your regular hourly rate," he chides.

"I'm not a hooker, Mr. Holtz." I've had other clients who have tested my patience — most of them do — but no one has ever come at me quite like this. I worked at a small firm right out of law school that took on petty criminals. Those cases we could make a few bucks on without having to do much discovery. Some of the men would stare at me, especially if they'd been in lock up for more than a few days. River Holtz is different. Power and money sway.

"Your husband told me you're the best. I want the best, and I'm willing to pay for it," he adds, softening his expression. His rebel-like good looks probably haven't hurt either.

I can practically hear Cole telling him that on the phone...hear his voice. It boils up some of the memories from this morning, but I quickly bury them away.

"My husband is a smart man."

"Prove it," he says, obviously baiting me.

Cole is going to hear about this tonight. He's knocked me so far out of my comfort zone it's not even funny.

"Where and what time?" One side of his lips curl; he wins.

"I'll pick you up at ten."

"Ten?" I ask, almost falling out of my chair. Court starts at eight tomorrow.

"That's what I said. He'll meet us at 10:30 after the opening festivities." I pass him a piece of paper and a pen.

"Write down the address. I'll meet you there."

"I said I'd pick you up," refusing to take them from me.

"And, I'm meeting you halfway. I'll go to the club with you, but I'm driving myself. Take it or leave it."

Shaking his head, he grabs the pen. "He didn't mention you were stubborn."

"He didn't tell me you were so difficult," I hit back. He passes me back the pad of paper. The address is familiar, but it's at least a half hour from my house.

Tomorrow is going to suck.

"Don't be late," he says as he stands. "Or you'll see how difficult I can be."

"Goodbye, Mr. Holtz. I have a client waiting."

"Don't you need me to sign some sort of a contract or something?" I force a smile, crossing my arms over my chest.

"Let's see how tonight goes. I get to pick my clients the same way you get to pick your lawyer." His thumb runs along his lower lip, drawing my attention.

"This is going to be interesting."

"Yes, it is," I answer back, opening the door for him. If that isn't enough of a hint, I don't know what is. He reaches his hand out before crossing the threshold. I take it, reluctantly. He uses his strength to draw me in close—on the edge of too close.

"Wear something nice," he whispers, his warm breath hitting my cheek.

Speechless, I watch him walk out the door still feeling where his fingers touched mine. I wonder if he noticed the waiting room is empty. I wonder if he felt my eyes on him the whole way out. I wonder a lot of things about River Holtz.

"Beatrice!" I shout from the doorway.

"Coming!" she yells back. Her smile falls when she sees my face. If stress were a spring trend, I'd be wearing it like Gisele.

"I need you to gather everything you can on Mr. Holtz. Everything."

"Anything else?" she asks.

"Yeah, can you call Laurel and tell her I'm not going to make girls' night?" She reaches forward as if she wants to take my temperature. Wine is my religion.

"Is everything okay?"

"I've been better," I say honestly. "Do you know when Cole's plane lands?"

"He booked his own flight. Should I try calling him?"

Shaking my head, I reply, "No, he's only been gone a couple of hours. He's probably in the air. I'll try him before lunch."

"Good idea."

As she walks away, I stand in the same spot watching her but not really seeing her. Life has never been this lonely. To an outsider, I have it all—the job, the husband, and the house—but inside I'm nearly empty. Hell, I've been running on these fumes for over a year.

I can't go on much longer...not like this.

ACKNOWLEDGEMENTS

FIRST, I HAVE TO THANK the one person who made this—and ever other book I've written—possible: my husband, Michael. If it weren't for you, I wouldn't have the courage to keep at this, or the time. Thank you for everything you do to keep the household going while I'm "working".

To my kids, I love you more than words can ever express. Thank you for understanding when Mommy has to work instead of play. It just makes every moment I get to spend with you that much better.

To my assistant, Melissa, thank you for everything you do for me. You're not only my assistant but a great friend, even if you do "meh" me every now and then.

To my Laura, Lisa, Allison, and Kara, thank you for helping me shape this book into what it is. Even if your "team" didn't win, you will get your happily ever after in the novella.

I also have to thank my editor, Chelsea, for keeping me away from clichés. My formatter, Kassi, for always making the pages pretty. Regina for giving me a cover that I love. And my agent, Jill Marsal, for supporting me along the way.

And last but not least, the bloggers and readers who have been with me over the last couple years ... you helped make my dreams come true. THANK YOU!

35676607R00140

Made in the USA
San Bernardino, CA
30 June 2016